White
Glove Life

White Glove Life

M. L. Wright

Ms. Blueberry
PUBLISHING

Published by Ms. Blueberry Publishing, Ms. Blueberry Limited
Published in Hong Kong

Edited and designed by Girl Friday Productions
www.girlfridayproductions.com

Cover Illustration: Erin Wallace

ISBN (paperback): 978-988-74557-8-3
ISBN (ebook): 978-988-74557-1-4

First edition

To the joy of my life, Darren

CHAPTER ONE

New York, New York

"Three million!" the auctioneer barked, whipping his right hand out towards the seated bidder.

A telephone bidder immediately shot his hand up and shouted anxiously, "Bidding, sir! Three point five million dollars!"

Must be a first-time bidder.

"Four million, not with you," the auctioneer, quickly catching his breath, countered.

The overzealous telephone bidder stood in a boxed-off area at the far side of the room, one of a slew of other telephone bidders dressed in head-to-toe black-tie outfits, each talking incessantly on the phone. Without a doubt, they were all trying to persuade their clients on the other end of the line to place a bid.

By the time the telephone bidder relayed the development to his defeated client, a few dozen hands and paddles had sprung up in earnest, obstructing the flat-screen TV hanging on the back wall that broadcast real-time online bids.

Amidst all the commotion, Madeleine, seated at the back of the saleroom, glanced down at her catalog and phone.

Sigh . . . I'll just wait till all the commotion dies down.

This was the last lot at D's Magnificent Jewels sale in New York City. Wired from multiple shots of caffeine or simply hanging on to their last thread of adrenaline, everyone in the room was clearly on edge. Not only because after ten hours, they had reached the final and most expensive lot of the sale, but also because it was the largest fancy vivid blue-green diamond authenticated by the industry's diamond authority, the Gemological Institute of America (GIA), to date.

Mad was at the auction bidding for her patron, who happened to be one of the princes of the illustrious Qatar royal family. A chance meeting between Mad and the prince's personal assistant, in addition to a highly publicized exit from her jewelry specialist job at the prestigious auction house Minos, had led her to this current position.

Despite it being a year ago, it seemed like a mere blink of an eye since the prince offered her a job that shined a light on what Mad could really do with her talents. For all her life, Mad's passion had been jewels and gemstones. The prince gave her an opportunity to live her passion without having to compromise her morals and integrity. She held full control over the prince's personal jewelry collection, and her only goal was to make it one of the top in the world.

Which was why she now traveled all around the world chasing rare gemstones and jewelry.

"Four point eight million!"

The same number of hands, if not more, waved frantically in front of Mad.

Not yet.

The prince already possessed many diamonds in an array of pure rainbow colors, intensities, shapes, and sizes. "Pure" meaning that the diamond was graded by the GIA as having no secondary hues. The assortment of these diamonds was so extensive that a geological director at any prestigious museum would swoon over the opportunity to showcase the extraordinary display of nature's finest. Nonetheless, it was also because of this quintessential model of a collection that Mad was here bidding for a 5.68-carat fancy vivid blue-green triangular-shaped diamond. The prince—and frankly, Mad—had grown blasé about His Highness's perfectly immaculate display of exquisite diamonds.

"It's the combination of impurities that make a gemstone unique. Those could be even rarer and more stunning," Mad had suggested a few months ago.

The prince, his curiosity spurred, had asked, "Tell me more."

"Classic beauty is what many strive for. But how many times have we fallen into that trap, only to be bored too soon? Unique beauty is something different, and, in many cases, imperfection is what makes it so intriguing—and infatuating," Mad had replied, flashing him an enormous smile.

The prince countered with a grin, "What do you propose?"

Mad knew the prince was going to love this new endeavor.

"Instead of looking for perfect pure stones, classic beauties, perhaps it's time to acquire some outside the box. One with more character, engagement, a little *je ne sais quoi.*"

Mad remembered the prince looked pleased, and so began her quest of finding stones that captivated her attention and lingered in her thoughts.

The prince is going to like this one.

"Five million!" someone shouted, snapping Mad's attention back to the sales scene before her.

Out of the corner of her eye, she saw a flurry of hands.

Not yet.

Mad pulled out her Tom Ford lipstick in Ruby Rush and a pocket mirror from her red Chanel bag. Slowly and carefully, she reapplied the lipstick and adjusted her 3-carat old cushion-shaped diamond ear studs, hoping that by the time she was done, she could actually start bidding. She checked her blazing-red lips reflected in her mirror.

A year ago, Mad wouldn't have been caught dead in such an intense shade. She had always been a minimal makeup kind of gal. Likely because subconsciously, she didn't want to stand out and was happy having someone else bask in the limelight. But after her life-altering stint at Minos, she felt like a phoenix rising from the ashes. It was time to stand out from the shadows, reap the seeds she sowed, and unapologetically become who she wanted and was meant to be.

"I will take five point four million!"

Jesus Christ! How much longer?!

Although Mad loved auctions and enjoyed the occasional drama, this one had been on the excessively slow side. More so because the auctioneer was blatantly trying to drag out each lot and bring in as many bids as possible. Unfortunately, Mad had a dinner reservation to make, and the harsh East Coast winter weather outside combined with the blaring heat from the indoor vents was not putting her in an amicable mood. Her red cashmere sweaterdress and black tights had been irritating her skin for the past hour or so. Her toes were aching from being stuffed in her high-heeled black suede boots. Mad looked down at her phone; it was already 7:45 p.m. She couldn't take it any longer.

With full force, she flung her paddle up into the air. The intensity of her flick and the fiery red of her ensemble instantly caught the auctioneer's weary eye.

"Five point five million, with the lady in red," the auctioneer announced.

Mad shook her head and gave him a piercing look, visibly displeased with what he said.

Clearly mystified, he asked, "Excuse me, my lady?"

Mad took a deep breath and spoke clearly, "Six million, sir."

A telephone bidder audibly gasped at the same moment people in the room spun around and stared at the audacious new contender in the back.

Let's get this over with.

It took the stunned auctioneer a few seconds to recover from the shock. Clearing his throat, he finally repeated Mad's bid as professionally as possible. "Six million dollars with the lady in red!"

Everyone started whispering and waited to see if the previous bidders were going to challenge her. However, the few in the room shook their heads in dismay.

Stoney-faced, Mad started typing a message on her phone.

Maybe I can make it to dinner on time!

That sweet thought quickly dissipated when a telephone bidder shouted out, "Six point one million, sir!" Mad closed her eyes but quickly snapped them back open. She could feel the auctioneer anxiously watching, waiting for her next move. Annoyed, Mad flipped her paddle up with a quick twitch of a hand, signaling that she would follow suit.

Hardly hiding his glee, the tux-clad auctioneer standing up on the rostrum for the past ten hours squeaked uncharacteristically, "Six point two million against you, Tony."

Tony, the telephone bidder, quickly bellowed back, "Six point three million!"

Claps and cheers exploded from the spectators in the room. Mad quickly flicked her paddle again, unintentionally elevating the excitement in the room by tenfold.

"Six point four million, not with you, Tony," the auctioneer declared gleefully as he, no doubt, calculated in his head how much buyer's premium the house was going to profit out of this lot.

"Six point five million," Tony faithfully repeated his client's orders.

Mad flicked her paddle.

"Six point six million, still not with you, Tony, but with the lady in red!" the auctioneer sang. He grinned wildly and even more so when Tony flapped his paddle, indicating another bid.

"Six point seven million!"

Flick!

"Six point eight million!"

Again, Tony rebounded with another offending bid.

"Six point nine million!"

Annoyed beyond words, Mad sternly swung her paddle up to reach an awe-inspiring price of "Seven million dollars!"

Hysteria exploded in the room. Though Tony appeared drained, it did not deter him from swinging his paddle up confidently for "Seven point one million dollars."

Every head in the room automatically swung towards Mad's direction, eager for her next move.

But she didn't.

After a few seconds, which probably felt like eternity to the auctioneer, he ventured with uneasiness, "Would you like another bid, my lady?"

Mad glanced down at her catalog. She knew, from her private diamond and gemstone database, which she'd built and maintained since her Minos days, that the diamond was worth $7.7 million before hammer. So, she still had leeway in terms of how high a price she could comfortably bid up to. Nevertheless, she needed to change the pace and alter the mood. She needed to put the competitor and the auctioneer on edge, take advantage of the situation, and win the lot once and for all.

Slowly, Mad, indulging in her own jest, looked up at the auctioneer's face, which had changed to a blatantly distressful shade of grey. By then, the room had gone silent, and not a muscle moved as they waited desperately for her response.

Without lifting her paddle, Mad casually, as if ordering a caramel macchiato from Starbucks, announced firmly, "Seven point five million dollars."

The auctioneer released a great sigh of relief and incautiously blurted, "Oh, thank god!"

The eyes that were a moment ago glued on Mad shifted at lightning speed to the silhouette of a sweaty, exhausted Tony, who had yielded to the stress and was unceremoniously loosening his tie. The spectators waited for his next move, which could potentially cause a tsunami of emotions.

Slumped in his chair, Tony talked quietly on the phone. He seemed to be mouthing terse words to the tenacious bidder behind the line. As hopeful as everyone in the room was for a prolonged show of a bidding war, Mad could smell victory. Eventually, Tony gave up and shook his head dismally.

"Very well then. All done?" the auctioneer asked as he held his gavel up and scanned the room before hammering it down.

A thunderous applause broke out and echoed throughout the room. The telephone bidders and auctioneer shed their austere faces and hugged each other vigorously as the surreal moment dawned on them. Simultaneously, champagne bottles popped open in celebration of the auction house's huge achievement. It was a white glove sale, a *perfect* sale, where every single lot in the auction had been sold. An extremely rare feat, considering the only other time Mad remembered this happening was the Elizabeth Taylor jewelry auction, ages ago.

Mad smiled at their undeniable accomplishment; her thoughts flashed to a few joyful moments during her former auction house days.

That's right . . . only a few.

Whipping herself back to the present, Mad hastily gathered her catalog, paddle, and bag in one hand and called her chauffeur with the other. There was no time to reminisce, nor had she wanted to; she had an important date to make.

♢　♢　♢

Screeching to a halt, Mad's town car arrived at her destination much sooner than she had expected. She had told her chauffeur that she was in a hurry, which clearly meant he was automatically given the green light to accelerate and haphazardly maneuver through traffic in Manhattan like a renegade yellow cab. At some heart-stopping moments, where they were just millimeters away from the next car, Mad wished she hadn't told him she was in a hurry.

Mad grabbed her bag, hurriedly freed herself from her safety belt, and bounced out of the car. As she passed the streak of emblematic green and red neon lights, Mad glanced at her watch. It was 9:00 p.m.

Not too late!

Auctions were intense, long, and so draining that Mad usually needed to recuperate afterwards with some heavy, hearty food. Tonight, the Italian restaurant Carbone certainly fit the bill. Barging through the doors, she breezed past the hostess and made a beeline towards the back room. Through dimly lit lighting, she could see a dark figure seated at a table. As Mad approached, the man instantly smiled brightly. Clad in a crisp white shirt unbuttoned at the top, a fitted blazer with trendy satin lapels, and tailored blue jeans was her husband of six months, Steve. He stood up and instinctively gave Mad a kiss on her mouth. Kissing back, Mad inhaled his delicious body scent mixed with fresh citrus cologne. She debated if she should prolong the moment, but her growling stomach advised otherwise.

"How was your day?" Steve asked, pulling out Mad's chair.

Flopping down on her seat, she took out her phone from her bag and threw it onto the table. "I'm so sorry for being so late! The auctioneer was really trying to milk every single possible bid!" As she talked, she inhaled the pungent smell of the garlic bread placed on the table. She reached for a slice, happy to find it still warm.

"I'm famished!"

"You could have telephone bid, like I always do," Steve said, motioning to the red-tuxedoed captain that they could start serving.

"You know I prefer to see and feel the room. Get my pulse on things. Plus, I don't like them knowing the interest level beforehand. You can't depend on the telephone bidders. What if they try to affect my decision? Some of them can be so pushy," Mad lectured like an expert, which, considering her extensive experience in the auction business, she was.

Mad took a big gulp out of her water glass, before taking a pleasurable sip of chilled champagne. Now she felt relaxed.

Just what I needed.

"Who would be foolish enough to try to manipulate you? As I recall, the last person who tried doing so ended up in prison," Steve smirked, taking a sip from his own champagne flute.

It was true. The last person, "the Boss," did end up in prison. After Mad left Minos, the Independent Commission Against Corruption (ICAC) in Hong Kong enlisted her help to obtain crucial evidence incriminating the Minos jewelry department. There were certainly no loyalties between crooks. Once the interrogation commenced, the Boss and her two accomplices began eagerly pointing fingers at each other for pushing up auction prices, taking kickbacks and bribes, and engaging in other nefarious acts. When cornered, the Boss's right-hand man, Ronald, threw her under the bus in exchange for a shorter prison sentence. He even exposed that the pink Golconda diamond that he and the Boss placed in their last sale didn't actually belong to their vendor, but was stolen property. Everyone thought Louis, her other accomplice, who was always the weaker of the two, would be the first to break down and confess. But it was Ronald that gave the agency just what they needed.

Mad thought Javier, the Minos auctioneer extraordinaire who tried to seduce her and steal an all-important client list, would be condemned for his acts. But he didn't even get a slap on the hand. The sneaky little snake came out of the scandal unscathed! During the ICAC interrogations, Javier instantly fled to London to meet up with Minos's board of directors and assert his innocence. He cunningly drew a line between himself and the Boss and placed the department's depravity solely on her. The board of directors were eager to accept Javier's version of the story (and too apathetic to verify if it was true or not) and distance themselves from the scandal, making sure with their powerful lawyers and newly hired PR firm that they had nothing to do with the Boss.

In the end, it wasn't Old Testament justice, but the Boss, Ronald, and Louis were ultimately implicated for corruption, and all received five- to six-year prison sentences and additional community service hours. Rising up from the rubble, Javier positioned himself as the company's savior from all the embarrassment. He was then promoted to the Global Head of Jewelry and had everyone else in the Hong Kong jewelry department fired, except for the vacuous specialist trainee, Veronica, no doubt saved by her ass-kissing skills. But Mad knew Veronica's days were numbered too; as soon as she was of no use to Javier, she would be forgotten as well.

Mad paused her thoughts as their favorite dishes arrived: meatballs in red sauce, spicy rigatoni, and veal parmesan.

"A cheater will always be a cheater," Mad eventually replied. "Still have to be careful. You never know how many more are out there."

That unscrupulous woman and her underhanded sycophantic allies certainly deserved it.

Mad's experience at Minos changed her without a doubt, but made her a stronger person. Not only did it have that effect on her, but her friends as well. Liam, from the Chinese works of art department, decided he needed a break from all the toxicity and went on a sabbatical, studying old Buddhist cave paintings on the Silk Road. Susan, from the Chinese paintings department, decided it was time to leave as well. She became a painter, and a pretty good one too. She was about to open her own gallery. Henry, from the watch department, who had left Minos before everything went down to become the head of the watch department at Colux auction house, had been doing so well, it seemed like his department would be the market leader this year. Everyone had moved on to much bigger and better things—but their success meant packed schedules, and managing to have a meal together was as hard as winning the lottery. Their attempts always started with a round of enthusiastic messages, followed by rigid, conflicting schedules, then dwindled to silence.

Mad's phone buzzed. She quickly flipped it over. It was from Luna, one of the world's finest producers of South Sea pearls. Based in Australia, the company had single-handedly made cultured pearls in fashion again. In addition, they were the only company in the world producing large enough pearl sizes combined with top-quality luminosity that could interest the prince. Mad quickly read the email, which was from the youngest of the three Luna brothers, Logan.

> "My dearest Mad,
> How have you been? We have a new pearl harvest—many extraordinary ones. I'm sure you will be pleased. Over 18mm in size. When can I see you?
> Love always,
> Logan"

The Luna brothers had always been polite to Mad, especially the youngest and the most flirtatious, Logan. Mad replied as pleasantly as possible.

> "Dear Logan,
> It's always nice to hear from you. I should be able to meet you in Australia in two months and will let you know as soon as I have my schedule set.
> Take care,
> Mad"

Mad threw her phone back down on the table and dove into the meatballs.

"I don't see why 'the lady in red' needs to be that cautious," Steve slyly quipped. "She seems like someone who has the whole auction room eating out of the palm of her hand."

Lady in red?

Mad stopped trying to maneuver a meatball onto her plate. Steve was grinning from ear to ear.

"That was you, wasn't it?!" Mad yelped. "On the telephone! You wanted the vivid blue-green too?"

She could not believe it. "Why didn't you tell me?!" Mad squealed.

"Why didn't you *tell me*?" Steve imitated her astonishment and laughed.

Yes! Why didn't we tell each other what we were bidding for?

In retrospect they really should have. This was not the first time they had gotten into this predicament; they could have lowered the hammer price and saved a few hundred thousand dollars!

"I didn't even know you were going to be bidding!" Mad exclaimed. "We really have to stop doing this to each other. Can you imagine how much more we're paying these auction houses, just because we forgot to tell each other what we're going to bid on?"

"And how many jobs we're supporting at these auction houses just because instead of talking when we see each other"—Steve grinned and continued—"we choose to do something more, shall I say, interesting?"

Mad instantly blushed as she remembered that morning. They were both jet-lagged and really should have been getting ready for their back-to-back morning meetings, but they ultimately succumbed and made love—twice. Once in bed and once in the shower, to be exact. Their busy work schedules and business travels had *made* them make the most out of their time together.

In actuality, they were still newlyweds, having just married six months before in a beautiful ceremony in Mallorca. Close friends and family had attended, which was easily a little bit more than five hundred in attendance. It had been a glorious *Tatler*-worthy three-day event of teary speeches, free-flowing alcohol, fireworks, and late-night soirees. Guests who had been dressed in skimpy swimwear (or nude) by day were decked out in designer gowns and tuxes with scintillating gemstones by night. When the wedding ended, guests left with a signature Spanish tan and a "whatever happens in Mallorca, stays in Mallorca" adage.

Mad and Steve then took a brief honeymoon in South Africa, where their days were filled with safaris. Until they got bored with seeing animals that all appeared the same to them anyways and managed to alter their itinerary to visit a diamond mine instead. After the vacation, it was back to curating the prince's collection for Mad and international real estate development for Steve. They promised to support each other in their careers, but would not allow themselves to be apart for more than two weeks at a time. Before their rendezvous in New York City, it had been more than a week since they'd been together.

Mad's phone buzzed again, disrupting her thoughts. She quickly picked it up and scanned the email. It was Logan again.

"Babe! Two months? I'm afraid that's too long! You know we always want to give you first choice, but we have a few Chinese buyers coming this month and it will be hard holding them off. And you know how much I miss you!"

She placed her phone facedown again.

I'll see to my schedule later.

Returning to their conversation, Mad insisted, "It's not only you, but I also barely have time to talk to Jackie, and she's my best friend! When was the last time I saw her? Gosh, I don't even remember!" Mad flipped her phone over and studied her calendar. She scrolled down the last few days, then weeks, but couldn't find what she was searching for.

"I give up! I can't even find 'Jackie' on my calendar!" Mad surrendered. "And did I just say 'gosh' again like a pathetic gullible little girl?"

"Yes, you did say 'gosh,' and you know I love it when you do. Don't stop saying what you feel like saying," Steve answered. He took a sip of champagne and added, "We saw her and her new boyfriend, Stuart, a little more than two weeks ago for dinner."

"Yes, she introduced him to us! I quite like Stuart, I must say. He seemed . . . different from the others."

"Let's see how long this one lasts," Steve said indifferently. "I'm surprised I still remember his name."

"You remember because you actually, even if you don't want to admit it, agree with me that this one might be the—"

Before Mad could finish her sentence, her phone buzzed, interrupting their conversation once again. She turned the phone over; it was from Logan. She quickly skimmed the email.

> ". . . but of course, if you can't make it sooner,
> I will hide the best away until you visit me. You
> know I will do anything for you ;)"

Mad smiled. He was young and unabashedly charming. And knew just how to get her to reply.

"I'll try my best. His Highness is looking forward to your new harvest. Having said that, we sure don't want to cause any bloodshed within the Luna dynasty just because you would do any-thing for me. Will update you soon."

While Mad was typing, she could hear Steve say some-thing to her. But she couldn't make out the exact words.

"What were you saying?" she replied when she finally looked up from her phone.

Steve appeared annoyed but repeated, "*I said* there's a lady sitting over there with a red diamond ring, heart-shaped, just like yours."

Mad snapped her head around. There was no "lady" in sight. Instead, she saw a group of men at the table. It took a moment, but Mad realized her husband was just playing around with her because he knew as well as she did that her 2-carat fancy red diamond engagement ring was one of a kind. The likelihood of finding one as beautiful and exquisite was almost impossible, and it would have certainly caused quite a reaction if indeed there was one located right next to her at that very moment.

"Hey! That was not cool!" Mad protested as she turned her head back.

"What other way to get your undivided attention?" Steve asked, stroking her hand, the ring finger glowing with her fiery-red engagement ring.

Gazing at her hand, Mad confessed, "You know, it would be nice if I could find one similar for the prince. After all, he so kindly let go of this treasure so that you could ask me to marry you."

"Yes, but it wouldn't be that special if there was something similar," Steve replied with his signature mischievous smile, "and I was saying that we will be seeing Jackie and Stuart at Courchevel. So, we can decide then if he's any different from the others."

"When are we going to Courchevel again?" Mad asked, honestly unable to remember.

"In two weeks," Steve replied quietly. "I'll see you in two weeks."

Steve's words punched Mad in the stomach, but she tried to hide her disappointment. A wave of melancholy swept over her. The next two weeks, Mad was scheduled for a jewelry-hunting trip in Italy and Switzerland. There were a multitude of Tuscan villas filled with antiques and treasures that she wanted to visit. Then it was off to Geneva for the biannual dizzying onslaught of jewelry auctions from the different houses. The first time Mad went to Geneva, she remembered being knocked off her feet by it all. The number of decadent jewels on display and the elegant clients circulating the rooms took her breath away. Now instead of her selling the jewels, the tables had turned, and she was one of those chic exquisite creatures. This time around, she could finally enjoy the spectacle—but there was something else on her mind.

I won't see you for another two weeks.

She pursed her lips ever so slightly. Sensing the change in mood, Steve took Mad's hand and smiled warmly.

"We'll make it work. And you know if you ever feel lonely, and you really can't stomach another sight of a diamond or jewel anymore, I could . . . I could . . . send a life-size cutout of myself to your hotel room!" Steve burst out chuckling.

Mad instinctively threw him a playful punch on his arm and feigned annoyance.

"OK, *OK*! All jokes aside, you know very well what I wouldn't hesitate to do if it comes to that moment."

Mad knew. Mad knew Steve would stop whatever he was doing, jump on the next plane out of wherever he was, find her, and wrap himself protectively around her. He would sweep her off her feet and bring her back home to their lovely apartment in Hong Kong. Yet, Steve knew that this job was Mad's dream, her passion. So, no matter what, he would be supportive. Until *that moment.*

Mad studied his kind face and thought to herself, *How did I get so lucky?* She remembered the day they met, which was also her first day at Minos. She'd been so naive, but somehow had managed to intrigue this unsuspecting ultra-VIP client, Steve Lam. From that day on, Mad had bumped into Steve on several occasions, not knowing that he had already been completely enamored by her ever since their first meeting. After a particularly nasty episode between Steve's niece, Clarisse, and the Boss, they'd started officially dating. And were married six months later. To some, it might have seemed like a short amount of time, but they both believed they had found their soulmate. That was not to say that Mad knew everything about him; she discovered new tidbits every day. Never had she thought that this stern-looking man, with premature creases between his eyebrows, was so mischievous. According to Clarisse, Mad brought the fun side out of him.

"Yes, I do know." Mad smiled sweetly and leaned across the table to give him a prolonged kiss, something she had wanted to do when she first arrived at the restaurant.

"Shall we? I can think of something better to do than dwell on the next two weeks. And it involves going back to our hotel room this instant," Steve said playfully.

Mad burst out laughing. "Well, do tell me more, Mr. Lam!"

"Actions speak louder than words, my dear Mrs. Lam."

Giggling like schoolchildren, they stood up from their table and walked out of the restaurant hand in hand. Once on the pavement, a cold blast of frigid wind hit Mad's face, momentarily halting her laughter as if to remind her that something was still amiss. She held Steve's hand tighter, and he automatically gripped hers reassuringly. The wave of melancholy returned, and her imminent travels boomeranged back to her thoughts. But she didn't want to tackle whatever was bothering her, especially right at that moment.

Perhaps it's just a passing feeling . . .

She wasn't sure. But she knew for certain that she had Steve by her side, her partner in crime, her till-death-do-us-part, her husband. So things should and would be all right.

CHAPTER TWO

The Tuscan Hills

The brutally early 5:00 a.m. flight the next day to Florence did not dampen Mad's spirit at all. She was her usual assiduous, enthusiastic self, though physically she needed her sunglasses to shield against the vicious daylight glare and also to hide her puffy bloodshot eyes.

On the plane, after drinking two iced cappuccinos and a shot of espresso, she was ready to examine her schedule for the next few days. Scrolling down her phone, she knew it would be an aggressive four days of visiting at least two villas a day in the Tuscan area of Italy. Tuscany had an abundance of old estates still owned by prominent Italian families. Families who'd accumulated a treasure trove of jewelry from their bygone days. No jewelry-hunting trip would be worth it without visiting as many of them as possible.

Mad recalled when she was working at Minos. Each time their Italy representative returned from Tuscany, he'd have in hand a bonanza of old Italian jewelry, many branded from the world-renowned Mario Buccellati, of the eponymous family, and Bulgari. Her mission was to acquire these vintage pieces manufactured when Italian craftmanship was king and each piece made was unique in its own way; nothing like the heavily marketed commercial pieces readily available nowadays. Although the prince certainly did not lack these pieces, he also did not mind acquiring more. He had vaults and vaults of—

"Would you like another coffee?" the flight attendant interrupted Mad's thoughts.

Mad knew she really shouldn't, but . . .

"Yes, please," she answered. "Iced cappuccino, thank you."

Just a few sips. I don't have to finish it.

She looked out the plane window and flashed back to the unforgettable moments when she saw the vaults around the world where the prince had his collection stored. At first, like a child in a candy store, Mad was beyond delighted. But it hadn't taken long to become overwhelmed by the sheer mass of gemstones and jewels he'd collected over the years. A few sleepless weeks of shuffling through countless boxes and trays were required before Mad had found her bearings and confidently accepted the title of Head Jewelry Advisor.

The prince owned an eclectic mix of jewelry ranging from antique and vintage, to modern contemporary pieces. In one vault, he kept a glorious display of Mughal jewels, rich with necklaces, bracelets, and earrings mounted in 22-karat gold, inlaid with precious gems and back-to-front vibrant floral enameling. Carved emeralds, spinals, and multiple strands of natural pearls in different shapes and sizes dazzled. Mad had thought the jade bejeweled daggers and feathered *sarpechs* were the climactic highlights, until she'd opened the appropriately named box of "Pandora." Inside the monstrous case was the most extensive exhibit of colorless diamonds she had seen in her life! Their unmistakable luster, limpidity, and old-cut meant they weren't ordinary colorless diamonds; they were all Golconda diamonds! The famed Golconda mines might have been depleted, but Mad had a hunch that 80 percent of the mines' supply was inside Pandora.

In another equally amazing vault was a collection of European pieces. Crowns and tiaras from monarchs laced with old-cut diamonds and pearls, which could be easily manipulated into necklaces and bracelets, adorned glass showcases. Jewelry from famed designer houses garnished the ocean of endless trays. There were the newer collections of Cartier tutti fruttis, panthers, and tigers, Van Cleef & Arpels mystery-set sapphires and rubies, and Chopard Happy Diamonds. However, the ones that made Mad's heart beat a mile a minute were the ancient Egyptian-motif Art Deco brooches with wonderful geometric circles, squares, and rectangles, the Belle Époque floral garland *devant-de-corsages* of platinum finesse, and the Art Nouveau Lalique glass cloisonné and plique-à-jour fauna and flora masterpieces decorated with signature opals and mother-of-pearl. As if that were not breathtaking enough, the prince also had a few 1960s Van Cleef & Arpels turquoise and diamond necklaces and brooches thrown in for good measure.

A surprising vault revealed a collection of contemporary pieces from current designers such as JAR, Cindy Chao, Bhagat, and even some names Mad had never heard of before. Fun and modern, these pieces were of fantastical inspiration but expertly manufactured with modern technical skills and pliable metals that made each even more sensational than the last. This collection was rather on a smaller scale, though, and mysteriously, Mad also found objects of vertu, such as carved jadeite ornaments, Cartier mystery clocks, and Fabergé eggs mixed within the collection. Obviously, this was a vault that needed more development.

The flight attendant returned with a fresh iced cappuccino, placing it on the seat table. "Can I get you anything else before serving the first course for breakfast?"

"I'm good," Mad replied, smiling. "Thank you."

Business travel had certainly upgraded to a more luxurious level since her Minos days. She took an appreciative sip of her perfectly brewed iced cappuccino before reminiscing about her favorite vault and pieces.

Although each and every vault was exceptional, Mad's favorite was one where feature gemstones systematically covered every single vacant surface area available. This was where the other colorless diamonds (non-Golconda) were kept. Each were categorized according to their whiteness, carat weight, cut, and clarity. The infamous colored-diamond collection was also padlocked within these walls, when not on display at some exhibition. Arranged merely as a rainbow arc akin to those prevalent in pre-nurseries (albeit valued at "priceless"), it never failed to put a smile on Mad's face. Other prized gemstones such as Burmese pigeon's blood rubies, Colombian Muzo emeralds, and Kashmir sapphires lavishly littered the space as did phenomenal stones such as cat's-eye chrysoberyls, color change sapphires, alexandrites, cat's-eye alexandrites, padparadschas, and more.

Personally, she couldn't help but adore the pieces with provenance. The stories behind the glitz and glamor were what made any jewel infinitely more desirable. During her auction house days, Mad saw countless jewelry bid up to astronomical prices just because the piece evoked emotions that led to an indescribable carnal need to own it. The Jackie Onassis faux pearls, the Eva Peron Argentina brooch, the Spanish royal family/Joseph Bonaparte/Duke and Duchess of Abercorn/ Elizabeth Taylor La Peregrina natural pearl; all sold at well above high estimate prices. The prince had plenty of pieces once owned by royalty or celebrities and had asked her to help him acquire more, which Mad was more than happy to do. She herself was always on the lookout for jewelry with a little story behind it. If she saw something rapturing or inspiring, something that spoke to her heart, she then knew it had to be acquired.

Mad's Mercedes sedan sped through the palette of orange, brown, and greens that were the landscape of Tuscany. Olive trees dotted the rolling hills and patches of lined vineyards. Through a dusty avenue flanked by carefully manicured cypress trees, Mad arrived at her first appointment. Her car scattered a family of chickens strolling on the pebbled pavement as it stopped in front of a large villa with citrine-yellow outer walls and a terra-cotta tiled roof. Rustic bushes and potted plants lined the facade, while vines covered the side of a wall. Linked by the vast farmland, smaller replicas of the main house spread across the estate.

An elderly couple in their eighties and a little boy about ten years in age stood waiting outside the front door. The woman wore a generous beige pencil skirt along with an ivory cashmere twinset. Her perfectly coiffed hair was white mixed with a few strands of grey. Framing her face was a pair of circa-1966 René Boivin white and grey cultured pearl and diamond Algues ear clips, and a strand of matching grey cultured pearls hung around her neck. The man wore a pair of beige pants, a sky-blue shirt, and a dark-blue jacket topped with a beige newsboy cap. In a similar ensemble, the little boy looked like a miniature version of the old man. With the quintessential Tuscan background, all three appeared to have just walked out of a Brunello Cucinelli advertisement. Mad assumed they were the owners and quickly got out of the car to shake their hands.

"Buongiorno," the couple said in greeting.

"Buongiorno," Mad repeated. "You must be Mr. and Mrs. Russo. I'm Madeleine. Thank you for meeting with me."

With a slew of Italian words, the little boy quickly translated what Mad said to the couple. Mad could only decipher her name.

They seemed satisfied and nodded, giving the little boy permission to introduce himself.

"Thank you for coming today. They are Massimo Russo and Francesca Russo. I am Lorenzo Russo, their grandson, and I will help with . . . eh . . . how do you say . . . ah . . . translation in English today," Lorenzo explained.

Francesca spoke a few words in Italian and motioned for Mad to step inside the house.

"Please come in," Lorenzo said.

Mad and Lorenzo followed Francesca and Massimo inside the house. They walked through a hallway, passing by several shut beige doors until they reached what seemed like a living room. Other than the brick walls, exposed wooden beams, and a cozy fireplace, there was nothing stereotypically Tuscan about the room, though. A plush trio of white sofas surrounded a sleek white coffee table that was centered in the middle of the room and illuminated above by a huge Baccarat crystal chandelier. Mother-of-pearl mosaic vases containing delightful flowers and fruits, and beige candles of all heights and sizes spread throughout the space. Huge mirrors hung on the walls, next to the slightly opened floor-to-ceiling French doors, which ushered in an aromatic breeze of lavender and herbs. A little white cat with black spots, snuggled on a cushion next to the fireplace, glared at Mad, watching her every move.

From behind, a woman slid Mad's coat off as if she had done it plenty of times before.

Francesca spoke, and Lorenzo subsequently asked, "Would you like something to drink? Tea? Coffee?"

"Coffee would be great, thank you."

Lorenzo instructed the woman, and she left with Mad's coat in hand.

Francesca pointed at a rectangular wooden table with a chair set up near one of the windows. Lorenzo didn't have to translate; Mad knew this was going to be her workstation. She automatically walked over, set her bag down, and took out her phone, notebook, and tool bag. Francesca and Massimo disappeared from the room, but Lorenzo assured her that "they will bring the jewels."

"Thank you," Mad politely replied and took a seat at her designated table. She checked her phone to see if anyone had contacted her, and indeed there was a message.

Steve:

The only thing I did today was miss you

Mad grinned. She was about to reply when the Russos returned with a stack of trays and placed them in front of her. There were five trays of brooches, each lined neatly with plush velvet cushioning. She used her phone to take pictures of each so she could file them in her database later. Then, slowly, her eyes scanned the pieces to see what would fit in the prince's collection.

There were brooches in all shapes and sizes, mostly in yellow gold and of flora, insects, or a whimsical animal motif. Some of *en tremblant* design and some shell cameos in typical coral and white relief. One whole tray of Buccellati brooches— textured white and yellow gold floral sprays with circular diamond accents, textured gold butterflies with pierced openwork wings, and various pendant brooches centered on a ruby, emerald, or sapphire with rose-cut diamond accents that resembled little twinkling stars. But the prince had too many of these already. Mad stacked the trays and placed them on the side of the table. Francesca instantly understood and left the room, only to return with several more.

This time around, the trays held rows and rows of rings with various gemstones. Once again, she took pictures with her phone, then scanned the trays to see if there were any that fit the prince's collection. There were gemstone solitaires in shapes of ovals, rectangles, sugarloaves, and cabochons. A handful of pierced Buccellati two-toned gold bands centered on a sapphire, ruby, or emerald. Various Art Deco pieces with old-cut diamonds and pierced plaques. Nothing really caught Mad's eye at first, but a second scan proved her wrong.

On the lower right-hand corner of a tray, something red beckoned. Mad held it up for closer inspection. It was a ruby for sure. Approximately 8 carats, deep-red color, and the most amazing sparkles of fire. She yanked her loupe out of her tool bag and ran towards the window. Under natural white light, Mad's extensive experience told her instantly that the material of the stone was different. She lifted the loupe and ring towards a ray of light and looked inside the stone.

Clean.

Other than a tiny little crystal on the side (meaning that the stone was unheated!), it was perfectly clean. Mad smiled. She hurried back to the table and took the UV light from her tool bag. She dropped down on all fours and huddled in a dark corner under the table to see if the ruby glowed in the dark. It did!

Red! It's Burmese for sure.

Mad leapt up in excitement and grabbed a yellow pocket light. The light illuminated the treasure as she smiled and admired it.

"Do you have any certs for this one?" Mad finally inquired.

Francesca quickly emitted words at what seemed like a hundred miles per hour and swung her hands around in animated gestures.

Lorenzo tried to catch up but managed to only loosely translate that "no papers for this one . . . but one of the people from the auction house came here before and gave us a price of eight hundred thousand US dollars."

What?!

Mad could not believe her ears! If this piece was what she thought it was, which most certainly was an extremely rare, top-quality Burmese, nonheated, pigeon's blood ruby, then it meant that it should be ten times the price the auction house had offered! Mad postulated that the "auction house people" were from Minos. They were infamous in the industry for giving ridiculously low estimates to unassuming owners with no idea what the market prices were. Many clients had complained on numerous occasions, but Minos continued to attempt the cheating scheme.

Mad shook her head. "I can offer more, please set it aside for me."

Lorenzo hastily translated.

Upon hearing this, Francesca and Massimo both looked extremely pleased. Smiling broadly, Francesca hurried out of the room. Within seconds she scurried back with a box in hand.

She spoke as fast, if not faster than she did before. This time little Lorenzo couldn't keep up. Without waiting for him to translate, Francesca unlocked the decrepit brown box, revealing something splendidly unexpected. It was an unmistakable 1960s Bulgari bib necklace with amethyst and turquoise cabochons, mounted in gleaming yellow gold. Scintillating circular diamonds encircled each gemstone, further accentuating the divine specimen.

Mad couldn't help herself. Without asking, she swiftly plucked the necklace from the box. Her skilled hands instantly found the hidden clasp and unfastened it. She gently placed the necklace on her neck and secured the clasp with a swift click. She dashed over to the nearest mirror and gazed at her reflection. The necklace rested perfectly on her neck; the superb craftmanship and fine articulation allowed it to hug the curves of her shoulder and collarbone. Mad slid her fingers over and then underneath the necklace. As hoped, it was smooth as silk.

Exquisite.

After Mad took a photo of the necklace, she took it off her neck. Using her loupe, she checked each gemstone and found an authentic Bulgari maker's mark. Thoroughly satisfied, she placed the necklace back in the box and looked at the three anxious bystanders, who were gazing back, grinning earnestly.

"Please put it aside for me." Mad beamed.

Francesca's eyes glistened with elation. She left the room in a flash. Within seconds she returned with another tattered old box. Mad braced herself for what could possibly be another brilliant discovery. Francesca grinned as she handed the cubic box to Mad. She wanted her to do the honors. Mad slowly opened it and gasped. A pair of mesmerizing emerald eyes stared back at her. They belonged to a turquoise scaled Bulgari Serpenti bracelet/watch in yellow gold. Mad took the sensational creature out and wrapped it around her arm three times. The sprung body coiled effortlessly.

Ahhh . . . Bulgari craftmanship.

She flipped open the head to reveal the circular gold dial and diamond bezel. The dial was signed "Jaegar-leCoultre," and the body signed "Bulgari." It had the essential pedigree.

The prince could add this to his Serpenti collection.

Mad placed it back in the box and put it next to her pile of treasures. Glancing up, she smiled so profusely that her teeth shone.

I will take that as well, thank you.

Massimo, who had been quiet all along, suddenly dashed out of the room.

Another box? Yes, please!

Instead, he returned a few minutes later with a bottle of red wine! The woman who took Mad's coat followed closely behind with a tray of wineglasses. A jubilant Massimo hummed as he poured the wine generously in each glass. He handed one each to Mad and Francesca, abruptly clinked them, and shouted, "Salute!"

This did not need translation at all. Mad laughed and took a sip of her wine. How could she not? It was indeed a celebratory moment. Even the cat that had been so antagonistic was now purring next to her feet.

Francesca and Massimo both talked profusely at the same time while poor Lorenzo tried to translate to no avail. Mad couldn't stop laughing at the comical spectacle. She gazed over at the treasures on the table. She was scheduled for four days in Tuscany, but if in the next few days, she couldn't find anything else to add to the prince's collection, she would be happy with what she had found already. She had hit the jackpot on her first appointment.

She scanned the trays and boxes a second time to make sure she didn't miss anything. Then something caught Mad's eye. It was a little yellow gold brooch sculpted as an hourglass with wings. The bottom was engraved with the words:

Tempus Fugit

"How peculiar. What is this?" Mad voiced out loud.

Francesca looked at the brooch and blurted out something before she grabbed the trays and scurried out of the room.

"Oh! So sorry," Lorenzo explained. "It's not branded and has no gemstones on it, definitely not what you are searching for."

She was even more curious about the piece now. "Oh, I see. But what does it mean?" Mad asked.

"'Time escapes,'" Lorenzo replied. "Is that how you say in English?"

"Time flies?" Mad proposed.

"Yes! That's what it means!"

Mad opened her mouth, but before any words materialized, Massimo barged in, interrupting the conversation.

"Drink!" Massimo urged as he poured more wine in Mad's glass, cascading down like a crimson waterfall. He didn't stop till it reached the brim. Precariously clinking her glass, he shouted "salute!" and downed his portion.

Trying not to spill, Mad cautiously took a sip, but an unsatisfied Massimo motioned for her to follow suit. Francesca returned and without a word emptied her glass too. Defeated and not about to upset her hosts, Mad obliged.

"Salute!" she repeated, reminding herself that she could loosen up a bit. She didn't work for Minos anymore!

The impromptu party lasted well past dark. By the time Mad left, she and Francesca were happily inebriated, whilst

Massimo had passed out on the sofa. Outside under the beautiful starry night, Mad gave Lorenzo a peck on each cheek before her chauffeur helped her into the car. Though she collapsed on the seat and passed out moments later, she knew it had been a very productive day.

CHAPTER THREE

Lake Geneva

Mad sashayed into the lobby of the Mandarin Oriental, Geneva with her jet-black sunglasses on and indispensable phone in hand. It had been a fruitful four-day hunting trip in Tuscany, and the success of acquiring several important pieces had undeniably fueled her ego. She was confident and ready to slay the coming days of jewelry auction furor. From the corner of her eye, she spied a trio descending upon her.

"Bonjour, Madame Lam, we've been expecting you!" the manager sang as he waltzed in front of Mad with his leather-bound VIP file.

"Bonjour," she replied as if expecting to be greeted, even though she was actually taken aback by the welcome bestowed on her.

"I hope you had a wonderful trip to our hotel," the manager continued. "Please, may I help you with your bag and offer you a drink?" Mad handed him her Louis Vuitton Keepall. Without breaking eye contact, he gave the bag to one of the attendants behind him and swiftly handed Mad a glass of chilled champagne in return.

They must have done some research beforehand.

"Your suite is ready for you, and your suitcases have been sent up; may I escort you to your room?"

Mad nodded and followed him to her room located on the top floor of the hotel. The manager opened the door to a suite doused in shades of beige with pops of turquoise and oranges. She placed her glass on the marble coffee table, where another bottle of champagne was being chilled beside an assortment of elaborately decorated welcome chocolates. Fresh lilies, Juliet roses, and orchids ubiquitously decorated and perfumed the whole room.

"Madame Lam, would you like the curtains opened?" the manager inquired as he pulled the sheer fabric to the side, revealing a vast balcony and the magnetic view of the iconic snowcapped Swiss Alps.

Mad's face beamed with delight as she made a beeline towards the balcony. As if perfectly understanding what she wanted, an assistant and the manager slid open the double glass doors, and a gust of fresh crisp air embraced her. Under the panoramic, Toblerone-inspiring mountains was the charming old town of majestic houses and orange roofs. Artisan chocolate shops and fondue restaurants trickled down to the pristine lake of Geneva, where jewelry shops lined the banks and swans swam in the waters.

A year ago, she would not have pictured herself here. The last time she was in Geneva, Veronica booked her into a grim, eerie hotel that she later found out had been a morgue. She rushed off each day and slaved away behind the showcases, afraid to even use the toilets, as she watched fabulous clients flutter about. But now she was back, and under very different circumstances. Like the many dealers who congregate in Geneva for the biannual auctions, she was here to source jewelry for her patron. Auctions were an excellent and efficient way to find valuable pieces. The specialists at each house, like little ants, scoured the world discovering and negotiating rare jewelry that would satisfy the rich. It took at least six months to curate a Magnificent Jewels sale, and anticipation was always high. From the catalogs, Mad had already chosen a few hundred items that she would have to sift through and examine. It would be difficult for some, but for a specialist like her who knew the ins and outs of the auction world, it would not be a problem at all. Knowing the next few days would be hectic, Mad decided on a long, pleasant bath because, this time around, she could.

"Mad! I've missed you!" Louise cried as she offered a hug and gave her the customary triple cheek kiss greeting. "What brings you here?"

Mad had just walked into Minos's preview room after admiring the signature grandiose flower display at the hotel lobby. The delectably vibrant flowers and piercing aromas of roses and peonies welcomed her back to another streak of auction hysteria. It was the calm before the storm.

"I've missed you too, Louise!" Mad returned the pleasantries and was truthfully elated to see a friend at Minos. "Well, I've come to see a few items for my client."

"After all that they have done to you?!" Louise exclaimed. "You're still going to bid here?!"

"Well, it's strictly business, you know," Mad answered matter-of-factly. "Plus, there might be some things worth it this time." Truth be told, she did hope there would be nothing to see at Minos so she could skip the preview and avoid the anticipated awkwardness of facing her ex-colleagues. She had brought down their whole Hong Kong department, after all. But unfortunately, there were a few interesting pieces, and she had come to terms with the fact that she would need to face them someday.

It's a public preview. What are they going to do? Kick me out?

Louise stared at Mad with disbelief and amazement. "You are truly a professional. Let me help you get the lots then. I'm now head of the helpers. The girls will get the lots for me, and I'll tell you which ones are 'worth' bidding on," Louise said with a wink.

When Mad was in Geneva last year showcasing lots from the Hong Kong sale, she was lucky to have Louise as her helper. Without her saying, Louise knew what Mad needed, even if Mad didn't know herself!

"Plus, I'm a big fan of yours!" Louise chuckled. "How you took down the Boss is legendary! You have so many fans here, you know. Now, would you like a coffee? And some chocolate thins for old times' sake?"

Mad couldn't help laughing. Last year, the only substances she had time to ingest were water and the complimentary Swiss chocolate thins placed in bowls throughout the preview room. Each chocolate was an essential sugar rush that had literally saved her from collapsing out of sheer exhaustion.

"Yes, I'll have an iced cappuccino, please, and make it several pieces of chocolate."

Louise laughed and instructed one of the helpers on the side. "Now, tell me, what do you want to see?"

Mad handed Louise a handwritten list of the lots she wanted to examine from the sale. She started to head over to the dealer's room when Louise stopped her.

"No, no, no, that will not do. Come with me." Louise handed the list to another helper and led Mad to a little private table next to the window behind an empty booth. "You can have the table all to yourself. And look, you have the Jet d'Eau as your view."

"Thank you," Mad said to her appreciatively.

"Of course! You're VIP!" Louise chimed as she left.

Mad sat down at her private table and admired the water fountain in the lake. The sunlight shone at the perfect angle, creating a rainbow effect.

How much more comfortable is it this year?!

Louise brought back the certificates and condition reports with Mad's iced cappuccino and a whole bowl of chocolate thins.

"I made sure it's not poisoned." Louise giggled.

As Louise placed the cappuccino on the table, her eyes locked on Mad's engagement ring, and she froze. "Is this the famous red diamond?!" she asked.

"Famous? You mean my engagement ring?" Mad said as she turned her head and peered down at her hand.

"It's beautiful! It's like a ruby, but the luster and those flashes really confuse you. You think it can't be a diamond, but it actually is!" Louise exclaimed excitedly as she held Mad's hand up to get a closer look at her ring. "How spectacular! Yes! It's infamous! Your husband bought this from the prince of Qatar to ask you to marry him! *C'est romantique!* Is he here? All the girls can't stop telling their boyfriends about your husband, and of course all their boyfriends can't wait to murder your husband!"

Mad laughed. "Unfortunately, no. He's working on the other side of the world. I won't see him until all the auctions are over."

"And you don't miss him?" Louise's eyes widened.

"Yes, I do, but we promised we would support each other's careers, and we don't stay apart for more than two weeks."

Louise frowned. "It's hard, huh?"

"It is, but we've got to do what we've got to do."

"Well, you two are what we all aspire to," Louise yielded and smiled. "The perfect love story and couple."

"Gosh, you're making me blush!" Mad laughed humbly. She didn't think her and Steve's love story would have that effect on people—or that people knew about them. A sense of pride swept over her. She took out her phone and typed a quick message to Steve.

Mad:

> Miss you
> Love you

As if expecting her message, Steve instantly replied.

Steve:

> Every second that passes by, I find myself
> missing you, loving you infinitely more

She was so absorbed with the message that she didn't notice a helper placing a tray of rubies in front of her, until she felt a breeze leaving the table. The ruby rings in all shapes and sizes were lined up in a row with a brooch and pendant placed underneath them. Mad only wanted to see the Burmese nonheated rubies. Unless it was truly spectacular, she could not be bothered. Noticing how the rubies were assembled, Mad smiled. Louise had the helper place all the rubies that she wanted to see together so she could compare their colors and clarity side by side. Still, no sooner had Mad scanned the tray than she found herself frowning.

Not that great of a selection.

"The clarity is not that good this time," Louise agreed with Mad. Although it was quite common to find included rubies, Mad was on the lookout for something similar to the 8-carat she had found in Tuscany.

"Some have the color, but the inclusions and the fire are quite disappointing," Mad explained.

She wondered if she should give the other rubies a chance this time.

Perhaps I'll be pleasantly surprised.

"You have a Madagascar this time. How's that?" Mad asked.

"You won't like it," Louise warned her.

"Oh," she replied with disappointment, then placed the tray of rubies to the side in time for a tray of sapphires to arrive. These were separated by the three most important origins: Kashmir, Burma, and Ceylon. The cornflower blues of the Kashmirs, the darker-toned Burmese, and the fiery Ceylons lined up separately in three rows. Mad scanned the tray to see which one would fit the prince's collection.

She held up a Kashmir ring and flipped to the corresponding certificate copy. "Why is this Kashmir labeled 'royal blue' in color?"

Louise shrugged her shoulders. "Apparently, that's what the dealers are looking for."

"I much prefer the classic sleepy ones. You know what I mean?"

"I know what you mean. Those are super rare nowadays."

Mad pursed her lips and put the ring back in the tray. She glanced over at the Burmese sapphires. A few royal blues and a few a bit overly dark in tone. The Ceylons had the fire, but were a little light in tone. Mad let out a deep exhale and sat back in her chair, taking a sip of cappuccino.

"You didn't even examine one with your loupe! It's that bad this time, huh?" Louise uttered.

Mad nodded in agreement. It was more than evident now that Minos had trouble finding consignments. After the Boss's illicit activities came to light, many had chosen to shun the auction house—and rightly so. Minos would have to rebuild their reputation if they were to survive this dog-eat-dog industry. Anyhow, it was none of her business, and she was sure Javier, impervious to anyone else's suffering but his own, would figure a way to claw his way up again.

Another tray arrived, this time with yellow diamonds. Mad took a quick scan and picked up an exceptionally saturated oval-shaped yellow diamond. She was sure it was a fancy vivid yellow.

Finally! Something worth looking at!

She flipped her catalog to the corresponding lot number while Louise helped her find the certificate and condition report. As predicted, the certificate verified that the 7.53-carat diamond was indeed fancy vivid yellow in color and a favorable internally flawless in clarity.

Mad held it next to the window, directly under natural sunlight. Fancy vivid came in different saturations, and this was a pretty good one.

"You're lucky this stone was certified recently," Louise commented.

"Can you believe some people don't even check the date?" Mad asked in reply. "How can you buy IF stones that weren't recently certified?"

"Of course! Have you heard of that specialist in charge of displaying jewelry every morning at Kronos auction house's gallery? He would just transport all the diamonds in one open tray and let them roll around scratching each other! Can you imagine how many are no longer IFs?" Louise asserted, clearly appalled. "You won't believe how many lots we have old certificates for."

"Oh! I believe you!"

"I almost forgot I'm talking to an expert!" Louise laughed. "Sometimes I just shake my head when I have to show clients those lots. I can't tell them, 'No! I forbid you!'"

Mad looked at the stone under her loupe. It was clean inside. She took out her gauge to make sure the dimensions matched the certificate. They did. She read the condition report to see if there was anything alarming. Nope, all was good. She read over the description in the catalog:

COLORED DIAMOND RING
Fancy intense yellow cushion brilliant-cut diamond
of 7.53 carats, gold, ring size 6
GIA, 2019, report 5202692974: 7.53 carats, Fancy Vivid
Yellow color, IF clarity

"You have a typo in your catalog," Mad notified Louise.

"Let me see. Ah yes . . . it should say 'fancy vivid yellow,' not 'intense'!" Louise groaned. "I'm not surprised. Guess who cataloged this piece?"

"Who?"

"Veronica."

"What? Why her?" Mad voiced with astonishment.

"She was given the catalog job, and the specialists are now regretting it. I've never seen someone so prone to mistakes! It's like her head is not attached to her body!"

"Oh gosh, it's good that you're only legally liable for the catalog heading, or I don't know how many people would sue Minos this year."

"You would think that would protect us. But she even managed to mess up the final lot!"

"What did she do, write that it was a colored stone instead of a colored diamond?" Mad snickered.

"No! Even worse. With spell-check, she still managed to spell 'colored' wrong!"

Both Mad and Louise roared in laughter at the absurdity of it all. They laughed so hard they had tears streaming down their faces.

"Unbelievable! I love how chaotic and unprofessional things can be behind-the-scenes at one of the most prestigious auction houses in the world, and how little clients know!" Mad said as she wiped the tears away.

"It's all about the brand."

Mad pulled out her phone to calculate the price per carat.

Louise took out a little note card from her pocket. "You want the per carat price for this? I have it here."

"You have it after buyer's premium?" Mad asked.

"I can't help you with that." Louise grinned. "You know more than I do, it's better to give clients a more attractive PPC."

"I know, I know. The tricks of the trade for those unassuming clients."

Mad picked up a few other rings but placed them back in the tray as soon as she saw the mounting. All of them had their pavilions covered with gold, which was a trick used to intensify the diamond's color.

"No good?" Louise questioned.

"They're all covered. I'm a bit skeptical."

"I know what you mean. A couple of years ago this dealer complained that he bought a green diamond from the Boss and that the mounting and the pavilion of the stone were both painted green, so it appeared even more vivid than it really was. No one believed him at that time . . . but now I wouldn't be surprised if she used that goldsmith nephew of hers to do it."

I wouldn't be surprised either.

Mad held up another ring that, according to the catalog, was by Cartier. She looked at it under her loupe to make sure there was indeed a maker's mark.

"The maker's mark is a little tricky for this one." Louise pointed at one of the corners of the shank. "It's on the side, do you see it?"

"Oh yes . . . this is a little tricky, but at least it has a stamp."

"You have to double-check these things. I heard once a specialist brought a ring back thinking it was by Mauboussin, but he misread the last letter. It was actually stamped Mauboussim!"

"That's hilarious!" Mad chuckled. "It's one of those real diamonds, but fake designer!"

"There's so many of those around! There's also plenty with the real designer mounting but somehow the original stone changed. You really have to know your stuff or you're screwed!"

"Like natural pearls and their clasps. It's so easy to restring the whole strand and change to a designer clasp. Who would know?" Mad giggled.

"No! For real?"

She winked at Louise.

"Let me ask you a question then." Louise huddled closer. "I never understood why you put 'Property of a Gentleman,' or 'Property of a Lady,' or 'Private Collector' on the catalog. I can't tell the client who the consigner is, so why would they believe me?"

"That's why you can only buy from a trusted source," Mad replied. "Of course, I've seen cases where the property doesn't belong to anyone notable but was labeled as such just to boost the salability."

"Mon dieu!" Louise cried. "It's a wicked game, *n'est pas*?"

"Mais oui, mon amie, mais oui."

"It's good that the prince has you. I don't know how many more dubious items he would have bought."

A helper placed a tray of emeralds of varying sizes and shapes on the table. Emeralds were fragile stones and were typically included and visible under the naked eye. But it was generally accepted, as eye-clean emeralds were extremely rare. Oil or resin were added to stabilize these emeralds and enhance the clarity. However, Mad was only interested in the ones that were naturally inclusion-free with no oil needed.

"These are all Colombian, no oil?" Mad asked.

"Of course! I didn't think you would want to see anything else."

Still, nothing stood out or stunned Mad.

"I heard you have one from Afghanistan this time?" she inquired.

Louise smiled. She uncovered a tray below her hands, revealing an emerald ring.

"You mean this one?"

"You know me so well." Mad smiled.

"Well, and almost every dealer here. They all want to see this one."

Mad looked up from her table. By now the preview room was filled to the brim with dealers and private buyers circling about and chatting. The room was getting too crowded. She needed to finish up soon.

She quickly flipped her catalog to the corresponding lot number. According to the description, this was a 10.21-carat non-oiled stone. Under the natural sunlight, the rectangular-shaped emerald was an amazing lush-green color. Not as dark as the high-quality Colombian ones, but very close indeed. The most wonderful part was that it was eye-clean and the fire was exceptional. Mad studied the certificate copy. It had a certificate and appendix from SSEF that read:

> ... possesses exceptional characteristics and merits special mention and appreciation ... saturated green color ... finest emeralds of Afghanistan from the Panjshir valley ... were historic places for gemstones ... size and quality are rare and exceptional ...

Mad grinned.

Finally, something worth bidding for.

She took some pictures with her phone. Satisfied, she placed it back on the tray.

"Anything else to see?" she asked Louise.

"Something fun," Louise replied and unveiled a Cartier panther bangle.

Mad twisted the swivel bangle and secured it on her arm. The bangle had the classic head of the iconic Cartier panther with emerald-green eyes. The diamonds were pavé-set all

45

throughout the body, and unique onyx spots further decorated the piece—no silly demantoid eyes and sapphire spots the new Cartier bangles were made of. It was a truly classic piece. Nonetheless, she felt something wasn't right.

Mad took a sip of her cappuccino and furrowed her brows.

"What's wrong?" Louise asked softly.

"Do you know where they got this piece from?"

"This one? Funny story! I heard it just came from a FedEx box! How odd, right? Such an important piece, but they shipped it via FedEx instead of Malca-Amit."

"I see," Mad said as she started to comprehend what was wrong. "Do you know if this was shipped from Russia?"

"That I don't know. Why?"

"There have been fakes made—especially these Cartier panthers—mostly from a Russian group. The workmanship is spectacular, and they have been known to target quite a few auction houses," Mad explained. "The worst part is, clients buy from auction houses and then resell at another auction house, so you don't know where the item originated from."

"Can't Cartier authenticate it?"

"Even Cartier doesn't know. They can check the workmanship and the serial number, but if that matches, what can they do? There could be a few legitimately well-made pieces with the same serial number floating about in the world right now."

"And you think this one could be fake?"

"Highly likely," Mad said as she sat back in her seat and crossed her arms.

"You think I should tell the specialists?"

"I don't think they care," Mad answered matter-of-factly.

"That's true; they have a budget to meet. I just won't show this to anyone anymore. It's not right."

Mad nodded in agreement.

"Let me get the next tray of items for you," Louise said as she left to put away the counterfeit.

Sitting alone at the table, Mad thought about how many people had fallen into these traps—and how many of these lots she had unwittingly sold to her clients. The notion gave her chills, and the sudden ringing of her phone startled her. It was Jackie.

"Hellooooo!"

"Hi, J."

"Are you ready for truffle pizzas and champagne showers?!" Jackie screamed exuberantly on the phone.

Mad instantly hunched over and covered her mouth so no one could hear her conversation.

"By the way, where are you now?" Jackie asked.

"I'm in Geneva."

"Doing what?"

Mad rolled her eyes. "At the auction previews! I've mentioned it to you about a million times!"

Mad and Jackie had been friends since their boarding school days. Their family backgrounds could not have been more different; Jackie was well known in the *Tatler* circuit, while Mad didn't even know what that was before she met her. Yet, they were each other's inner circle and would do anything for one another.

"Oh yes! How much longer will you be there for?"

"I just started!" Mad tried hard not to yell.

"Just?! Why does it always take you that long? Can't you be a normal human being and buy from a store?"

"What? And let them cheat me with those racked-up prices? No way! You know that's why I have a GG degree—so that I don't have to buy from the stores!"

"So, you won't be in Courchevel this weekend? It will just be me and Stuart?"

"And Steve."

"What?! You're leaving your husband alone in party central? Do you know how many hot Russian girls will be there? And how many other girls would jump on your lonely husband who's known for his big fat bank account and awesome jewelry collection?"

Situated in France, Courchevel was one of the largest ski resorts in the world and probably the most prestigious and glamourous. Known for bending over backwards for its über-rich clientele, Courchevel boasted an army of five-star hotels, Michelin-star restaurants, top-notch ski instructors, and a slew of designer boutiques. You didn't have to ski if you didn't want to; the notorious après-ski scene started at lunch, and dancing-on-top-of-tables parties did not end until the wee hours of the morning.

"Well, I've got you, right? I don't expect you'll miss out on anything. You have people telling you every bit of gossip."

Plus, I trust Steve.

"That's true. I do have eyes everywhere!" Jackie giggled.

"If I know you, you'll be reporting every thirty minutes. Where he is, what he's doing, who he is with, when he used the toilet—"

"Nonsense! So, I'll have my PA contact his and see when he would like to join us for dinner." Jackie cut Mad off.

"Sure," Mad said, though she suspected her husband might not like the idea of being the third wheel. "I'm sure he would like to see you and Stuart majorly PDA-ing."

"Did we do that last time?"

"Sure did." Mad's thoughts flashed back to when she'd endured them acting like a bunch of hormonal teenagers.

"Well, too bad. Can't stop the love! When you're in the mood, you're—" Jackie crooned.

"Which is every second of the day for you! Just try to control yourself, all right?"

"Right, right, anyhow, Clarisse is opening her atelier soon. Did you get the save-the-date yet?" Clarisse used to work at Minos with Mad. After she stood up against the Boss for Mad, she left the auction industry and built her own jewelry brand. Now, she was back with revenge, about to open her own atelier.

"I have it in my inbox, but I haven't checked it yet. I will be there for sure."

"Yah, I will be there too. We have to support our fellow women! Can't believe how much she has matured since having to endure that crazy psycho bitch."

"You mean the Boss?"

"Right, whatever her name is. Who calls themselves the Boss? Can't believe she terrorized so many people! So, when are you going to be in Courchevel again?"

Mad rolled her eyes.

"After the auctions are over," she managed to say.

"Which is?"

"After the weekend."

"Right. Can you explain why again?"

Exasperated, Mad replied plainly, "No."

"Riggghhhhtttt . . . whatever, I'll see you in a few days."

The man's eyes looked like they were about to pop out of his head. His jaw had practically dropped on top of the showcase glass. Mad tried to ignore the man who was now unashamedly staring at her, with his mouth still wide open in disbelief.

Is he still staring at me?

Mad had just walked into D's Geneva preview room and already felt like people were staring and whispering about her. Did she have something on her face? She would have steered clear of that man, who by now had discovered the decency to close his mouth, but she wanted to see the showcase directly beside him. Mad pretended he was invisible and quickly scanned the jewels. But she could still feel his gawking eyes as he slowly crept over, huddling next to her. Mad braced herself for the inevitable.

"Buongiorno! I'm Luigi, jewelry specialist at D's," he announced with an Italian accent.

Visibly annoyed, she slowly gazed up at a man wearing a fitted suit and skinny tie with groomed stubble on his face.

Mad tried to be polite and flashed him a megawatt, albeit fake, smile.

"Hi," she said plainly and hoped he would get the message and leave her alone.

"You're the infamous Mad!" he cried excitedly. "Sorry for being so audacious, but you're a superstar here! You're *my* hero! One day, I want to be just like you. Leave this auction house world and chase magnificent stones for the ridiculously rich and famous! Can I pleeeease help you with anything?"

Physically and mentally taken aback, she took a step back to create some space between her and his animated flailing hands.

"I'm just looking around," Mad said, resisting.

"Well, just let me know what you want to see, and I'll help you with it!" Luigi chirped blissfully like she had just made his day, which by the sound of it, she did.

Mad ignored him and continued browsing around the preview room as Luigi relentlessly followed closely behind like a lost puppy attached to his newfound master. He kept dropping comments here and there and suggesting which lots she should or should not bid on. The other specialists and helpers stole glances of her as she walked past them. If what Luigi said was true, it meant that they weren't hostile, but rather intrigued. Which made Mad feel vaguely strange and uncomfortable. But D's did have a much better collection this sale than Minos, and that benefitted everyone here.

"You know what?" She turned around and took a chance. "There are a few things I need to see, could you help me with it?"

"Yes! Of course!" Luigi cried delightedly. "Come sit at this table, and I'll go get them for you! Would you like a coffee?" he asked, but his tone sounded more like a statement.

"Umm . . . sure," Mad said. She took out a list from her bag and handed it over to Luigi.

He led her to a table towards the corner of the room.

"Super private, and the lights are all set up for you. I'll be back," Luigi whispered as if he were telling her a secret.

Mad sat down at the table and took out her tools and D's catalog. A helper brought over a nice hot cup of cappuccino and sugars on the side.

Not bad, at least they know I like cappuccinos.

After taking a sip, Mad instantly felt more relaxed. Luigi returned shortly with the first tray of lots. She expected him to leave her to her work, but instead he sat in the chair directly next to hers. He was so close, Mad could smell his musky cologne.

Very well then.

She held up a brooch designed as a camellia flower head. It was pavé-set spectacularly with different sizes of blazing-red rubies. Each petal elegantly overlapped each other, resembling the flower at its peak of beauty and grace. It could only be made by the jewelry maestro JAR. His masterpieces were sold to a distinguished few and only once in a while appeared at auction.

"Exquisite! What a beautiful piece," Mad praised. Luigi promptly answered, but instead of agreeing, he simply went in a whole different direction.

"You know you're a legend here. I mean, we all knew there was something fishy about the Boss and those minions of hers, but we didn't know it was so bad that they were on the Hong Kong anticorruption agency's radar. I mean, how many clients avoided KYC through her? Talk about money laundering on another level! I wonder how much they made under the table too. How is it possible no one ever said anything before? You're the first, and you brought them down. You're amazing!"

Mad stayed quiet as Luigi rambled on. He spoke so hastily, she thought he should really consider a career as an auctioneer.

"The working environment there must have been so toxic! Is it true that the Boss grabbed this marketing department girl by the arm at the subway station and wouldn't let her go until she agreed to lie about this other girl in an upcoming 360 individual evaluation?"

Mad wouldn't be surprised. She remembered how the Boss viciously yanked her arm when she ran out of that much-publicized final auction. The Boss even told Mad that she'd broken her heart. But Mad knew it was all a guise and had answered that was impossible, since she didn't have a heart. The Boss's stunned, defeated face was still freshly cemented in Mad's mind, probably never to be forgotten.

"I also heard the Boss was so stingy with your salaries and bonuses. You had no commission unless you were part of her 'gang.'" Luigi emphasized with four of his fingers held up as air quotes.

Without losing momentum he continued. "The most hilarious rumor of all was that sometimes she wouldn't even let you claim expenses! I heard she made this girl work over the weekend and wouldn't let her claim her lunch expense because it had a tiny bit of abalone in it! That the Boss told everyone and mocked the poor girl for treating herself."

Mad flashed back to once when the Boss boasted about a dinner she'd enjoyed the night before with her husband at a Japanese teppanyaki restaurant. She showed Veronica, Lisa, and Florence images on her phone of the delicacies they enjoyed: a South African abalone, which was as big as her palm, and an oversize Australian lobster made partly as fresh sashimi. The girls' obnoxiously high-pitched "oohs" and "aahs" still echoed like nightmarish shrills in Mad's thoughts.

"She did love those abalones," she blurted out unintentionally, but Luigi was so busy talking that he didn't hear her.

"I heard the Boss wouldn't let people take certain public holidays. But she did! Try doing that in Switzerland!" he said with his eyes widened. "She would say that she had to meet clients outside the office, but once she got caught going on holiday with her husband in Taiwan! Can you imagine, while everyone was slaving away back at the Hong Kong office."

I sure can. She would do anything to keep her husband from leaving her.

Luigi paused as if waiting for Mad to give him some confirmation. She instantly shook her head and rolled her eyes, indicating her continued disbelief of the Boss's bad behavior.

Satisfied, Luigi proceeded.

"I heard she had a crush on the president! *Mio Dio!* She got so jealous of this gorgeous girl in the client advisory department that she forbade her from traveling to previews where she knew the president would be!"

He's right. The Boss does have a crush on the president.

"I heard she insisted on using this most uncreative photographer who never made deadlines. He was so bad, even the president complained about him! He was so slow, the boys working in the panic room had to wait for him after hours every night and even had to work multiple weekends. Turns out the Boss was getting little gifts from the photographer, that's why she insisted on using him."

"Is *that* why?!" Mad cried. She'd always wondered why they had used the inept photographer who only caused trouble and lacked any originality in his work.

Unbelievable!

Luigi had definitely piqued her interest. She placed down an incredibly rare ring carved entirely out of one piece of emerald and asked, "What else did you hear?"

Delighted at finally capturing Mad's undivided attention, Luigi took one deep breath, then cracked open like a broken dam. "Well! They didn't tell you about the vendor terms and conditions on purpose because they were afraid of you getting ahead of them. They kept trying to steal your clients, and they would call and message them behind your back and wouldn't tell you when your client showed up at the office. They all ganged up on you to advance their careers. Everyone knows about Veronica and how in your face she would flower you with pleasantries just to get what she wanted, but when you're not looking, she would stab you a million times in the back!"

"Wow," Mad whispered, astonished, under her breath. She was frankly shocked at how much Luigi knew.

After taking a big breath, he resumed his rant. "Your ex– auction house was toxic. You know, there's a reason why Minos is associated with hell and the devil."

"How so?"

"The toxicity is rampant. Everyone knows," Luigi declared like a wise man. "One of the business managers, who shall not be named, didn't do her job during one of the press conferences. When she was confronted about her incompetency, instead of taking responsibility, she went straight to HR and claimed that her colleagues caused her extreme anxiety and excessive stress. Talk about excuses for not doing your job right!"

"She should be fired!" Mad exclaimed.

"No! She should not have been hired in the first place!"

That's true. Minos's HR department had been known to be quite useless.

"Unqualified yet self-justified," Mad whispered under her breath. She had met a handful of those before.

"How about that guy who was caught on CCTV? What's his name again? Anyhow, that disgruntled ex-colleague of yours had to work over the weekend. He was handling all these jade-ites in a cart, and he must have thought he was an F1 driver. He sped through the hallways and into the panic room, flinging the whole cart over!" Luigi took a deep breath for dramatization. "He goddamn broke a few pieces! *But* he picked them up and pretended he had nothing to do with it. He denied it! Only to be told that it was all captured on the CCTV."

"You're bullshitting me!" Mad was aghast. "Surely, no one could be that dumb. Of course, CCTV is everywhere. If what you're telling me is true, that guy is definitely beyond stupid!"

"My sources tell me that working at Minos was so bad, people threw things at each other!"

"No way! Where did you hear this from?" By now, Mad was fully immersed in the conversation, and not only was she ignoring the jewelry on the table that was piling up, but also the constant buzzing of her phone alerting her of messages. She took a quick glance. They were from Steve.

Steve:

Thinking of you constantly

Let me know when it's a good time to call

She should message him back, but she also didn't want to miss out on this once-in-a-lifetime chance of devouring the most delicious exposé ever. "Which department?"

"From which department? Of course, the jewelry department! Books, consignments, garbage bins! You name it! Not even that, I heard the Hong Kong jewelry team stole those fancy devil-red jewelry boxes from Geneva and New York, so that they could save a buck or two on expenses! How cheap! And clients think auction houses are elegant and professional; behind the scenes, people are savages!"

He's right.

Mad revisited scenes in her head of the constant chaos. How whatever did not fit the brand was covered up and polished over with insane amounts of marketing money.

That's where our salaries, bonuses, and commissions went!

Mad knew she should resume working, but Luigi had begun talking about even juicier tidbits of the industry. Like who had gambling debts; who sold their kidney to repay their debt; which dealer had a daughter as an escort; which dealer was certifiably insane; which dealer's wife ran away with which dealer; who slept with whom to get a promotion; clients and their most outrageous demands, etc.

She ended up staying for four straight hours of cappuccinos, pralines, and tantalizing gossip. Did Susan, Liam, and Henry know about these stories? If they did, how come none of them had told her? Surely Liam, who knew everything, would have. She'd ask him the next time she saw him.

But for now, much to Luigi's delight, she'd need to come back to D's tomorrow to finish up her work. And guiltily, she knew she had to reply to all those messages from Steve before he thought something horrible had happened to her.

Let me give him a call at the hotel room.

As she rushed towards the exit, a dealer in a large overcoat stopped her in her tracks.

"Hello, Ms. Madeleine," he said as he put his hand out, wanting to shake hers.

"Hello?" Mad repeated questionably. She kept her hands to her sides and instead stared rudely at the dealer's prominent oil-slicked hair speckled generously with white dandruff.

Undeterred, the dealer soldiered on, "I'm Antoine; here is my business card. If you need anything, please give me a call."

"Thank you, I will," Mad said as she took his business card.

Catching sight of the security guard moving towards them, Antoine quickly scurried away. It was common courtesy that you didn't solicit clients at someone else's place of business, and he obviously knew he wasn't welcome. Mad had had her fair share of dealing with these scumbags during her auction house days.

"Madame, is he bothering you?" the security guard asked as he approached.

Mad ripped the business card in two and tossed it in her bag.

"Not at all, not at all," she replied and turned around to leave. But not before catching a glimpse of the security guard's faint smile.

Mad dove into her Bellini as soon as the bartender placed it gingerly in front of her. It had been a long day two at D's, trying hard to fight off Luigi's gossipy tangents and reviewing all the important pieces at the same time. But with immense concentration and perseverance, she'd finally finished her work. The Four Seasons's bar was exceptionally busy tonight, but Mad still managed to find a seat at the handsome mahogany bar table, in direct view of the rows and rows of orderly liquor bottles, framed black-and-white pictures, and two nimble bartenders. The cacophony of cheerful clientele banter and jingle of clanging glasses and silverware created the white noise she needed to drown out the clatter in her head, while the dim chandelier lighting put her at ease. She could finally have her moment of peace before meeting up with Henry for dinner. Mad lifted her flute for another gratifying gulp but froze midway when she heard an abhorrently familiar voice.

"Hello, my dear."

Seeping with unwarranted haughtiness and confidence, the voice threw flashes of the most undesirable memories through her head. Tamping down the disgust rising in her throat, Mad slowly turned her head and took in the creature spewing those words between his forked tongue.

"Ja-vi-er." She cringed as she enunciated each syllable. If his name gave Mad butterflies in her stomach last year, it most certainly sounded like fingernails on a chalkboard at that very moment.

Javier, clearly unfazed by her obvious displeasure, smirked and leaned in to give Mad the customary triple cheek kiss greeting.

Having learned a few tricks this year, Mad swiftly tilted her head, marginally escaping Javier's lips, before holding her drink up for a victorious sip.

Although taken aback at her quick rebuke, Javier's thick skin did not allow him to surrender just yet. Relentless, he propped himself onto the conveniently empty seat right next to Mad.

Why did I think he was Adonis before? Was I really that blind?

His perpetual golden tan had vanished. Most likely from the lack of hedonic holidays he once had the pleasure of taking every month. His eyes looked tired, and the bags betrayed his age. But the most revealing sign was his thinned and receding hairline, the bane of men's ego. Like a lion who had wrecked his prideful mane, there was no longer a vibrant glow nor twinkling stars reverberating off him. He was all along just a carbon atom developing into feeble graphite, and not the prized diamond that everyone thought he was.

The bartender arrived just in time to keep Mad from lingering too long on Javier's deflated appearance.

"I'll have a dry martini, and for the lady here . . ." Javier gazed at Mad and gave her the finest smile he could manage. "May I get you another drink?"

She peered over at Javier but did not utter a word. The bartender waited patiently as Javier sat uncomfortably in the ensuing silence. Droplets of sweat appeared on his forehead before Mad finally ended his torture by simply replying, "No."

The bartender nodded professionally and briskly left the scene.

"So, what have you been up to, Mad?" Javier asked, refusing to acknowledge rejection. "It's so nice to bump into you here!"

"Is it?" Mad returned, deadpan.

"Of course, I've been thinking about you ever since we last saw each other!"

"Really?" she replied with annoyance.

"Yes! Mad, you're one of the most intelligent women I've met in my life. And I love what you've done with yourself. No more boring monotone outfits. Your red lipstick. Your aura. When I met you, you were a little girl, but now you've become a very attractive *and* perceptive woman."

And much more use to you, for all you really care.

Javier waited for her reply, but to no avail. Nonetheless, he persisted. "You know, I've always had a soft spot for you. I thought we shared such special moments together . . . moments I would never forget."

Mad couldn't contain herself and burst out laughing so loud people in their vicinity stopped what they were doing and, to Javier's horror, directed their attention at the source of the commotion. His distressed appearance showed that he most likely did not expect this reaction from her.

"For real, Javier?!" Mad cried out sarcastically in between her bouts of laughter. "Paaa-lease! What other cheesy lines do you have? Continue! *Please* continue! You're too funny!" She placed her right elbow on the bar table and propped her chin on her right hand. With a sly smile and daunting eyes, she waited for the court jester to amuse her.

"Well . . . ummm." Javier gulped as more sweat formed on his forehead. "Um . . . I thought what we had was special. The chemistry between us is undeniable. We should reconnect."

Mad melted into an exhilarating uproar! She laughed obnoxiously louder and deeper, tears forming in her eyes. Even the bartender who had just placed Javier's drink in front of him tried hard not to react, but a small smirk gave him away.

His face blazing hot with embarrassment, Javier gulped down his martini in one long drink.

"Go on, Javier. I would love to hear how we could 'reconnect,'" Mad scoffed as she blotted the tears away from her eyeliner.

His mouth hung open. He appeared reduced to something irrelevant, unimportant, and worthless. His figure and poise shrank further.

Mad grinned with delight. She was much enjoying this.

"Yes, I would like to know as well," someone said from behind. Both Javier and Mad swung their heads around and saw Henry.

As if someone had thrown him a life preserver, Javier exhaled with extreme relief.

"Oh! Your friend is here!" he cried ecstatically. "You won't be needing me anymore. Please excuse me, I'll let you two catch up!" He shot up from his chair and quickly placed some Swiss francs on the table. He was about to either give Mad a hug or a cheek kiss, but her glare and what she said next abruptly stopped him midtrack.

"Boy, bye."

Stunned, Javier turned around and fled, melting into the crowd.

"What did he want from you?" Henry asked as he sat on the empty seat.

"To reconnect," Mad chuckled.

Henry raised his eyebrows.

"Come here, you!" Mad jumped out of her seat and gave him a big hug. She'd missed her dear friend a lot. Friends were a rare commodity in the auction world, and Henry had been one of the few who had unselfishly supported and advised her. "What would the market leader like to drink? I'm buying tonight!"

"Hey, hey, hey! We're close, but we're not certain yet. We'll know tomorrow," Henry replied modestly, even though both of them knew his sale would be another record breaker. "Let me get dinner then."

"Of course, I was expecting it!" Mad said with a wink as she returned to her seat.

"Always my pleasure." He waved for the bartender and ordered a gin and tonic.

"So how have you been?" she asked. "It's so hard to catch you, now that you're the most important person in the watch industry."

"What?!" Henry exclaimed. "You're even harder to catch, Mrs. Lam. You're practically in a different time zone every day!"

"That's not true. I'm going to be in this one for more than a week! Plus, you know how much I enjoy this new job. So many new places to go, jewels to see, new experiences, and for once I feel like I'm in control. No politics, no cat fights, no ulterior motives, just plain old work."

"Look at you when you talk about your job! I can see stars in your eyes!" Henry laughed. "So how is Steve doing? Where is he now, by the way?"

Mad paused. She actually wasn't sure. She'd spoken to him on the phone last night, but she had been so tired she'd actually fallen asleep midconversation. Was he still in Asia, or was he on a flight already?

Mad furrowed her brows.

"You don't know?"

"I'm not sure if he's on the plane yet," she answered hesitantly.

"You know, you can't spend too much time away from your husband."

"Yes, that's why the most we spend apart is only two weeks."

"Two weeks?! Are you two Hollywood celebrities? That's an eternity for Irene and me! You have to get your priorities straight. What are you going to do when you have a kid? I try to be with my family as much as possible. Kids grow up so quickly, and in a blink of an eye they're not going to hang out with you. You have to treasure whatever time you've got with them."

"We're barely at your stage yet! We just got married!"

Henry shook his head. "What you two are doing now might work for a while, but you could become the Boss! All work, no family!"

"I would never become her," Mad snorted.

"She probably never thought she would end up like that either. Broken family, broken relationships—"

"Yes, because she has no regard for anyone but herself!" Mad cut in.

"She's too self-centered to care for anyone else in this world," Henry clarified.

"Which I'm not at all!" Mad defended herself.

"I'm not saying you are. You're far from it. But as a friend, my duty is to make sure your fate does not end up like hers."

Mad smiled. Henry was a genuine friend, but he worried too much. Many women juggle the demands of balancing work and family. She wouldn't be the first—and she would succeed. She was sure of it.

I'm wise enough to not fall into the Boss's predicament.

"Thanks, Henry. I'll keep that in mind."

His face softened.

"Now, show me pictures of that little squirt of yours!"

Henry pulled out his phone, but Mad's phone buzzed at the same time.

"Maybe it's Steve," he said hopefully.

She scanned the message. "It's not him. Remember Doreen from Minos's client advisory team?"

"Of course!" Henry sneered. "That awful woman treated you like an indentured servant and only knew how to steal other people's clients."

"Yup. She just wrote me a very pleasant email inviting me to tea." Mad grinned.

Henry rolled his eyes. *"Now* she wants to be your friend. You've got to give it to her. That woman can smell money from halfway around the world."

"My friends all know I don't drink tea," Mad scoffed and pressed "block" on her phone.

Henry raised his glass. "To tea."

She laughed and raised hers. "To tea!"

A few days after her dinner with Henry, Mad found herself scrolling down her last email and placing her phone on a table. She scanned the scene at the hotel café. Most of the dealers that had congregated thirty minutes ago had left for the Minos evening auction held upstairs. A few lingering souls sat at the corner table. From their somber faces and physical rigidity, they looked like they were disagreeing on some important business matter. The auction had already begun, but Mad was not in a hurry. She only had one lot to bid on, and it was not her time yet. In actuality, she was only going to bid on a total of three lots in Geneva. There just wasn't much that caught her discerning eye.

She had been scouring the smaller auction houses for potential acquisitions. She went through hundreds of lots, and the specialists all tried their best to persuade her to bid on almost everything. Regrettably, there was nothing she liked. Mad ended up revisiting the Big Two to finalize what she would ultimately bid on: the Afghanistan emerald ring at Minos and the ruby camellia brooch and carved emerald ring at D's. She was exhausted by the end of each day. She'd relished room service in her hotel bathrobe and her favorite noise-cancelling TV channel, CNN. At first, she enjoyed the time to herself, but by the night before the auctions, she felt a little restless. That strange feeling that something was amiss crept back.

Perhaps Henry was right. This kind of life is not sustainable. But I shouldn't be complaining! Hell! I'm having room service in a great big fancy suite in a five-star hotel! Albeit alone . . .

She did miss Steve and wished he was there with her at that moment so she could just talk to him about her day. She knew she would see him soon, but that feeling lingered.

Is it emptiness? No! How absurd! I'm not depressed!

That feeling crept up again as Mad sat alone in the café. She immediately shook it off and glanced down at her watch. It was time. She grabbed her bag and catalog and headed to the auction room.

"One hundred thousand . . . one fifty . . . two hundred . . . not with you . . ." Javier bellowed as Mad reached the familiar room. The imposing high ceilings, chandeliers, and glittering lights all reminded her how mesmerizing this industry could be, especially to the outsider. In-room bidders, in their suits and cocktail dresses, worked with their catalogs and paddles, concentrating intently as they sat in the multiple rows of blue velvet chairs flanked by the raised telephone-bidding podiums. Dully dressed telephone bidders spoke anxiously on the phone as they relayed the proceedings to their clients. Reporters with their cameramen crushed in the back corner of the room, waiting in anticipation for an auction record, their lenses all focused on Javier, who stood in the middle of the stage, elevated on a courtly rostrum.

Ding!

Mad checked her phone.

Mr. Jain:

Your 2 o'clock

Mad looked up and instantly saw Mr. Jain, the largest natural-pearl dealer in the world, waving at her with an empty seat next to him. She smiled and walked towards her dear friend.

"Mad, how have you been?" Mr. Jain said as he gave her the routine triple cheek kiss greeting.

"Good, good. How's the sale going?" she asked.

"Most sold under the estimate. You know what that means."

"That they're hemorrhaging profits, so the sold-by-lot percentage looks better on paper."

"It's like watching sharks circling and taking bites," Mr. Jain snickered.

"Got anything you like?"

"You know, natural pearls. I got a few already. The prices are quite good. I hope you are not competing with me!"

"Don't worry about it. I'm only here for one lot, and pearls are not what I need."

"Let me guess, you're here for the Afghan?" Mr. Jain chuckled. "Like what everyone else is here for."

"Is that so?" Mad raised her eyebrows. "That bad, huh?"

"I've only heard the whole world talking about it the last week I've been here! Good luck."

"Thanks. We'll see how it goes; I have a sense of how much this should go for."

"Lot 1143, the Afghanistan emerald ring," Javier interrupted their conversation.

Mad turned her attention to the front of the room.

"We can start at five hundred thousand. Five hundred thousand Swiss francs!"

A sea of hands shot up from the seats, and a flurry of paddles flapped wildly on both sides of the telephone podiums. This lot was indeed as popular as rumored.

As if a renewed confidence surged through him, Javier exuberantly called out the bids.

"Five hundred fifty thousand Swiss francs! Six hundred thousand! Six fifty with the gentleman in the back! Seven hundred! Seven hundred fifty! Eight hundred! Eight hundred fifty thousand with Lucia on the phone, thank you!" Javier beamed.

The commotion slowly abated but not Javier's spirit. "Nine hundred thousand, not with you, Lucia," he cried as he swung his gavel dramatically, pointing towards a man seated in the middle of the room. Mad recognized him; it was the jewelry agent, Hari, bidding for one of the big international jewelry brands.

In return, to match Javier's theatrical act, Lucia waved her paddle spastically.

"One million, thank you, Lucia," Javier said as he again swung his gavel back towards the telephone podium. Hari shot his left finger up, indicating that he would follow. His right hand grasped his cell phone tightly as he mumbled to his client on the line.

"One point one million, not with you, Lucia," Javier grinned.

This time, Lucia flung her paddle up with such force that she almost knocked the specialist on the right off her seat.

"One point two million! Careful there, Lucia!"

Hari held his finger up.

"One point three million? Yes, thank you!"

Lucia swung her paddle again.

"One point four million, thank you, Lucia."

Only to be overshadowed by Hari's response.

"One point five million, not with you, Lucia."

Lucia spoke quickly on the phone, trying to convince the client it was worth it to bid once more. Clearly, she was persuasive, because she flipped her paddle lightly.

"One point six million, Lucia!"

The price was already over the high estimate. Mr. Jain looked over at Mad, wondering when she would bid.

Mad did not budge. Neither did Hari.

"One point seven million?" Javier asked Hari hopefully. But Hari had his head down as he mumbled on his phone. He was so preoccupied with his conversation that he was oblivious to Javier's genuine concern.

"Yes? No?" Javier pleaded, more anxiously this time. Hari was still in his own world.

"Sorry, sir," Lucia choked as she broke up the awkwardness. "Sir, I misheard my client. One point six million not with us." She blushed vibrantly as she announced the mistake.

Javier looked to be gritting his teeth and smiling forcefully. He tried, despite clearly being angry, to show that he was managing the situation.

Taking a deep breath, he barked, "One point five million then, with the gentleman in the room." He glared at Lucia as she shrank expeditiously in her seat and collapsed into an even darker shade of red.

Regrettably for Javier, Hari was still fully immersed in his phone conversation and didn't notice the change of events— particularly, the change in mood in the room. A visibly distressed and sweaty Javier waved his gavel back and forth as he tried to grab Hari's attention, but to no avail. As Javier tried to engage Hari, others chuckled and whispered gleefully at the debacle.

The corners of Mad's mouth curled up into a wide broad smile. If there was one thing she liked, it was bidding in the midst of chaos, when the almighty auction house has unhinged itself.

It's time.

As clear as a conductor's baton, Mad lifted her paddle and announced her bid, "One point six million." The room fell silent as everyone craned their heads around to see where the voice was coming from.

"It's her . . . the prince's advisor . . . it's her" echoed throughout the room as they discovered the identity of the new contender. At first, Javier's facial expression erupted with relief, but as soon as he too craned his neck and narrowed his focus on the source of his redemption and realized it was Mad, he plunged back in. His face cringed with pain as he tried to suppress his shock, but the paleness of his skin tone betrayed him.

Mad smirked.

Let's have some fun.

"Um, yes, ma'am, one point six million with Mad—I mean at the back. I mean in the room! Yes! One point six million," Javier managed to say with as much poise as he could muster.

Hari, who had finally poked his head up from his phone and realized that he didn't have the lead, shouted, "One point seven million!"

Javier turned to see if Lucia would be able to pull off another bid, but she shook her head. Returning his gaze to Mad, he waited for her response. As did everyone in the room, who all knew perfectly well that she represented the prince and had access to endless funds.

However, none of them got what they expected. Instead, they watched as Mad chatted with Mr. Jain, blatantly ignoring everyone around them.

"Um, madam, would you like to bid?" Javier inquired.

Mad didn't even glance up. She simply lifted her index finger at him, commanding him to wait for as long as she wished.

Javier stood stunned on the rostrum. This was surely the only time in his auction career that he had been publicly belittled and embarrassingly paralyzed. A round of snickers and giggles descended upon the room.

A delightful minute later, Mad, fully satisfied, finally turned her head around to face the gravely scarlet-faced Javier. Sweat dripped from his forehead as she haughtily flicked her paddle. Mute, Javier turned to Hari for a response.

"One point eight five?" Hari asked.

"Um, sure," Javier muttered, losing his command and forgoing his authority.

With dread in his eyes, he turned back to Mad just in time to see her shoot daggers at him. He quickly dropped his head down, to avoid further eye contact presumably, and picked up a glass of water.

"I'm afraid one hand might not be enough to lift that *enormous* glass of water," Mr. Jain whispered amusingly into Mad's ear.

Mad laughed, but enough was enough. She was ready to end the game.

"One point nine million," she called out.

Hari finally surrendered and shook his head solemnly.

"Right," Javier said as he unceremoniously wiped the gathering sweat off his forehead with his jacket sleeve and hammered his gavel lightly on the rostrum. Exhaling a breath of relief, he looked like he had just survived an execution.

"Will you be going to D's tomorrow?" Mr. Jain asked.

"Yes, will I see you there?"

"Yes, but just a word of advice, Mad. You might want to think of a way to bid more discreetly tomorrow. You're too conspicuous. You don't want people to know your cards."

Mr. Jain was right. Mad could feel it too. Everyone knew she was representing the prince and how deep her pockets were. She needed to be more subtle.

"Thank you, Mr. Jain. I'll have to figure out something."

But she wasn't sure what yet.

The next day, Mad walked into D's auction room ready to bid for the camellia flower brooch and the carved emerald ring. The room was bursting with people as she recognized dealers, clients, and specialists from yesterday's Minos auction; some of them spotted her instantly, and she could feel them watching her every move. From the corner of her eye, she could see a jittery Luigi scanning the room, most likely for her. He had been messaging Mad nonstop the last few days. Reminding her when her lots would come up, that he would save seats in the auction room for her, that she could call him or message him anytime of the day she needed anything, etc. . . . As Luigi's laser-sharp eyes moved towards her direction, she dove out of the room, just in time to avoid a lengthy, suffocating encounter.

This is not ideal at all for me.

Mad slowly stepped away, walking towards nothing in particular. She needed to assess the situation, *pronto*. As she strolled along thinking about what to do, she found herself in front of the hotel bar. Her eyes lit up.

Brilliant! At this hour of the day, I'm sure this would be the last place anyone would expect to see me!

Smiling broadly, she made a beeline towards the empty bar table and sat herself down on a stool farthest away from the entrance. The bartender, who had been standing alone wiping a cocktail glass, glanced up at the untimely guest.

"It's happy hour somewhere," Mad explained. "I'll have a blanc de blanc, thank you."

The bartender nodded and went to work straight away. Mad pulled out her phone and logged into D's live-auction website. The auction had just begun, and it was a good twenty lots before her first one. Her drink arrived, and she relaxed as she waited. Fifteen more lots. Ten more lots. Raised voices and claps from the auction room trickled into the bar. Five more lots.

Ding!

Luigi:

Where are you?!

The carved emerald ring is coming up
NOW!!!

Mad ignored the message. She was waiting for something else.
One more lot.

Ring!

Ring!

Ring!

Mad smiled. This was what she was waiting for. She picked up the phone.

"Hi, Henry, are you in position?" she asked.

"I sure am, right where you want me to be," he replied.

Last night, Mad knew she needed to devise a plan ASAP if she was going to bid as discreetly as possible. So, she enlisted Henry's help. He would be Mad's eyes and ears as he bid on her behalf. She knew he would excel as her telephone bidder because Henry knew her temperament and auction lingo. Plus, with him, people probably thought he was bidding for an Asian tycoon and not, for a second, the prince.

"Are you ready? It's the carved emerald ring," Henry alerted Mad.

"Yup, you know what to do."

From her phone, Mad heard the auctioneer spitting out the prices as fast as a bullet train. Henry hummed as he waited for the right moment.

"Where are you, by the way?"

"You would never guess."

"The toilet? No, can't be."

"The bar."

"Nice choice! Oh! Heads up. Fifty thousand, Mad; it's way over the high estimate," he reported.

"Let's do it!"

"Fifty-five with us," Henry relayed. "Sixty with a dealer in the room."

"Bid," she said.

"Sixty-five with us . . . and still with us, annnnnnd . . . it's ours."

Mad smiled and took a celebratory sip of blanc de blanc.

That was easy.

"Get ready, it's the camellia brooch now."

"OK," Mad replied.

The price quickly reached the low estimate of one point one million dollars. But Henry didn't say anything, indicating that it was not time. The background cries of frenzied bidding continued until the pace inevitably slowed down.

"Three point five million, Mad. Shall we enter the ring?" Henry finally asked.

"We shall."

Loud gasps and claps erupted. It was so sudden that even the bartender shot his head up and glanced towards the doorway.

It must be Henry's bid.

"It's with us," Henry reported.

He had no sooner spoken than exuberant cries exploded once more.

"Three point seven against us. With Edwin—Singapore," he said sternly.

"Bid," Mad instructed.

"Three point eight million with the gentleman in the back," the auctioneer barked, confirming Henry's bid.

"Still with us, but he's talking incessantly on the phone. He's really trying to squeeze this out of his client. I don't think he'll be giving up yet. Oh, and here he goes."

"Three point nine million, thank you, Edwin," the auctioneer shouted with elation.

"He managed. Shall we?" Henry asked.

Before Mad could reply, her phone alerted her of a message.

Ding!

Mad read:

> Stop bidding

She instantly understood the urgency of the message.

"No, don't bid!" Mad promptly instructed Henry.

"You sure?" he asked hesitantly. "He might give up if we throw in another bid and—" He barely had time to finish the sentence when excitement erupted from the other side of the room.

"Someone just bid four million. Edwin is definitely out. He's shaking his head. You want to—"

He was interrupted by the deafening sound of the gavel hammered down on the rostrum followed by an eruption of wild applause. It was over. For a split second Mad's heart stopped as she questioned her judgment. Holding her breath, she didn't dare let go until . . .

> Ding!

Mr. Jain:

> It's done

Mad smirked. Her plan worked.

Mad:

> Thank you for your help! I'll have the
> payment transferred to your account today

Mr. Jain:

No problem

That was the most fun I've had in ages

Let's do it again next time

Mad chuckled and flung her phone down on the table. She had also enlisted Mr. Jain to help her divert attention and bid on her behalf.

As she took a sip from her drink and savored her ingenious scheme, Henry plopped down in the stool next to her.

"Did he message you?" he asked hastily.

"Yes, he did. Four million is a record price, but nonetheless it's worth it."

"Was I good or not? If this auction thing doesn't work out for me, I should consider a career in acting! You should have seen Edwin's face! He was exhausted by the time he persuaded his client to bid once more against me, then when Mr. Jain swung his paddle up and Edwin saw the hesitation on my face, he just withered and gave up."

"I see you and Mr. Jain are both enjoying this a bit too much!"

Henry laughed. "Yes indeed! Enlist me next time, please! Now, where is my drink?"

CHAPTER FOUR

Courchevel 1850

"Are we there yet?" Mad asked, her eyes squinting at the excruciatingly bright white landscape outside the car window. Like white opals, the sun's rays hitting the snow produced a dazzling iridescence, as if to welcome her up the mountain. If only she wasn't so hungover, she could have enjoyed it.

"*Mais oui*, madame! About forty-five more minutes," the chauffeur replied, or rather chirped a bit too annoyingly for Mad's current state of mind.

She drowsily pulled out her phone. 4:30 p.m. She had passed out for a full two hours after popping in two Panadols to alleviate her debilitating headache. Instead of going to bed last night at a decent hour, Mad and Henry had been celebrating, or more precisely, drinking excessively, in jubilation of their successful bidding scheme. One drink became two, two drinks became a bottle, and the next thing she knew, Mad woke up to a tingling hot sensation, which turned out to be a hot ray of sun, simmering down on her face. She realized she was lying flat on her back, on the bed, in her hotel room, wearing her out-fit from the night before—even her boots. The bedside clock had alarmingly informed her that it was already 11:30 a.m.; she should have left for Courchevel two hours earlier to make it for lunch with Steve! Her head thumped from dehydration as she blindly used her hands to find her phone and message both the chauffeur and Steve that she would be late.

Begrudgingly, she slid off the bed, slowly crawled into the bathroom to shower, painstakingly packed her luggage, headed down to the lobby to check out, then grabbed something to eat. She had only managed to take a few sips of the chicken broth before surrendering to her nauseous stomach.

"We just passed Saint Bon. It's 1100," the chauffeur reported.

The ascent up the beautiful villages of Courchevel had begun. Located in Les Trois Vallées, the largest ski area in the world, Courchevel encompassed six villages, which occupied different altitudes on the mountain. Each village had a name paired with a number that indicated the altitude above sea level. The farther up you went, the more glamourous, flashy, and glittery it got. Saint Bon, the lowest village that they'd just passed, was located 1,100 meters above sea level.

Hovering on the side of the road, a ginormous ski jump came into view.

"This was built for the 1992 Albertville Winter Olympics. Now we're at Le Praz 1300," the chauffeur said.

Shortly after, a charming rustic French village with snow-covered roofs emerged from seemingly nowhere. Mad admired the storybook scenery before snow again engulfed her view; then in the horizon, wooden storied buildings and chalets loomed ahead.

"In front of us is Le Tania 1400. It was built in 1992 for the Winter Olympics. The dormitories are now converted to apartments. Very family friendly."

More chalets dotted the landscape as the road became narrower and steeper.

"This is Courchevel Village 1550. Not as exciting."

Finally, they drove past a village lined with shops, restaurants, and far more people and traffic.

We must be close.

"Moriond 1650. We're almost there."

Moments later . . .

"And here we are. 1850."

Mad tried not to gasp as they entered Courchevel 1850, the apex of all the villages, the shiny beacon of luxury. What appeared before her eyes was nothing like what she had seen in the other villages. Flanked ubiquitously on either side of the winding road were ritzy designer brands the likes of Hermès, Chanel, and Fendi. Jewelry ateliers Moussaieff and Chopard sat housed in brightly lit wooden boutiques, catering to laughing clients with glasses of alcohol in hand. Erected in the center of the village, the main gondola and lift hub served a swarm of skiers in fancy outfits followed by the famed world-class Courchevel ski instructors in discerning red.

A horse-drawn carriage carrying a group of children and their nanny in gleeful spirits overtook their car but made a left turn on a forked road as they made a right. The echoing peals of laughter dissipated as they went even farther up the mountain, following a slew of private hotel and Scott Dunn cars chauffeuring their guests about. They passed by countless opulent hotels and chalets housing fine-dining restaurants and bars. Mad half expected a dozen popping bottles of champagne and a flurry of golden confetti on arrival at L'Apogée Courchevel.

Instead, they stopped at a rather charming traditional wooden chalet, albeit on a much larger and majestic scale.

Directly beneath a protruding snow-covered arch, a line of bellboys in swanky dark wool pants, fitted sweaters, and chili-red scarves were assembled. Each smiled zealously upon the arrival of their guest. Amidst the French version of this Banana Republic–like advertisement stood Steve, waiting patiently for her.

"I'm so sorry for being late!" Mad croaked hoarsely as she got out of the car. Clearly, she had not fully recovered from her hangover.

Steve kissed her on the lips and peered at her dark eye circles.

"Looks like someone had a rough night. I'm guessing your hunting trip went well?"

"So sorrrrryyy! Henry and I were celebrating," she answered sheepishly.

"Yah, until 3:00 a.m. last night!"

"How did you know?!"

I'm not even sure myself!

"Henry reassured me that you got back to your hotel room safely last night," Steve added sternly. "That is the least he could do."

That's how I got back to the hotel . . .

"I see," Mad said, wanting to explain why last night called for celebration. "Well, you see, we were—"

"Excuse me, would this be all?" one of the bellboys interrupted. Mad's luggage was already unloaded from the trunk and on a golden trolley. She nodded.

"We'll send them right up to your room," the bellboy said, still smiling. The whole group swiftly disappeared, leaving Mad and Steve alone.

Mad was about to continue her explanation, but Steve gently took her hand in his. "Shall we?" He smiled.

She loosened up and smiled back. She didn't need to explain herself. Steve understood.

He led her into the hotel, where the doors opened to a pristine marble-clad lobby with golden light fixtures. Upon seeing Steve, the manager instantly lit up and ushered them through a hallway, leading into a sleek bar filled to the brim with beautiful people in posh après-ski outfits. Sitting on the leather sofas and velvet armchairs next to jet-black coffee tables, women wore trendy designer brands such as Bogner, Moncler, and Fendi—the brand names and logos boldly emblazed on their fur-trimmed jackets, fitted pants, cashmere turtlenecks, fur hats, and snow boots. With their sleek makeup and gorgeous blown-out hair, they sipped on sexy martinis and hot toddies. They didn't look like they'd skied today but rather just woke up for the après-ski scene. Without any makeup on and still dressed like she had just rolled out of bed, which in hindsight she had, Mad felt extremely out of place. She wished she'd at least put some lipstick on. Fortunately, they were seated in a private corner, away from the bustling crowd; a bottle of champagne chilled at the side of their table.

"So how were the last few days?" Mad asked as she stopped staring and turned to her husband. "Did you ski? Did you see Jackie?"

Steve sat ever so handsome and suave on the dark-green velvet armchair in front of her. The black turtleneck and heather-grey pants he wore amplified his broad shoulders and swimmer's physique.

How is it that he can look so good just sitting there?

"Just a few runs here and there. I had dinner with Jackie the other night, and we've had drinks a few times. Really, I've just been sitting around and waiting for my wife to arrive so I could tell her in person that I miss her a lot."

Steve leaned closer for a kiss, putting his hand on Mad's as she gazed intently at him. As their lips touched, all thoughts of the past auctions, jewelry, and the feelings of loneliness melted away and made room for warmth and security, which then shifted wonderfully into dizzying temptation. She closed her eyes and inhaled the scent of citrus and faint sandalwood undertones from the cologne Mad loved. Desperate for more, she took another deep breath of the intoxicating fragrance, but a waft of floral that exuded intense femininity pierced her senses and knocked her out of her reverie. The gradual realization of an odd heaviness to her side slowly pulled Mad's eyes open and Steve's lips away.

Jackie had sat down right beside her.

"How long have you been here?" Mad asked, stunned and feeling a little vulnerable that her best friend had been staring at her in the midst of an intimate moment.

"Oh, I'm not sure," Jackie said nonchalantly, in her chic white pants, purple turtleneck, cropped grey mink jacket, and matching boots. She brushed her hair back casually with her hands, revealing a pair of pear-shaped amethyst ear studs the size of costume jewelry, as she asked, "How long have we been sitting here, love?"

Mad swung her head in the direction Jackie was looking at. Stuart had been sitting right next to Steve all along too!

She looked at Steve, but oddly enough, he didn't seem flustered at all. He actually appeared aloof and collected.

I'm learning something new about my husband every day . . .

"Maybe a few seconds—or a minute," Stuart replied. "I'm not sure. But hey, how are you, Mad? We've missed you this weekend!" He jumped up and gave her a hug and two kisses on the cheek.

Mad liked Stuart. Moreover, she liked that Jackie was going out with Stuart. Jackie had dated all sorts of guys; most of them Mad couldn't have cared less about and didn't even attempt to remember their names. Some she even overtly disliked. The vast range of Jackie's boyfriends, be they models, celebrities, or bankers, all had one thing in common—they were always at her beck and call. There was one who had been so enamored by Jackie, he followed her around all day long, carried her bags, fetched her this and that, and incessantly took photos of her. It wasn't long before she got bored and disposed of him. They all treated her like a princess, and whatever she wanted she got from them. None of them had a distinguishable personality. None of them stood out. None of them were special.

Except for the last one, Eddy. If there was one thing Mad learned from her auction days, it was that first impressions could be deceiving.

Eddy was a horror. He started out just like all the other boyfriends. He worshipped the ground Jackie walked on. He was an "artist." He sketched, painted, wrote poetry, and showered Jackie and friends with pleasantries. Yet, there'd been something off. His dark, angry side eventually surfaced. The culprits, sadly classic, were childhood traumas stemming from abusive, narcissistic parents.

Things were worse when he drank. He became defensive, jealous, and obsessive. He mimicked what his parents did to him and mocked, belittled, and lashed out at Jackie. She'd stayed with him for all the wrong reasons and above all else because she pitied him. Finally, through Mad's forceful persuasion, Jackie knew the relationship had to end. Eddy didn't need Jackie; her actions only fueled the monster within him.

Eddy needed professional help. Jackie eventually left him, filed a restraining order, and hired more bodyguards. Those were grim days; Jackie vowed to take a break from the dating scene—until Stuart showed up.

Stuart was different. In him, Jackie had finally met her match. He had his own ideas, could stand his ground, and didn't let Jackie push him around. And, Jackie actually listened and paid attention to him. In many ways, they complemented each other. Mad didn't know much about Stuart before they met, but she did hear through the grapevine that he had a reputation for being a money-burning, make-it-rain, self-indulging playboy. But again, like first impressions, reputations could be deceiving too. And she was willing to trust her gut on this one.

"Mad, don't worry, you and Steve can kiss as long as you want." Jackie giggled. "I'm sure we've taught Steve a few moves over the weekend."

Steve closed his eyes, knitting his brows as Stuart patted his back in playful sympathy. "Sorry, pal."

"It's just a little creepy the way you stared at us without announcing your arrival!" Mad said as she hugged Jackie.

"You've got a lot to catch up on! We've got a table tonight at La Mangeoire," Jackie announced.

Mad's eyes widened.

More drinking?!

Completely comprehending Mad's expression, Jackie quickly pointed out, "Nothing too wild."

Mad took a sip out of her glass of water.

I don't remember a time when it didn't get too wild with Jackie.

"I'm sure you're going to want to do some skiing tomorrow morning," Jackie continued. "So, we have lunch at Pilatus booked for one thirty. Let's do that toboggan run together tomorrow too! And we've got to go to Pierres for the dessert buffet! I've been craving that! I've booked Chabichou for tomorrow night. When do you want to go to Cap Horn for some truffle pizzas?"

Mad scanned Steve's face, hoping that he might hesitate at the notion of going to a club tonight.

"Do you want to go to the club?" Mad asked.

However, Steve didn't get it.

"I don't mind, it's up to you."

"Come on, you guys, don't be party poopers!" Jackie interjected. "Loosen up a bit. When was the last time we had fun together?"

"A few weeks ago?" Mad said.

"Exactly, too long!"

As the girls bickered, Steve turned to Stuart. "How was your second drop this afternoon?"

"Not as great as our first drop this morning. I think the ski instructor was getting a little tired after the shot we fed him!" Stuart laughed.

Overhearing their conversation, Mad shot Steve an inquisitive look.

"We went heli-skiing this morning," Steve explained. "But I only went for one drop so I could make it back in time to the hotel."

"I didn't know you heli-skied!"

Note to self: so, turns out my husband is a daredevil too!

"I didn't, until Stuart asked me to join him," Steve said. "He told me it would be fun and that I would be able to handle it."

"There's always a first!" Stuart added. "And you handled it like a pro!"

"I have to say, that was quite fun indeed. Thanks for making me do it!"

"No problem! Thanks for accompanying me!"

Baffled, Mad gaped at Jackie, searching for answers.

"Don't stare at me, of course I didn't go! Crazy male testosterone! I went to the spa and popped into Hermès and Chanel. Honestly, they've been inseparable! I have felt like the third wheel these last few days!"

"When did this bromance strike up?" Mad asked, bewildered.

Didn't Steve have doubts about Stuart the last time they talked?

"I don't know." Jackie smiled. "But it's nice to have Steve's consent. He is my best friend's husband, after all. It means a lot to me."

Mad smiled back.

It sure does.

A tray of shots carrying clear liquid arrived at their table. Mad hadn't realized that they ordered yet. She turned towards Steve.

"Don't look at me," Steve said and pointed at Stuart.

"Welcome shots from Courchevel!" Stuart cried enthusiastically.

"Yes, come on, you have to catch up!" Jackie joined in the enthusiasm.

Still feeling queasy from the night before, Mad hesitantly took a shot glass and chucked the abhorrent liquid down her throat, hoping that she wouldn't throw up in the process.

Oh, not as bad as I thought it would be!

Mad set her empty shot glass down, and Jackie placed a new one in front of her.

"For being late!" Jackie stated.

I do deserve this one.

Caving in, Mad scrunched up her eyes and again threw the shot into her mouth. She hoped the second time would be as harmless as the first, but quickly abandoned the thought as it burned its way down her throat. Gasping for air, she grabbed the lemon wedge chaser and sucked on the juices until they alleviated the revolting aftertaste.

Ring.

Ring.

Ring.

Mad glanced down at her phone. It was Fiona, the prince's personal assistant and most trusted confidante. The combination of beauty and brains, she was the reason Mad had met the prince and found this current dream job of hers.

"Hi, Fiona."

"Hey, Mad, I hope I'm not disturbing you."

"Oh no, I'm with Jackie, Stuart, and Steve."

"Oh! Please say hi to them for me. And please thank Jackie for the exquisite perfume she sent over. It's absolutely amazing! Lasts an eternity!"

Mad looked up. "Fiona says hi," she said, turning to Jackie, "and she thanked you for the perfume. She said it lasts an eternity?"

"My pleasure." Jackie winked.

Mad made a mental note.

Must ask Jackie what perfume Fiona is talking about.

"She said 'my pleasure.'" Mad returned to the call. "So, how are you doing?"

"Oh, pretty good, we're enjoying some cooler weather finally. Which is nice, but nothing beats skiing. I absolutely crave the cold, freezing weather!"

Mad didn't recall it being chilly when she arrived. "Oh, it's not too cold here in Courchevel, might not be cold enough for you then. But there's snow."

"I'm thinking Harbin. I heard it gets to negative-thirty Celsius. That's what I'm talking about!" Fiona exclaimed.

"Gosh, that sounds cold! They have the annual ice festival; I heard it's pretty amazing. It runs until late February, so you can go before it ends."

There was silence on the line.

"Hello?" Mad asked.

Fiona finally spoke again.

"Do you mind stepping aside for a moment? For a bit of business talk?" Fiona's tone was stern.

"Not at all." Mad stood up. "Give me a minute."

Automatically, Steve handed Mad her coat. She flung it on her back as she charged out of the bar, through the lobby, and out the hotel entrance.

Once out of earshot, she asked, "What's going on?"

"Congratulations on the latest acquisitions! We love the ruby ring you found in Tuscany. Beautiful fiery red, and the old material is extraordinary. The JAR camellia is wonderful! The craftmanship is superb. The Afghanistan! How peculiar! Absolutely love! The carved emerald ring? Now that is a special find. Who nowadays would dare waste so much material for one ring? Absolutely unique! Very good prices too. We knew you were the best for this job!"

"That's great. I'm glad you like them already—and only from the images I sent you! I can't wait till you see the real pieces; they will be great for the prince's collection."

"Talking about the collection, I actually have something to tell you."

"Yes?"

"The prince has decided to exhibit part of his jewelry collection in Venice and would like you to curate the pieces. We need a few hundred, and they should range from traditional to modern masterpieces. The theme naturally is 'unity.' We want to show that beauty comes from a partnership of people all around the world. The origin of the gemstone, the expertise of the craftsman, the creativity of the designer . . . all put together to create something beautiful."

"That's a wonderful idea! Imagine! The Burmese miner who dug up the sapphire rough; the Thai cutter who meticulously added facets and fire into the stone; the French designer who created the jewelry masterpiece; and finally the Swiss craftsman who mounted it all together," Mad said as she envisioned the whole process in her mind. "And that's just a Burmese sapphire! Think of other gemstones, like diamonds, pearls, and jadeite!"

Mad really loved the idea. In actuality, it was the unity of everyone, from different places around the world, that contributed to the beauty of a masterpiece.

"You know how we strive to educate and promote the marriage between jewelry and culture, nature, and human craftmanship," Fiona continued. "Exhibiting in Venice will increase the awareness of our mission and elevate us on a world platform. All proceeds will go to funding the education of jewelry students with no means of getting into the industry."

"Such as gemological courses?"

"Yes. You know more than all of us do how expensive the courses at GIA, SSEF, and Gübelin can be. How could anyone even start a jewelry business after spending all that money on those diplomas?"

"So, scholarships for people with no industry or family background?"

"Yes! Who wouldn't want a 'GG' next to their name? It instantly gives you credibility."

That was indeed a great idea. People from the outside didn't know how nepotistic the jewelry industry was, and many with no background had no other choice but to start off at auction houses. If you were lucky, the auction house would fund your exorbitant gemological courses. And if you weren't? You ended up somewhere like Minos, with the Boss who cared nothing about your future.

"I can only imagine how many people you could help with this scholarship and how it would change the whole jewelry industry for the better!" Mad said excitedly. "Oh, Fiona! This is wonderful news! There are so many highlights we could use already!"

"Yes. The prince wants it to be a strong exhibition, and you know the weakest part of his collection are the modern pieces."

"Yes, I know. I'm going to need to acquire some new jadeite, rubies, and sapphires, pearls . . ." Mad dictated her thoughts out loud. "I have to go to Burma! And Bangkok! Hong Kong! Australia for pearls! Logan will be happy about that. Recut the diamonds in New York! Gosh! There is so much to do! I'll email you the pieces I think would be good from the current collection and other pieces that I would like to add to the exhibition."

"That sounds great. I'll work with the production and marketing agency so we can start designing and promoting the exhibition."

"Perfect!"

Mad was thrilled. This was something big and meaningful for the industry—and for her too.

"One thing, Mad." Fiona paused as Mad sensed a change in tone.

"Yes?"

"The exhibition is in less than two months—a month and a half to be exact."

Mad's heart skipped a beat.

"*What?!* You're kidding!"

"No, I'm not. I'm very sorry about this."

Mad collected herself from the initial shock and calculated in her mind. If she were to gather all the missing pieces, including recutting and recarving stones, shipping, and showcasing plus buffer time, it meant she would have to leave Courchevel tomorrow. She gulped.

"I'm so sorry, Mad," Fiona said as she deducted Mad's line of thought.

Mad knew this exhibition was important. No, essential. It was a chance to show the world the prince's collection, promote the industry, unify cultures, and most important, support people passionate about jewelry and gemstones. It was a project that anyone who cared about jewelry would cherish, *but* she dreaded telling Steve and Jackie that she would have to leave tomorrow.

"Mad? Let me know what I can do to help out. My team over here can—"

"No, no, Fiona, I can handle it. I truly am very excited about this exhibition, and I think it is for a very good cause. It's a great opportunity to showcase true beauty to the world—not what salespeople or specialists claim and dictate. It's about time we did something for the industry. I would be a fool not to spearhead it."

It will be a challenge too.

"OK, Mad. But do let me know if there is anything we can do here to help out and take some of the weight off your shoulders."

"Are you kidding me? You already have! I'm depending on you for the logistics, designing—"

"Yes," Fiona interrupted, "but I have people who can help me here. So just let me know if there is anything you want us to help you with."

"Thanks, Fiona. I'll let you know. Could you email me the details and the deadlines? I'll send you the list, and let's work from there."

"OK! Thanks, Mad. I'll send it to you in a few hours. And Mad?"

"Yes?"

"Thank you so much for helping us out with this."

"It's my pleasure, Fiona. Please send my regards to His Highness."

Mad hung up the phone and watched skiers ride the magic carpet up the slope. She had been strolling as she talked and ended up at the back of the hotel, directly in front of the ski room. Hotel staff were helping guests take off their ski gear while laughing children tobogganed down the slope. Her mind was somewhere else. She mentally mapped out her coming trips and estimated how long she would need to stay at each place.

I definitely have to leave tomorrow.

That would mean disappointing Jackie, and most of all Steve. She cringed at the thought of having to tell them.

They're not going to like the news.

The cold breeze that was blowing gently at Mad had gradually become stronger, forcibly whipping her hair across her exposed face. The sky was dark, and it was getting solemnly colder. Even the children that were tobogganing a moment ago were now gone. It was time to return inside and face the music.

Mad dragged her feet towards the bar. As she approached, she heard Steve's voice and a sudden burst of laughter coming from Jackie and Stuart. They were still laughing when Mad flopped down on the sofa.

"Are they happy with your acquisitions?" Steve asked.

"Um, yes, they are very happy."

He gave her a look indicating he knew something was wrong. Mad gazed at him, thinking about how she should disclose the unfortunate news, then at Jackie, who was by now quiet and staring at her. The silence was unbearable. Mad broke off eye contact and peered down at the table, but not before catching Stuart staring at her too. Seconds that felt like an eternity passed; Mad took a deep breath, faced Steve, and let it out.

"I have to leave tomorrow."

Jackie gasped audibly. "What?! Why?!" Being best friends with Jackie for such a long time, Mad easily predicted that she would be the first to react—and with the most dramatic reaction too.

"They're having an exhibition in Venice in less than two months, which means that I have to make preparations now in order for it to happen in time."

"Can't someone else do that for you?" Stuart asked.

"I'm afraid not."

"Mad!" Jackie yelled.

Mad scrunched up her face.

And here it goes!

"You have no idea how upset I am at you!" Jackie squeaked, her enlarged bloodshot eyes, wrinkled forehead, contorted face, and angry raised eyebrows fully displaying how distressed she was. "I've got so many things planned for us, and now you're leaving?!"

"I know, and I'm sorry," Mad tried explaining. "But it's such a great opportunity for showcasing the prince's collection, setting industry standards, and promoting culture, knowledge, and unity through jewelry. All proceeds go to jewelry scholarships! Talented people can't afford to work in this industry. It's time we do something about it. It's time people stop sacrificing their morals to pay for their education—for their future."

Mad thought she'd given a pretty good argument, but Jackie did not seem convinced at all.

"I'll make it up to you . . . I promise!" Mad added.

Instead, Jackie looked like she was going to have a meltdown. Mad held her breath as Jackie morphed into a thunderous volcano, with ominous black smoke steaming from the hot red core, seconds from an epic eruption. Mad was certain Jackie was going to forget all decorum and shout in this fancy bar, in a five/six-star hotel at the summit of the most glamorous ski resort in the world (which she was sure Jackie was fully capable of). But she didn't. Instead, the anger dissipated, and Jackie's face transformed into a sea of calm. There was something brewing in her head. Her facial expression reminded Mad of something she recognized from their school days. The narrowing of her eyes and slightly raised right corner of her lips, the unmistakable aura indicating that Jackie had devised something cunning and uncanny.

Slyly, Jackie asked, "What did you say you had to do?"

"I have to visit a few countries," Mad said cautiously, unsure of what Jackie was concocting. "Have gemstones recut and carved. That is why I need to go now and get the process started."

"But after you hand the gemstones over, you don't have to sit there and wait for them to get recut or carved, right?"

"That's right."

"And I'm guessing it'll take a few weeks?"

"Yes."

"Then perfect; you and I will go on a girls' trip together . . . to . . . to . . . the Maldives!" Jackie squealed. "How's that?! That'll only take a few days, and we can catch up on everything there."

"Ummm . . ." Mad thought it through.

"You can't say no!" Jackie cried.

"Right. I guess that is doable?"

It would take a few weeks to get the gemstones recut or carved, and she didn't need to arrive in Venice until about two weeks before the opening. Factoring in travel time and buffer time, it actually was possible. The fact that Jackie chose the Maldives meant that they would be in the middle of the ocean, on an extremely small island, which she wouldn't be able to escape from conveniently.

Well played, Jackie. Very shrewd of you.

"Then naturally, after that we will go to Venice and attend the opening of the exhibition together. Perfect plan!" Jackie's eyes were as big as saucers and glowed wildly.

Stuart clapped his hands. "Babe, that is a wonderful plan!"

"Right?" Jackie wasn't asking, she was proclaiming.

Mad ran Jackie's plan through her head again. It did seem possible, and most important, it got her off the hook.

Jackie was giggling ecstatically, and honestly, at the end of the day, she just wanted to spend some quality time with Mad. What's not to like about that?

"Well," Mad said. "It's possible, and I'll work out my schedule and let you know—"

"—when we will fly to the Maldives!" Jackie finished Mad's sentence. "I'll handle the logistics and hotel! You don't have to worry about *anything.* Just give me the dates."

Mad nodded and slumped further down on the sofa, exhausted from the battle she'd just fought and barely survived. Extremely relieved, she grabbed the remaining shot on the table and threw it down her throat.

Jackie, oblivious to Mad's relief, mumbled ceaselessly about her plans and how utterly delighted she was about the whole trip.

Now that Mad had pacified Jackie, she only had to deal with one more thing—albeit a bigger and more important one. Mad turned her head towards Steve for the first time since she'd made the announcement. He hadn't said anything to her.

Chatting cheerfully with Stuart as he sipped on his whiskey, Steve seemed blissfully ignorant of his wife's imminent plans! The boys talked about their previous ski runs, compared notes, laughed, and nodded in agreement. All the while completely neglecting the elephant in the room!

Perhaps it wasn't such a big deal after all?

In fact, the subject was not mentioned again. The effects of the shots subsequently seeped in; Mad loosened up, reclined in her seat, and felt the tension in her shoulders release. Joining in the conversation, she managed to forget about her coming trip as she chatted and laughed. The queasiness in her stomach had long gone, allowing her to indulge in the hearty alpine dishes of raclette, pot-au-feu, and fries. By 10:00 p.m., their dinner reservation had been forgotten, and rather than heading over to the club, Steve and Mad decided to stay in for the night.

"I'll let you go tonight, but there won't be any of that when we're in the Maldives!" Jackie said as they walked out of the bar.

The very word *Maldives* startled Mad. She hadn't forgotten, she had just conveniently buried it somewhere deep in her head. A wave of shuddering dread washed over her, plunging her deep into that routinely familiar feeling of melancholy and gloom, this time compounded with guilt. She would need to talk with Steve tonight.

"OK, OK!" Mad laughed, hiding the stress from her voice. "Good night, and I will see you in a few weeks."

Stuart patted Steve on the back and gave Mad a hug before leaving with Jackie.

Steve and Mad walked to their hotel room in excruciating silence.

Why am I feeling this way? The exhibition is for work, and don't we have a mutual understanding? I'm not doing something wrong . . . but why this feeling?

Steve opened the door to an alpine chic room with lush green velvet sofas and scarlet curtains. The black-and-white plaid carpeting extended to the enormous bed covered by a luxurious mink fur throw. The marble fireplace illuminated the charming wooden ceiling and golden accents throughout the room. The inviting warmth beckoned and should have been calming, but Mad only felt more stressed. She couldn't take it anymore. Once the door closed behind them, she whipped around and looked Steve straight in the eye.

"I know you must be really disappointed or even angry at me for having to leave tomorrow," she blurted out and started reasoning. "And I'm truly very sorry for that, and you do know that I miss you a lot, but this is such a great opportunity! It would mean a lot if you could be supportive of me and—"

"Mad!" Steve interrupted. "Wait, wait, wait! I never said I wouldn't be supportive of you! I know this is something significant and an amazing opportunity."

"Really?" Mad was astonished. She did not expect this at all.

"Of course I'm upset that you're leaving tomorrow, but by no means am I upset with *you*." Steve pulled her closer and wrapped his arms around her. "I haven't seen my wife in two weeks, and now after barely seeing her again, she has to leave me! Poor me!"

She giggled. "Sorry."

"But I would be very proud of you for pulling this exhibition off."

Mad smiled.

How did I get so lucky?

"Come on, let's compare schedules and see how we can work this out."

She followed Steve to the study, where his laptop was set up.

"I'm planning to head to Burma tomorrow," Mad said as she scrolled down her phone. "Stay there for a few days, then to Bangkok to have the stones recut. Then back to Hong Kong to source some jadeite and have a stone carved."

"So, I will see you at home."

Yes . . . home.

"Yes, perfect. Then I'll head to New York City to recut some diamonds, before I go down under to Australia."

"Why are you traveling from Hong Kong to New York then to Australia? You're going around in circles," Steve said, acting like he was an expert in business travel.

"I have to get there first if I want to get the stones recut in time for the exhibition."

"All right then," Steve said disapprovingly, but there was nothing he could do about it.

"The gemstones will be recut, carved, and mounted simultaneously, which means that I will have more than enough time to go to the Maldives for a few days with Jackie before heading to Venice. I'll then have a good two weeks to prepare for the exhibition."

"Which also means that I could probably move my Sydney meetings to the same week you're in Australia. We could have some alone time at the Blue Mountains before you go to the Maldives with Jackie. How does that sound?"

"That's perfect!" Mad squealed with delight. "Broome to Sydney should be fairly close to each other. Let me ask Logan about it."

"You're going to see Logan Luna?" Steve asked in a slightly agitated tone.

"Yes, of course. I might as well go and collect those pearls he has been emailing me nonstop about."

"Emailing you nonstop?"

"Am I sensing a bit of jealousy?" Mad chuckled.

Steve raised an eyebrow.

"I know, I know. The Luna brothers are quite well known for their wholesome Australian Hemsworth-like tantalizing good looks. It just makes girls giddy and dizzy all over." Mad walked closer to Steve. "But it's just going to be a day trip to Broome."

He groaned.

"And as far as I know"—Mad inched closer—"there's only one man that could make me feverish . . . light-headed . . ." She slowly took her sweater off and dropped it on the floor. "Do you feel hot too?"

Instantly, Steve pulled Mad over to him, kissing her intensely. She kissed him back longingly as her hands tore his turtleneck off, exposing his broad shoulders and tight abs. His mouth moved to her ears, kissing, and tickling all her senses, rendering her weak in the knees. Without stopping, Steve carried her to the bed, where his hands unhooked her bra and caressed her breasts before moving down to touch her in places he knew she liked. Mad moaned as she felt Steve's pelvis push against hers. Before long, they were naked under the sheets, joined passionately in sync until reaching ecstasy and falling asleep, wrapped in an embrace.

In the middle of the night, the buzzing of Mad's phone woke her from her blissful sleep. She had left it on the table. Careful not to wake Steve up, she tiptoed over and turned it on silent. It took a few moments before her eyes got used to the shocking bright glare of the screen. She scrolled down her messages and shot off some quick replies.

It's too late at night. I'll give them a call tomorrow morning.

Her hands blindly found the charging cable and plugged it in her phone. Oddly, Steve's phone was nowhere to be seen. Mad checked the table and the surrounding floor area before realizing she actually hadn't seen it for months.

Is it true? How could that be?

The ruffling sound of twisting sheets interrupted her thoughts. Mad glanced over and saw that Steve had turned to his side but was still asleep. She should go back to bed. Quietly, she returned, slipping under the blanket slowly. She closed her eyes, thinking about Steve's phone before falling back into deep slumber.

CHAPTER FIVE

Burma or Myanmar?

"Sanda!" Mad hollered as loud as she could over the boisterous crowd. Her voice couldn't be more deafening than those emitted from the people around her, but it did, fortunately, catch Sanda's attention.

Sanda's eyes flicked across the Arrivals gate, locating Mad before she waved frantically in return. After more than twenty-four hours of traveling, Mad had just landed at Yangon International Airport. Previously named Rangoon, Yangon was the largest city in Myanmar and where Mad hoped to acquire a few important pieces for the exhibition.

Located in Southeast Asia, Myanmar, previously known as Burma, was sandwiched between Thailand, Laos, China, India, and Bangladesh. Even though the country had been renamed, the gemstone community and laboratories still referred to the prolific number of gems originating from this fortuitous country as Burmese. The legends and profound history of the gemstone mines had been so deeply and extensively recognized around the world that not much could alter its industry designation. As a matter of fact, the geology in Burma was so unique and rich in gemstone-forming marbles and rocks that, other than emeralds, almost every other gem had been found there. Even more remarkable was that only a few regions in the world have had such high concentration of mines that were able to produce such high-quality gemstones consistently throughout history.

Prized gemstones, such as the famed rubies from the legendary Mogok Stone Tract in Upper Burma, had been mined since the sixth century. Chromium, natural to the area, was found in these rubies' chemical composition, enhancing the redness of the stone and giving it a red glow under UV fluorescence lighting—the most saturated and highest quality earning the name "pigeon's blood."

Although not as esteemed as the rubies, Burmese sapphires are among the finest in the world, commanding prices second only to Kashmir sapphires. This is due to their intensely saturated blue hue, similar to a midnight blue. So majestic and dominant is the color that the highest quality is called "royal blue" in the trade. Indeed, these are extremely rare and highly sought after as commercial goods are commonly overcolored or too dark in color.

Much adored by Asians for centuries, jadeite is only found in a few places around the world, such as Myanmar. Not to be confused with jade, jadeite is a variety of jade that is rarer and more valued than the other variety, nephrite. As jadeite's unique crystal structure allows it to be more porous, light can easily pass through, making it even more vitreous than its cousin nephrite. The attained translucency gives it the valued "water," as the Chinese call it, producing greater luminescence. In addition, jadeite comes in a wider range of color and vibrancy than nephrite, making the former an exorbitantly prized gemstone. Similar to the western civilization's usage of marble, the two varieties are often carved into fantastical figures.

On her last trip, Mad had acquired a large jadeite boulder, which would be carved by a group of professionals in her next destination, Hong Kong. This made her new trip more manageable; she only needed to secure two strands of necklaces: a ruby and a sapphire. Although she was exhausted from her flight, she was ready for the task.

"Mad!" Sanda hugged her and magically produced an iced cappuccino from thin air. She had timed Mad's arrival perfectly; the ice was still intact.

"You are the best!" Mad said as she took a long and much needed sip. By now, she was so much defined by her iced cappuccinos that anyone who knew her well knew how often she needed it.

Sanda winked at her. "Our driver is waiting outside, let's go."

Mad had only met Sanda during her last trip to Burma, but they'd hit it off instantly and become fast friends. As Mad's agent, Sanda scheduled all of her appointments with the dealers and miners. Since Mad didn't speak Burmese, in addition to being her translator, Sanda also helped bargain. She had garnered quite a reputation for working miracles, and several big international buyers enlisted her services. Mad was grateful Sanda could drop everything and help her at such short notice. Her fantastic apple-green jadeite cabochon ear studs perfectly accessorized her ensemble, a yellowish-green Burmese blouse the shade of peridot gemstones and a matching long skirt. Her unceasing smile exuded a perpetually pleasant and nonthreatening aura. It was no wonder she was at the top of her game in the industry.

Sanda led Mad out of the comfort of the air-conditioned airport. As the glass doors opened, a wave of hot, tiring humidity hit their faces. They moved as quickly as possible towards a car parked on the curbside and climbed in, welcoming the blast of cool air and frozen towels.

"So, I managed to book a few appointments this afternoon starting at three," Sanda reported, "giving you some time to freshen up beforehand."

Mad greatly appreciated her efforts. "Thank you so much again, Sanda. I know I didn't give you much notice."

"Don't worry about that. It must have been very important if you needed my help immediately."

"It is indeed."

"But I'm telling you, those miners and dealers are cunning and calculating." Sanda gave her a heads-up. "If they know you are in a hurry, they will try to rip you off."

"I know what you mean, but I'll just have to try my best to fool them." In all honesty, Mad wasn't sure how she was going to pull it off. She was a hopeless actress.

"I'll help you, of course; but you know their tricks."

On her last trip, Mad was fortunate to have Sanda take her under her wing. With Sanda's vast connections, numerous dealers came to Mad's hotel to show her their collection of Burmese gemstones. Despite the number of appointments, though, the gemstones brought on the first day were mediocre at best. However, as the days progressed, the dealers offered finer gemstones, until finally the best qualities were presented. The whole process could best be described as "pulling teeth."

Predictably, each appointment started with small talk, then coffee, followed by smiling and awkward silence. Repeat a few more times, gemstones finally appear, negotiations may or may not ensue before a long-overdue exit. The time spent was unbearably excessive and painful; the Burmese relished dragging the whole process out to a point that if Mad didn't know better, she would have thought they didn't even want to sell anything at all!

And when they had narrowed down to a suitable piece, the negotiations took days as well. They didn't cut to the chase, there was no straight talk, just smiling, awkward silence, and coffee drinking. Frankly, the deal itself seemed secondary to the prelude, which was very much defined by a sense of limitless time and patience on their side. On several occasions, dealers brought the same exact pieces she'd seen from previous dealers, except priced differently. Talk about running around in circles!

Myanmar was an incomprehensible world. A trip that was planned for three days ended up being two weeks. By the time Mad could finally leave, she was exhausted from the inertia. She could not afford that sort of delay this time. She simply did not have the luxury to do so.

"Sanda, I *absolutely* cannot have what happened last time happen again!" Mad said sternly. "I've got a very tight schedule."

Mad hoped that her serious tone registered, but Sanda only softly replied, "I'll see what I can do."

It was not much in the way of reassurance, but more like pacification. All Mad could do at the moment was hope for the best. Yielding temporarily, she turned her head to the window and took in the distinctively contrasting scenery from her last destination.

Their car whisked by tall apartment buildings and old colonial houses bursting in between with chaotic foliage. Endless streetlamps and electrical cables guided pedestrians and traffic alike. Amidst the maze-like cement jungle, golden pagodas sprouted intermediately. Their car passed by the

Shwedagon Pagoda, one of the holiest Buddhist shrines in the world. Thought to be built during the lifetime of the Buddha, it contains sacred relics, compelling many to make pilgrimages to the site. The gilded stupa with a diamond-studded spire dominates the skyline of the city. At night, spotlights ignite the beacon, cementing its magnificence. Although Mad had never visited the pagoda itself, the sight of it during her last trip, and at moments like this, offered her much-needed serenity in this strange mystical city.

The peace, unfortunately, only lasted a few minutes.

"We're here."

Their car pulled up to a sleek white colonial building. A bellboy opened their door and welcomed them into a contemporary Bill Bensley–like lobby rendered in sleek black and white lines, vibrant pops of furniture, and splashes of greenery. This would be Mad's home for a few days only—hopefully.

"I'll see you at three o'clock at the private rooms," Sanda said as she handed Mad her room keys.

"Yes, thank you, Sanda." Mad grabbed the keys and walked briskly towards the elevators.

At 3:00 p.m. sharp, Mad arrived at the private rooms, where Sanda was already waiting for her. Mad had unpacked and freshened up. Donning her killer red lipstick, she was eager to start. As always, Sanda had prepared the room. A catered table, overflowing with enough petit fours and coffee to feed a village, was placed strategically next to plush sofas. Another table accompanied by a set of four chairs was placed next to the window where an abundance of sunlight flooded into the room. This table would be where the action unfolded.

"Are you ready?" Sanda smiled.

Mad was more than ready.

"Bring them in."

Sanda made a call to the front desk, and within five minutes a petite man in a buttoned-down short-sleeved white shirt and scruffy pants strode in. He was not carrying any bags.

Oh no! I sure hope he has big pockets then.

Conversing in Burmese, Sanda led him over to Mad. They shook hands and smiled at each other.

"Hello," Mad said.

"Hello," he replied.

Silence.

"Uh, would you like a seat here?" she offered, directing his gaze over at the sunlit table.

He nodded, and Mad subsequently found herself and the dealer staring at each other at the table instead—in excruciating silence.

Mad was desperately trying to think of some Burmese phrases she had learned on her last trip when Sanda, with a hot cup of coffee in hand, saved her from further embarrassment.

The dealer instantly grinned, showing his yellowish stained teeth.

While Sanda and the dealer engaged in small talk spoken wholly in Burmese, Mad tried feigning interest. But in all honesty, both knew she was completely clueless. They talked, then paused to take a sip of coffee, then after some silence talked again.

Same old drill.

It was not long before the chattering noises developed into a melodic, hypnotizing rhythm, luring Mad into a dangerously languid state. Her mind began to wander as her eyes drooped and her body floated towards a warm glow beckoning her to surrender. Ever so slightly, her head nodded forward, and she shot up from her seat.

I'm mortified! Did they notice?

Fortunately, they were still talking to each other, oblivious to her blunder. She exhaled in relief.

That was close.

Mad quickly made herself a double-shot expresso. Better to be overcaffeinated than risking falling asleep a second time. Finally, more than half an hour after his arrival, the dealer pulled out a small parcel from his pants pocket. He unfolded the brownish paper that had probably seen better days, revealing a sterile white package.

Damn it! It's so small!

As he unwrapped the package, Mad felt her spirit deflate. Within was an alarmingly small plastic ziplock pouch. The dealer opened the pouch and dropped an oval ruby, about 3 carats in size, in the previously prepared tray on the table. He looked up and smiled, clearly proud of what he had just delivered.

Utterly disappointed, Mad couldn't help blurting out, "Only one ruby?"

After more than thirty minutes of pointless chitchat?!

Sanda translated, sans the irate tone, to which the dealer nodded in return. Mad wanted to roll her eyes but thought wisely against it.

Why do they have to do this every time?! And now I have to act all interested and hope that he will bring me better stones tomorrow. They really have too much time on their hands!

Except, Mad did not have the time to entertain this trip. Nevertheless, she politely took the ruby and placed it in between her middle and index finger on the back of her hand. Tilting it left and right, she pretended that she was admiring the beauty of the ruby, but in actuality she couldn't believe how visibly included and pinkish the stone was. As if testing her mental strength and physical discipline, a distinct black crystal on the table of the stone further amplified the inferiority of it. Irritated, nevertheless immensely restrained, Mad smiled and placed the ruby back on the tray.

"Do you have any nice ruby and sapphire necklaces?" Mad said cautiously, suppressing an explosion of adverse emotions. "That's what I'm looking for this time."

Sanda translated, whereupon the dealer smiled, took a sip of his coffee, paused, then replied in a slew of slowly spoken Burmese.

"He says he can bring some tomorrow."

"You think they are any good?" Mad, exceptionally skeptical and upset, asked Sanda.

"Yes, they should be good."

Straining to hide her anguish, Mad said, "All right then."

When the dealer finished his coffee and was finally ready to leave, Mad shook his hand anxiously, then slumped down in her chair right after the door closed.

It was 4:30 p.m. An hour and a half and nothing had happened. She was drained.

"You OK?"

"I'm tired," Mad replied. "It's the same thing again. Could you just ask them if they have the necklaces first? So we don't have to go through the whole dance again?"

"I'll try, but you know what they are like."

"Yes, unfortunately, I do."

A female dealer came in next with an assistant holding a much more promising briefcase. Even though Sanda and the dealer chatted for more or less the bulk of the conversation, Mad managed to join in when they talked about the current weather in different parts of the world. Despite the size of the briefcase, the dealer only unveiled a few low-quality gemstones and swore she would come back with suitable ones the next day. By the end of that appointment, the sun had set and the natural light had disappeared. The artificial lighting in the room was inadequate enough that Mad didn't even pretend she could see the next dealer's faulty stones clearly; she simply invited the dealer to come back the next day with necklaces instead. Sanda still had to chat with the dealer, though, consequently ending all engagements and closing the private room doors at 9:00 p.m.

"So, I'll see you at ten tomorrow morning?" Sanda asked.

"Do you think we could push it to nine?" Mad questioned.

"I'll try, but it's going to be hard. They don't like changes, and . . ." Sanda looked hesitant, and there was no mistaking the uncertainty in her voice. She opened her mouth, about to say something, but closed it after a split second. Exhaling deeply, she eventually spoke.

"News travel fast."

"What news?" Mad was puzzled.

"They all know you used to work at Minos."

"So?"

Doesn't everyone?

"Are you aware of the recent news of the disgraced Indian jeweler? He has dozens of shops around the world. Hollywood and Bollywood stars regularly wear his jewelry."

"Ummm . . ." Mad pondered.

Do I?

"He turned out to be a fraud."

Reflecting on the past few days, Mad seemed to remember CNN news reporting on an Indian jeweler/designer/mogul wanted for the biggest fraud in India's banking history.

Apparently now a fugitive in the United Kingdom, he swindled US$2 billion from the banks and left India before the scam exploded publicly.

"Initially," Sanda continued, "he was involved in a corruption and fraud scandal with an Indian bank. Then the authorities found out that he also defrauded another Indian bank by conspiring with a rogue bank official who forged documents of unapproved guarantees allowing him overseas loans. He never paid a cent back, and of course there's money laundering involved too. And all of this is possible because of Minos."

"What do you mean?" Mad was now confused.

"He only shot to meteoritic fame, which granted him legitimacy, when his necklace was featured on the front cover of a Minos Hong Kong jewelry sale catalog. Remember a necklace with a 13-carat Golconda diamond? The pear-shaped one? The necklace set with argyle pink diamonds?"

Mad nodded. That necklace was heavily advertised in all magazines and billboards. The week of the sale, it was pretty much all that everyone was talking about.

"No one knew who he was before Minos," Sanda added. "Why would Minos feature a nobody on its catalog cover?"

A blanket of horrible dread loomed over Mad.

"It's not like Minos had a great reputation to begin with," Sanda further explained. "They've never been known to be pleasant. I mean, the degrading nicknames the Boss used behind clients' backs and the racism she overtly displayed for dealers and agents like us, people with different skin tones—it's plain disrespectful. Now, the question is not even if Minos was involved in any dirty business, but to what extent they were involved. What did they receive under the table?"

Mad held her breath.

"You worked at Minos. The Boss hired you. It begs the question of how clean you are."

"Nonsense! How preposterous! People here think I'm of the same dubious nature?" Mad cried in disbelief. "Do you? Do you think I'm complicit?"

"Mad, I've worked with you. You're so transparent. I know you're not capable of this," Sanda quickly clarified. "But they don't, and that sheds a bad light on you. It was hard making appointments for you this time. People think you may involve yourself with underhanded dealings."

"*What?!* I would never do that to the prince or anyone! I never compromise my moral rectitude!" Mad roared.

"That's just my deduction. Mainly I think they just need time to see if you're trustworthy or not. This scandal, it's fresh and just reminded them to be more cautious."

"Of anything in relation to Minos?"

"Relationships take time to build."

"Apparently, it takes longer when you've worked with notorious crooks."

I thought I'd left Minos behind me! Don't people know that I purged and overthrew the Boss and her cronies?

Sanda read her mind.

"You could do ten good things and have one bad thing, that you're not even involved in, ruin your reputation. That's all people will remember—that one bad scandal."

"I'll just have to show them that's not me, then," Mad said firmly.

In the limited amount of time that I have . . .

Mad tapped her fingers on the table, next to the two cups of coffee she had already ingested. It was 9:45 a.m. the next morning, and no one had shown up yet. She and Sanda had been waiting in the private room for over an hour. Mad peered at Sanda, who only returned an I-told-you-so expression.

Why are they making this so difficult for me? Do they really think I'm corrupt? That I'm all about money? And that I don't deserve any respect at all?

Mad shook her head and tried to brush all the negative thoughts aside. At 10:30 a.m., the dealers ultimately rolled in, and the whole routine repeated itself. There was chitchat, there was coffee, but no ruby or sapphire necklaces until 1:00 p.m. A dealer eventually produced a sachet of ruby and sapphire necklaces. Mad's eyes gleamed with hope that she no longer needed to leave Myanmar with her tail between her legs. Sanda gave her a wink.

Mounted in traditional Burmese 24-karat gold style, each necklace was set with oval and cushion-shaped sapphires or rubies. Most people would unmount the stones once they purchased it and reset them, but Mad wanted to keep them the way they were. She found the whole design rather charming and representative of the Burmese culture. Now, she just had to find a strand of top-quality well-matched stones. After that, she would have them repolished by an expert in Bangkok who could bring out the fire in any gemstone. Under a natural beam of light, she instantly eliminated the low-quality necklaces. Another ten minutes of intense scrutiny and she was left satisfied with a strand of sapphires with thirty-three stones totaling approximately 60 carats and a strand of rubies with thirty-nine stones totaling approximately 55 carats. Now came the task of negotiation.

"How much is he asking for these?"

Back and forth Sanda and the dealer spoke, before a reluctant Sanda replied, "Five hundred thousand US dollars for the
sapphire necklace and one point eight million US dollars for
the ruby necklace."

Mad smiled. She expected the astronomical prices, and the
dealer expected her to bargain; it was all part of the process. It
was time to put her acting chops to work; despite the comical-
ity of it, it was still expected. With her very best overly exagger-
ated facial expression, she bellowed out, "Wow! So expensive!
Can you give me a better price?"

Sanda followed with an excruciating pain-stricken face
as she pleaded. Of course, the dealer didn't flinch at all. He
expected all the drama; he would be worried if they didn't give
him such a reaction.

"He said, it's already very cheap," she translated with furrowed eyebrows.

"Oh, please! You know I don't come here often, and I have
so many friends around the globe. I will definitely tell them
about you if you give me a better price."

"He said, he really can't. He won't make any money out of
them already."

"Tell him, this will be the beginning of a long-term relationship. It's not about just one business transaction, but about
many more to come."

As Sanda and the dealer bickered back and forth, her face
scrunched up even more, displaying her dissatisfaction.

"He asked, what do you want to pay?"

As anticipated, Mad replied with utmost confidence, "One
hundred thousand US dollars and five hundred thousand US
dollars."

These were the current market prices, and she knew for
sure the prices were as fair as could be.

This time around, it was the dealer's turn to expel pain, disbelief, and agitation as he spoke.

"He said, it's not possible."

"Tell him to think about it then," Mad said firmly.

The dealer shook his head. After a moment of silence, he excused himself and left.

"He'll be back," she said quietly and hoped desperately.

The next day was filled with more appointments, but there was nothing suitable or close to what Mad was searching for. She was supposed to leave that day but was forced to alter her plans, which meant less time in Hong Kong with Steve. He'd been really sweet on the phone when Mad relayed her situation. He had been supportive and understanding, but she couldn't help but still feel frustratedly powerless. Her disappointment and anxiety were only alleviated slightly by a zen Japanese lunch before getting back into high gear when at 2:00 p.m. there was still no sign of the dealer from the previous day. As she paced around in the private room, Mad thought about a contingency plan.

If the dealer doesn't come, I'll call a dealer in Bangkok. Maybe, just maybe, Bangkok will have something. But prices will be quite high too! Should I call the Burmese dealer back then? That would be so embarrassing! Maybe I should just forget about the necklaces! No one would notice in the exhibition, right?

At 3:00 p.m., the front desk rang and informed them of a visitor, releasing Mad from her misery. Lo and behold, the dealer walked in. Mad hid her smile as Sanda offered him coffee and talked.

"He said the lowest he could go is one million US dollars for the ruby necklace and three hundred thousand US dollars for the sapphire."

"That's far from what I offered yesterday."

"He said there are others offering better prices, but he also wants to do long-term business with you, so he chose not to sell to those people."

"Who?" Mad asked, not even bothering to put up with the lie.

"Other people."

Mad knew she had to remain patient. Politely, she declined the prices and let the dealer leave again. As she slumped down in her chair, Sanda said reassuringly, "He will be back."

"Yes, I know he'll be back, but I'm out of time. I'm supposed to leave today!"

"Yes, but that's how they operate here."

"Do you think we could reach a deal tomorrow?"

Sanda frowned.

No longer in a pleasant mood, Mad kept to herself the rest of the day, only briefly responding when she was expected to. Still, the last appointment did not end until 9:00 p.m.

The later you stay at work, the more hardworking you look. Fake it till you make it.

The last thing Mad needed at this very moment was to have Veronica's words creep into her mind.

Why is Minos still plaguing me?! Mad, get your head together! This is not the time to have Minos pester your mental state.

She shook her head, getting rid of the dismal thoughts dragging her spirits down.

"Sanda?"

"Yes?"

"We could offer more tomorrow."

"You sure?"

"If it comes to that . . ."

"Let's see what I can do." Sanda frowned.

Mad nodded in silence.

What could she do?

Predictably, the dealer came back the next day and offered a slightly lower, yet unsatisfactory, price. It was still far from what Mad wanted to pay, but she was anxious to seal the deal.

"Could you go a little lower?" She tried pushing once more. "My patron gave me a budget."

"He said, tell your patron to give you a higher budget," Sanda said apologetically.

Mad was sure the prince wouldn't mind the current price; he trusted her, and even with such a limited amount of time, she was trying her best to secure the most favorable deal. Still, she just couldn't get over it herself. It was not a fair market price, and she knew she shouldn't allow the dealer to twist her arm like this. Nonetheless, she genuinely wanted—no, needed—the necklaces for the exhibition. The more unattainable they were, the more essential and irreplaceable they had become.

Very well then.

"O—" Mad started to say but was halted abruptly when the cup of piping-hot coffee in Sanda's hand enigmatically slipped and spilled all over Mad's dress. She shot up from her seat and sent the cup and the remainder of its contents flying off her lap and onto the dealer's white shirt. His chair toppled over as he attempted to duck unsuccessfully from the impact. Rather uncharacteristically, Sanda screamed and ran to get napkins to wipe everyone off.

"I'm so sorry! The coffee just slipped out of my hand. Are you hurt?" Sanda asked as she threw a bundle of napkins on the dealer and blotted Mad's dress.

"This is definitely not a good day! I never spill coffee, it's such a bad omen!" Sanda continued.

Did Sanda just wink at me?

Mad wasn't sure, but her gut told her to play along.

"You're right, Sanda. Something doesn't feel right. Spilling coffee is certainly not auspicious at all!" Mad concurred. "I hope you don't mind, but perhaps we should continue negotiating another day."

Sanda translated with a mixture of emotions that encompassed deep regret, apology, and a helpful pinch of drama. The dealer opened his mouth to say something but closed it instead and nodded his head. Reluctantly, he left.

Mad waited a few seconds, making sure the dealer was out of earshot, before bursting out loud with "What was that?!"

"You have to trust me on this one!" Sanda spoke hastily. "He knows you're in a hurry and has got you under his thumb! I absolutely won't let you pay that ridiculous price he's asking for!"

"Your solution is throwing coffee on me?!"

"If that's what it takes! I had to stop you from acquiescing. Sorry about your dress, though."

"Don't worry about that." Mad giggled. "That was quite funny actually. Perfect timing, I have to say. I was about to say OK! So, what is your plan?"

"You're to leave tomorrow."

"What?!"

"Trust me! I'll tell everyone I'm free tomorrow because you're leaving. And the dealer will find out, and he will most surely shit in his pants and come back with a much more agreeable price."

"You mean, we'll trick him into thinking I don't want it anymore and that I'm leaving?"

"*No!*"

"What then?"

"You *are* leaving tomorrow. I'm betting he'll look into your flight, and he'll get here in time before you leave."

"Well, OK. What if he doesn't?"

"You still have to leave, right? Aren't you in a hurry?"

"Well, *yes*! But I'm hoping with two necklaces in my possession!"

"Trust me then! There *will* be two necklaces in that LV Speedy bag of yours! Stick to your price, don't give in to him."

This time, there was no mistake in Sanda's voice. She exuded sheer confidence and certainty.

But Mad still had to ask, "You sure?"

Sanda's steely eyes answered her question.

"I trust you then."

"A ham and cheese omelet annnnnnd, oh, a double-shot iced cappuccino, please," Mad said to the waitress in the café. Her voice was so hoarse from the dryness in her throat, she must have sounded like a man. She hoped she was not coming down with anything, especially when that was not her only problem. Her stomach had been upset the whole morning, and she was sure it was not from hunger. She hadn't slept well last night. She tossed and turned until she finally fell asleep from exhaustion, only to be woken up covered in cold sweat. She couldn't manage to fall back asleep again, causing her mind to spin out worst-case scenarios, which of course incited a roller coaster of emotions ranging from anxiety to panic to hope.

What did I get myself into?

Yesterday, she stuck to her guns and didn't let the dealer call the shots, but that didn't mean that she could stop thinking about what happened. At her weakest moment, she almost surrendered, but thankfully was saved by Sanda's ruse. She trusted Sanda and whatever she had planned, but still, she couldn't help worrying, evident from the dark circles around her eyes and unsettled stomach.

Ding!

Mad took her phone out slowly from her bag as she chewed on a bite of her warm omelet. Breakfast was just what she needed. Which could not be said for what she saw next.

Sanda:

Your flight leaves at 1pm

Mad's eyes popped wide open. If she felt fatigued a moment ago, she most certainly was not now. Fully awake and with a surge of adrenaline, she immediately called Sanda.

"What do you mean, my flight is at 1:00 p.m.? It's already 11:00 a.m.!" Mad screeched. "I thought my flight would be in the late afternoon. I have to go to the airport now!"

Unbelievable! Sanda is getting out of hand!

"Are you having breakfast?"

"Yes!"

"Well, you're all packed, right?"

"Yes! But the dealer is not here yet!"

"Enjoy your breakfast. I will be there in ten minutes." Sanda hung up the phone.

Mad placed both hands on her throbbing temples and closed her eyes. They felt even more swollen than they had before.

Really? Enjoy my breakfast? How could I enjoy my breakfast? I still need to check out, get my stuff from my room, and most important, I need the two necklaces!

Like it was a vodka shot, she emptied her cup and swallowed the coffee in one gulp before gathering her belongings. She felt like she had just fallen deeper into a bottomless pit that was the depressing failure of this trip. She would have to leave Myanmar—defeated. Wallowing in her self-pity, she got out of her seat and was about to take a step when she froze in her tracks at the sight of a blazing white blur forcefully thrusting open the front door of the café. The waitresses let out a tiny scream as the door flew open and hit the wall so violently it looked like it was going to fly off the hinges and shatter into pieces. The commotion brought everyone in the café to a standstill as they gaped at the source of disturbance. Mad found herself staring at the dealer. She blinked her eyes, just to make sure she wasn't seeing an apparition of her imagination.

Is this a joke? How cruel if it is!

The dealer scanned the room and at once ran towards Mad when he spotted her.

"Madeleine!" he cried.

"Mr. Tin?" Mad stared at him in disbelief.

"Why are you leaving today?" he demanded to know—in perfect English.

"What? How do you know?" Mad said, astonished at what had just magically fallen into place. She didn't even bother to conceal the smirk materializing on her face.

Damn, he speaks perfect English too.

"Well, she has some urgent business." Sanda arrived just in time. Likewise, with a conspicuous smirk on her face.

"But what about the necklaces?" Mr. Tin implored.

Mad exhaled dramatically and replied with much regret in her voice, "I'll just have to come back another day. I really have to go! I'm so sorry, but thank you for everything."

Mr. Tin stood still, his face filled with shock.

"Very well then!" she said with impatience. "Let me get you a coffee, but I really have to go." She glanced down at her phone. "My god! I'm late!" She waved down the nearest waiter.

Mr. Tin grabbed Mad's hand firmly. "I can give you the price you're asking for."

"What?" She pretended she didn't understand.

Finally.

"For the two necklaces."

Mad slowly sat down in her seat as Mr. Tin loosened his grip.

"How much?" she said, as her confidence, power, and leverage crept back.

"Six hundred thousand US dollars and one hundred fifty thousand."

"Oh," Mad said disapprovingly. "Mr. Tin, I would have you know that I offered you five hundred thousand US dollars and one hundred thousand respectively the other day. I'm a woman of my word, and I know that's a fair price. I don't cheat, lie, or play games. I believe respect is earned, not bought. Now, would you like to take my offer?"

Stunned by her brazenness, Mr. Tin said nothing as his mouth dropped open.

"Mad, ticktock! We have to go! Traffic is bad," Sanda urged, again right on cue. That was all they needed to seal the deal.

"OK!" Mr. Tin shouted immediately.

He took two boxes out of his bag and handed them over to Mad.

Opening the boxes cautiously, she gave out a quiet sigh of relief. The vibrant reds and blues of the rubies and sapphires sparkled and danced under the light, scintillating with unfaltering intensity. Gently, she stroked her hard-won prizes. Satisfied, she snapped the boxes shut and shoved them in her Speedy bag before shooting up from her seat.

"Sanda!" Mad said, ready to deliver her instructions. Except, she didn't have to.

"I'll deal with the rest," Sanda responded intuitively.

"Thank you." Mad smiled with much appreciation.

She turned her head back to Mr. Tin, who was by now sweating profusely.

"Thank you for your business. I'll see you next time."

Mad strutted away, heart thumping, grinning from ear to ear. As she left the café, a drop of sweat rolled down her left temple, but she quickly wiped it off her face.

Thank goodness, he didn't see this.

Minutes later, she found herself seated comfortably in the car, heading to the airport. She couldn't stop smiling to herself. Sanda was truly a rainmaker, miracle worker, and most of all a dependable friend. Earlier, the day felt dark and abysmal, but it then made a dramatic turn; the skies had morphed into a vibrant blue, the sun gloriously bright; even the birds outside her window looked like they were singing in glee.

"Excuse me!" Mad said to the chauffeur. "Could you stop here for a minute?"

"Here?"

"Yes, on the side of the road, please."

Mad jumped out of the car and ran towards a woman with a big cage of swallows. Sanda had told her that the Burmese believe setting birds free imparted luck and granted the person merit in their next reincarnated life. Mad didn't believe in reincarnation, but she did believe in good karma.

"All of them." She handed the woman the remainder of the kyat left in her bag.

"All?"

"Yes, all!"

The woman grabbed the cash and laughed out loud. She was done for the day. Cranking open the cage door, she shook the birds out. One by one they were released, until they filled the whole street with blissful chirping. Aware of how lucky she had been, not only today but for the past year, Mad closed her eyes and prayed.

Please let things stay as perfect as they are.

Within a few hours, Mad found herself in a different country. She waited for a tuk-tuk to speed past before deeming it safe to push open the car door and jump out into a kaleidoscope of exhilarating smells, sights, and sounds. The stickiness of the air combined with a pungent aroma of spices from the nearby street vendor enveloped her as she navigated around the backpackers in their tank tops and shorts, towards the endless line of stores stocked with everything gem-related and imaginable: tweezers, loupes, microscopes, parcel paper, pen lights, loose gems, mounted gems, etc. If Antwerp was the diamond capital of the world, then Bangkok, Thailand, was the colored-stone capital of the world. Practically every rough colored stone was brought here to be processed, manufactured, and traded. Brokers, merchants, dealers, cutters, and laboratories congregated in the small but highly productive gemstone district.

Maneuvering with ease through one of the hidden alleyways, Mad headed up the stairs of a dilapidated building, housing one of the finest lapidaries in the world. This was where the ruby and sapphire necklaces would be polished.

"Mad! How are you doing, my dear?" Raj said as he swung open the second armed door to his lapidary and welcomed her with air kisses to the cheeks. "You got me all worried when I didn't see you strutting in here yesterday. You were going to be the highlight of my day."

Dressed in a fitted light aquamarine-blue suit, white shirt, a dark-blue pocket square, and glorious cushion-shaped sapphire cufflinks, Raj was the suavest lapidarist Mad had ever met. Not only that, but he was also probably the most skilled colored-stone cutter in the industry, known to be able to unlock the potential in any stone. His talent was legendary. He knew where to cut and where to polish, making sure at the same time the stone retained as much weight (and financial value) as possible. As famed as he was, he also unselfishly trained a new generation pro bono, passing on his skills, experience, and all that he knew. He always said, "The world would be an uglier place if no one could do what he could do." To Mad, he was a man of his word, which was paramount in this aspect of the industry. No broken promises and false aspirations; if he said he could do it, he could. If he couldn't, no one could. Mad had heard too many horror stories of overzealously earnest cutters damaging gemstones worth millions to consider enlisting anyone else but Raj for help.

"Oh, Raj! You know how much I hate disappointing you," Mad replied.

"Burma, right?" Raj said as he gave her an all-knowing look.

"Right. You know what it's like," she confirmed. "How are you, by the way?"

"Couldn't be happier to see you. Come, come! I have something to show you."

Raj led her past rows and rows of women seated at desks with old-school faceting machines fitted with grinding wheels, simple motors, and drip tanks. The machines buzzed with constant activity; none of the women looked up at Mad as they busily polished their stones.

Once in his office, Raj closed the door behind them, shutting out the noise.

Mad sat down at his desk and pulled out her two prized possessions.

"Very good eye . . . very nice, indeed." He examined the necklaces under his loupe. "But just as you mentioned on the phone, they do need some polishing."

"You know what to do. I need them fast, though."

"Don't worry. I can do it; my girls can do it. Don't you worry. I'll add the fire and some light in these stones."

"I want to keep the mounting."

"For sure?!" Raj clearly disapproved, frowning as he spoke.

"Yes, for sure."

"Very well then. If you change your mind, you know I can get it remounted easily for you."

"Yes, thank you. I just find these charming . . . and sometimes when it's good, why change it?"

"Because it could always be better."

Mad laughed.

Raj was always the perfectionist.

"Just try to hold back, OK! Don't touch the mountings!"

"Fine," he said, sounding reluctant.

"OK, what else do you want to show me?"

Raj swiftly pulled out a tray from the safe behind him and placed it in front of her.

"These are all nonheated and freshly cut for you to see."

Placed in neat multiple rows on the velvet tray were gemstones of all colors and shapes. Trying to outshine one another, they gleamed, glistened, and begged for attention. However, only one stone captured Mad's eye. Instantly, she knew, she had to have it. The oval-shaped pink sapphire glowed with such brightness, only an expert cutter, such as Raj, could have achieved it. What's more, it radiated flashes of purple that added another layer of complexity in the stone.

"Tell me about this." She slipped the pink sapphire into her palm.

With a twinkle in his eye, Raj replied, "Ohhhh, you're so good! I tried to use other stones to distract you, but you still found it." He laughed. "Good eye! It's Ceylon. We got it the other day, and one of our young cutters saw the purple under the dichroscope. So, she did her magic, sliced over here and there"—he indicated with his finger—"and voilà! Here we are!"

She really did her magic. The stone is amazing.

Sapphires are a pleochroic gem, meaning that when viewed at different angles of the crystal lattice, more than one color appears. When the cutter slices in the right places, it unleashes the purple hue, making the gemstone even more spectacular than it already was.

"Send it along with the two necklaces," Mad said as she stood up to leave. "I'll email you the address."

"Wonderful!" Raj smiled and shook her hand. "As always, great doing business with you."

The sky was dark when Mad left Raj's office. Although traffic in Bangkok was notoriously bad, the safest way downtown was still by car. She hopped into her waiting vehicle and headed through the mingled high-rises and narrow alleyways. Slowly but gradually, she reached the restaurant, Ma Maison, more than an hour later. Situated in the middle of a park amidst the hustle and bustle, the beautiful restaurant boasted floor-to-ceiling glass windows, voluptuous flower arrangements, and some of the best traditional Thai foods in the city. Mad was there to meet her college friend Vikram and his wife, Shari. Rushing through the doors, she quickly spotted them and ran towards their table.

"I'm so sorry for being late!" Mad gave both of them a hug.

"Don't worry. We already ordered, so just sit and eat," Vikram said.

"Sorry for being the third wheel!"

"Are you kidding me, Mad—if you didn't tell me you were in town, I would be angry at you. Plus, you can finally meet this little man."

Directly next to Shari was a Bugaboo carriage, holding a little cherub of a baby with Michelin Man–like arms poking out of a blanket.

"Awww, look at him! So cute!" Mad walked over and cooed at their six-month-old bundle of joy.

"Do you want to hold him?" Shari asked.

"Goodness! No! Not at all!" Mad jumped back as though the baby was about to grab hold of her. "I don't even know how to," she stammered.

"Here, it's really easy." Shari took the baby out of the carriage and was about to pass him to Mad, who again jumped another step back.

"No, no! I really shouldn't. My clothes are all germ-ridden from the plane."

"OK! OK! Calm down! Can't believe you actually jumped!" Shari laughed.

Relieved she didn't have to hold the baby, Mad walked to her seat.

"How are you, Mad?" Vikram asked.

"Oh, busy, busy. We're having this amazing exhibition in Venice, so I have to travel the next few weeks and source a few more items."

"Wait a minute, travel the next few weeks? I thought you were going to start a family soon. Like us!"

"What? I have a family," Mad said as she stuffed a Thai spring roll into her mouth. She'd known Vikram and Shari for such a long time, she was sure they wouldn't mind her table manners.

"You don't have kids. With all that traveling, how are you going to have kids?"

Mad had never really thought about that.

Don't kids come naturally? They need to be planned? Now wouldn't be the time to have kids, though . . . would it? We're busy with our careers and happy at the moment. How would we put kids in the equation?

"We've never talked about it. We're quite happy with our lives at the moment. We just got married! Come on, Vikram! Even my parents haven't asked me yet!"

"You've been married for six months already!" Vikram retorted. "Hey, I'm just saying, it's something you should think about. Even Anderson Cooper says it's 'a new level of love.' Unlike anything he's experienced. What are you waiting for?"

"It's true. You know how many of my friends go through in vitro nowadays," Shari added. "It's really not that easy to get pregnant—and the older you get, the more complications there are. The miscarriages, the pain, the heartbreak. Do you know how many women waited to get pregnant and then it doesn't happen? That hurts too."

"But there must be a perfect time for it, right?" Mad questioned.

"There's never a perfect time. But when it happens, it's going to be the best thing in your life," Shari said with a smile.

"And other things will fall into place. You will make it work." Vikram sounded like a philosopher.

"Well, I'm sure one day . . . but guys, these things should happen naturally, right?" Mad challenged.

"You can time it! All you have to do is—" Vikram started saying.

"Seriously, you guys?! You're stressing me out!"

"All right, all right, call me when you need—" he attempted again.

"Baby-making advice?" Mad said, her eyes threateningly large.

"All right, all right! Change of subject," Vikram said wisely, and raised his hands in surrender. "Let me show you something then." He took a box out of a bag.

"So, you know how I went to Bogota recently, and there were talks of revolution and unrest, and I really thought it would be my last time there."

"Right."

"And I know how you really wanted something nice to match the ring you got from me last time."

"Yes, the absolutely flawless emerald ring. I told you I wanted nothing less."

"But you've got to know, it's difficult. With the unsettling news, everyone rushed to the mines, and they were asking outrageous prices. It's so hard to source anything nice now."

"I get it, Vikram." Mad smiled softly with appreciation.

"So, this is all I could find." He opened the box.

Mad gasped.

Inside were a pair of flawless, intensely green, rectangular-shaped emeralds, roughly 30 carats each, dangling from an equally amazing emerald surmount of roughly 15 carats each. Simply mounted, but absolutely gorgeous in the way that they needn't have anything else to amplify their beauty.

"Aren't they ravishing?" he asked.

Vikram had done it again. He always pulled through and found the best gems for her. She was elated—and astonished!

"How could you pull this out in the middle of the restaurant! People can see them!"

"Oh, don't worry, the owner of this place wears bigger diamonds than the Queen of England. We're safe here."

"Right!" Mad rolled her eyes in disbelief.

Vikram laughed out loud. "Do you want it or not?"

"Absolutely!" She grabbed the box and snapped it shut. Before she could stash it in her bag, Vikram stopped her.

"On one condition!"

"What?" Mad paused.

"Only if you hold the baby."

"What?!"

"Come on, try it."

Hesitantly, Mad gazed over at the baby. Of course, Vikram wasn't going to force her to hold his baby if she vehemently refused to. But in all honesty, she wasn't 100 percent against it either. Shari handed her the little boy. Stiff as stone, Mad held him tightly, afraid she might drop their precious cargo.

"Loosen up!"

"OK! OK!"

She slowly eased her grip and cradled the little being. He felt so soft in his sky-blue onesie and smelled like sweet honeysuckle.

"How does it feel?"

Calming. Strangely calming.

Mad gazed at the sleeping child in her arms and felt like she had entered another world. She smiled.

So, this is how it feels.

"You want this too?" Shari asked lightly.

"Absolutely . . . one day . . . one day."

CHAPTER SIX

Home

When she pushed open the apartment doors to a grand duplex penthouse situated in the prestigious Mid-Levels in Hong Kong, Mad had the urge to shout out, "Honey! I'm home!" But stopped herself.

"What did you say, ma'am?" asked her chauffeur, Ben, who was dropping off her luggage in the foyer.

"Oh! Nothing. I'll be downstairs in a short moment."

Ben nodded and closed the front door as quietly as he had entered, leaving Mad staring at the magnificent floor-to-ceiling view of the glittering harbor and tangled skyscrapers of the Hong Kong skyline. Had she arrived earlier as planned, "Honey! I'm home!" would have been so much more appropriate; she envisioned the welcoming hugs, laughs, and kisses from Steve before he went to work. Instead, she found herself standing alone in the whiteness of their sterile living room that desperately needed a touch of hominess to make it more inviting. A black-and-white close-up photo of them on their wedding day, laughing at something outrageously hilarious, sat propped against the wall, waiting to be hung. Beside it, a momentous pile of wedding gifts, waiting to be opened. She'd told Steve that they would do it together, but it had been half a year and they hadn't had the time to do so, let alone enjoy their beautiful new home.

Not surprisingly, most of their time had been spent traveling. And when they were actually in Hong Kong together, they were hardly home. There were dizzying social events such as dinners, soirees, charity balls, and restaurant openings to attend.

Mad couldn't even remember the last time she'd taken in the spectacular harbor view. Or, when she'd last sat on their beige ultraluxe Italian sofa and lazed in the sea of matching cushions. Other than to make coffee, had she ever used their state-of-the-art kitchen? How about that fake fireplace? Yes, the one she had really wanted installed in their apartment. Had they used it yet? Mad gazed at the black hole underneath the sleek flat-screen TV and imagined the crackling fire warming up the whole room.

Would look good with Christmas stockings hung on top. How about a Christmas tree over there? Actually, where were we last Christmas?

Mad racked her brain but couldn't remember. Submitting to defeat, she turned her attention to what needed to be addressed more urgently: freshening up and running off to her meeting before having dinner with Steve and his family tonight. It had been a while since she'd last seen her in-laws. She was actually quite looking forward to spending some family time with them.

Dragging her suitcase up the stairs, she arrived at their bedroom, which had already been cleaned and tidied by their part-time housekeeper. Not that there was much to tidy; she hadn't been back for weeks, and neither she nor Steve were messy. Mad maneuvered around their California king–size bed, which occupied the better part of the room, and into her walk-in closet connected to her own bathroom. Someone had once told her that the key to a long marriage was having his-and-hers spaces. Was it from one of those tai tais, who loved giving her life lessons at the jewelry previews? She would be hard-pressed to remember. Regardless, those were wise words considering the boiling friction the toilet and closet space could cause any couple, especially when the honeymoon period was over.

Steve's wing was on the right side of their bed, making it conveniently separate yet not too far apart from Mad's. His closet was easily distinguishable, if one were to accidently step in. Whilst his was a palette of blacks, greys, and whites with hardly any signs of vibrancy, hers was bursting with a Pantone of lively colors that shouted celebration, glee, and elation, clearly compensating for her former dreary years of monotonous auction house attire. Amid the mirrored surfaces accentuated by automated LED mood lighting, a white multidrawer dressing table allowed Mad, an organizational fanatic, to hide an unlikely clutter of creams, makeup, and tools that she had yet to sort out. Hovering above the table was a giant vanity mirror, and unbeknownst to others, a built-in jewelry safe hid right behind the panel, equipped with a two-layer security system and a just-in-case panic button. That was where she placed her blossoming collection of jewelry and where she usually headed first upon arriving home.

Today, lying on top of the table was a note from sweet Steve:

I miss you.
See you at HK Club tonight at 7:00 pm.
Love, Steve

Mad smiled; but she couldn't help noticing a digital clock out of the corner of her eye, warning her that she was going to be late—again. Grabbing a Q-tip, she quickly cleaned the smudges of makeup off her eyes, reapplied her lipstick, grabbed her bag, and rushed down to the car. They made their way down the hill, through one of the cross-harbor underwater tunnels, and into the Kowloon side of the city. They turned onto a street dedicated to selling various jade items, where generations of jadeite dealers and highly skilled carvers convened. Stopping in front of one of the many unassuming storefronts, Mad hopped out of the car and made a beeline towards an entrance flanked by typical commercially ready jade ornaments and cheap touristy jewelry. No one would suspect that this place belonged to one of the biggest jadeite dealers in the world and that behind the mirage of a tourist trap, high-quality goods worth millions of dollars were stashed on the upper floors.

Inside the shop, a powerful odor of herbal oils mixed with some sort of cooked meal hovered in the air. Indeed, behind one of the showcases sat a woman with a newspaper in one hand and the other digging into a rice dish with meat of some sort. The woman barely gave Mad a look as she walked on by and ran up the stairs to the second floor, where she was to meet Hailey and Hazel, the next-in-line to this prominent jadeite family business.

Mad had met Hailey and Hazel while they were studying at the GIA school. The twin sisters did not need any schooling in the field of jade, but when it came to diamonds, Mad and the two bonded over the difficult task of mapping out the various microscopic inclusions on the diamond table and pavilion under 10x magnification. Funny how such excruciating torture formed lasting friendships.

"Mad! Finally! You're here!" Hailey said, swinging open the door to their workshop.

"I hope it's OK. The woman downstairs didn't stop me." Mad gave Hailey a hug. "I just walked on up."

"Don't worry about it," Hazel said as her head appeared from behind the door. "She knows who you are."

"Hey!" Mad gave Hazel a hug. "How are you?"

The identical twins were only born a minute apart; they were so similar in the way they acted, talked, and dressed that even their parents sometimes had difficulty differentiating them. Mad only figured out how to tell them apart by the way they parted their long black hair. Hailey *usually* had hers on the right side and Hazel on the left. Of course, Mad had made mistakes, but they always found it amusing and were quite forgiving.

"So, we didn't wait for you and started carving," Hailey said.

"Actually, we couldn't wait for you," Hazel clarified. "If you wanted to make that deadline of yours."

"I know, I know," Mad agreed as she was escorted by the women to a workbench. "You girls are the experts."

Placed on top of the workbench was the jadeite boulder Mad had purchased from Myanmar. It had been a gamble, since no one was sure what material or colors would emerge from within. As much experience as any dealer or miner had, no one could be 100 percent certain. Some stones appeared promising from the surface, but once cut open, it could be an entirely different story. She'd had it shipped over to the workshop months earlier so the women would have enough time to examine and study it before concluding if what Mad wanted carved was feasible at all.

"See." Hazel pointed at the behemoth of a rock that once had a weathered brownish layer of "skin" covering it. The layer had been stripped away and revealed the glorious shades of green underneath it. "We opened some windows here and there," she said, pointing with her finger, "and figured out where we could make the cut."

"You're very lucky," Hailey added. "The material and mottling are perfect for what you want carved. The translucency is more or less uniform throughout, and we can most certainly carve the people on the darker greens to accentuate it from the background."

"Like a relief. A shell cameo." Hazel chuckled. "Hated finding the RIs on those."

"For sure!" Mad said as she remembered their GIA days of finding the refractive index of different gemstones. Shell cameos were tricky and managed to stump them on numerous occasions. "So, when will this be finished?"

"Give us a few weeks. We'll make sure it arrives on time in Venice. I can't imagine your unity-themed exhibition without it."

Mad touched the side of the cold jadeite boulder and imagined what the finished product would materialize into. "Me either."

"Now!" Hailey took Mad's hand. "Follow me, we have something to show you."

The women led Mad into their office and quietly closed the door, indicating that perhaps they had something confidential and significant to show.

She sat down at their desk, hoping that they had found what she had asked for. It was not a secret that one area of the prince's collection that needed improvement was jadeite. Not only did she have to increase the quantity of jewelry items in this category; she also had to find truly spectacular pieces. Mad had easily acquired jadeite cabochons, carved pendants, and bangles of fantastic color and translucency in her first month of work. But the ultimate collector's item was a jadeite bead necklace, and in particular, one that could eclipse the most famous jadeite bead necklace in the world: the Hutton-Mdivani necklace, sold to Cartier for a record-breaking US$27.44 million.

In 1933 the necklace was given to Barbara Hutton of the Woolworth retail empire, the wealthiest heiress of that time, as a wedding gift from her father on her marriage to Prince Alexis Mdivani. Twenty-seven exceptionally carved imperial jadeite beads ranging from a stunning 15.4 to 19.2 mm, speculated to be from the Qing dynasty, adorned the necklace with a specially commissioned ruby and diamond clasp by Cartier. Well known for her impressive jewelry collection, Hutton had remarkable taste, and as a jade enthusiast sought out only the best. Naturally, not only were the beads of exceptional size (high-quality jadeite rough hardly yielded beads over 10 mm!) but they were all well-matched in bright emerald-green color with high translucency. This could only mean that all the beads came from one spectacular green vein in one slab of jadeite boulder. To this day, it was still known as the greatest jadeite necklace in the world. To acquire something of the same magnificence, if not better, would be one of Mad's greatest achievements.

"We thought you would be interested in these." Hailey presented a jewelry box big enough to store a bead necklace.

Expecting nothing less, Mad grinned from ear to ear as she hastily opened the box, only to reveal every type of jadeite jewelry *but* a bead necklace. Her heart sank. Despite the letdown, the contents were all old-material jadeite of superb craftmanship and intricacies reminiscent of the grand carving masters' work. Although the colors were a bit dull, due to the lack of "water" representative of the tastes of that period, they were nonetheless collectable pieces.

"You mentioned you wanted to find some old jadeite, right? We sourced them up and down this street."

"Yes . . ." Mad mumbled disappointedly. Her hand sifted through the rubble, eliminating those that had seen better days, before refining, landing on the keepers—carved jadeite pendants of auspicious animals such as dragons, fish, and phoenix, fruits and foliage such as pomegranates and bamboo, and dangling earrings of pea pods and chilis.

"I'll take these," Mad announced and slumped down in her chair.

"Oh!" Hazel pulled out another box. "We almost forgot to show you this one too."

"More?!"

"Yes, well, we found a collector from Honolulu. There's actually quite a bounty of old jadeite there!"

Mad dragged herself out of the chair and reached for the box, but she caught the women deliberately forcing down a telltale smile. Their lips unmistakably quivered as though they were trying to suppress convulsions of laughter. Mad instantly knew.

Snapping the golden buckles open, she grasped the lid, pulled it up, and feasted her eyes on a jadeite bead necklace of Flintstones proportions. Glistening splendidly, each and every bead was matched in vivid green color and naturally, of the highest translucency. Compared to the older material of the Hutton-Mdivani necklace, its color and "water" were simply unparalleled. The back of her hand grazed the surface of the beads, and a refreshing brisk coolness sent a thrilling electrifying pulse through her body. Taking a deep breath, Mad used her pocket flashlight to cast a beam of yellow light through each bead, uncovering any common flaws, such as mottling or black and white spots. Yet, there were none; *it was flawless.*

Heart thumping hard against her chest, she lifted the neck-lace up by the ends of the string impeccably strung through each hole. The beads ever so gently brushed against each other, ringing a crisp clinking chime, validating that it had not been impregnated with synthetic resin or color. The only thing missing was a clasp.

"In case you're wondering, twenty-seven beads, ranging from eighteen point two to twenty-two point six millimeters," Hazel whispered, careful not to disturb the rapturous moment.

Even larger than the Hutton-Mdivani necklace.

"I'm just going to assume you want it. Now tell me, what clasp?" Hailey asked confidently.

Without breaking eye contact, Mad replied, "I'll send you one."

"An Art Deco one like the Hutton-Mdivani? We can source one for you."

"No!" Mad said, slightly annoyed. "We move forward, girls. People try too hard, and they think it's all about emulating that necklace. But I'm not going to do that. I'm going to create something different—a legend."

The women looked puzzled.

"I'll send you a diamond star," Mad revealed. "It'll be per-fect for this."

"You mean like the Chanel ones?" Hazel asked. "Pavé-set with circular diamonds?"

"For real?! Chanel is for bags, not for jewelry." Mad shook her head and added incredulously, "Do you think I own one of those?"

"You can't mean one whole diamond?"

Mad smirked.

"No way!"

"We had a rough cut into a DIF star-shaped diamond and named the stone 'Superstar.' Cuz naturally it is a superstar!" bragged Mad.

"Carat weight?"

"Juuuussst over 50 carats," said Mad.

"Whoahhhhh! Only you could think of something like that!" Hazel grinned. "It's going to be the talk of the town!"

"We love it!" both women sang together.

"I'll have it sent over next week. Just make a simple mounting, less gold, OK?"

"Yes, *ma'am*! We know what to do. And we'll have everything shipped to Venice on time."

Mad couldn't help smiling as she took a picture of the necklace with her phone and sent it to the prince and Fiona. She knew when they saw it, they would be as ecstatic as she was.

She felt victorious as she left the workshop and walked down to the street. The sky had turned dark, but the street was alive with blazing neon lights perched perilously on the sides of the buildings. It had been a glorious and successful day. Things were back on track, the exhibition was turning out great, there was nothing to complain about. Just smooth sailing ahead.

Ding!

I heard you're back!

I have something for you to see

News travels fast!

It was Baron, one of the biggest collectors of contemporary designer jewelry, allegedly. Mad wasn't certain, but the rumor was he owned a pretty impressive collection. This was a good chance to see what he had to offer, and it was only 6:00 p.m. She *could* squeeze in a meeting before dinner. Even if she was late, she wouldn't be *too* late if she managed her time well. Steve would most certainly be fine with it. It certainly sounded feasible. Mad conveniently convinced herself that she should give it a go.

Mad:

> I'll come see you now

She jumped into her car and sped across the harbor, back onto Hong Kong island, up another hill, arriving at a house on Jardine's Lookout. As rare as houses were in Hong Kong, due to the aggressive effects of humidity, a well-maintained one was even rarer. If not varnished with a toxin-protecting nano-photocatalyst coating, structures, walls, and furniture easily wept with cancerous mold and bacteria. Now, Mad found herself in front of a perfect example. From where she stood, the house looked old, unkept, and burgeoning in black and dark-greenish contamination similar to the inclusions in serpentine gemstones.

"Mad! Glad you could make it," Baron said, walking out of his front door.

Clad in a Barocco-print Versace midlength robe, and from the looks of it, underneath, the pajamas of the same print as well, he swiftly held his hand out to shake hers, revealing a pair of yellow-gold Cartier love bangles pavé-set with circular diamonds. With his hair slicked back and feet in burgundy velvet loafers, all he needed was a cigar dangling from his mouth to complete the Hugh Hefner playboy persona.

"I just arrived in Hong Kong. How have you been?"

"Oh, you know, same old, same old," Baron said, ushering her into the house.

Fully aware of the limited amount of time she had, Mad pressed on. "So, what did you want to show me?" she asked hastily, cutting to the chase.

However, she didn't receive an answer.

Instead, he led her through a moldy hallway, passing several doors, into a room that looked like a study. Books, magazines, and unopened mail piled on top of an imposing wooden desk scattered with stationery and a three-quarters-finished cigarillo in an ashtray. The walls were plastered with framed photos of various sizes, many of which were Baron on a yacht with his friends, lounging in the sun, or catching a monster of a fish.

"Would you like a drink?" Baron offered.

"No!" Mad blurted out before realizing how forceful she might have sounded, then quickly tried mitigating. "I mean, no, thank you."

Overlooking her blunder, he turned to his helper standing at the doorway.

"The usual," Baron instructed.

The helper turned around and left, letting them settle into their designated seats by the table: Baron in a massive brown armchair which would fit seamlessly next to a fireplace with stuffed animal heads in a log cabin; Mad in a slightly precarious-looking swivel office chair. She should have known from her brief encounters with Baron that "the usual" was probably something unique. Half expecting water or coffee, Mad was surprised when two glasses of Hennessey XO cognac, each with a round ice cube, appeared before her eyes. Without a word, he took a sip. Normally, as a courtesy, she would too, but cognac was really not her thing, and she was not about to try to impress Baron when he hadn't even shown her any jewelry deeming him worthy of impressing.

"So, Mad," Baron finally said, placing his glass down. "You know how I'm quite well-known in the jewelry industry."

"Right."

"I'm not exaggerating. Everyone knows me! Of the vast jewelry collection that I have. Especially designer jewelry. I've been collecting jewelry from designers who weren't even famous yet, and now all of them are recognized and acclaimed jewelry designers and brands."

"So I've heard."

"I'm not tooting my horn, but before me, they were honestly no one. Just the other day, my friend was telling me how they overhead someone from the next table at the Jockey Club talking about my jewelry collection. They say I have 'an eye' for spotting the next up-and-coming designer, and I'm the jewelry industry's influencer!" Baron laughed out loud, obviously enjoying retelling the tale. "How funny! I don't even know who these people are! And they know who I am!"

"Well, yes, you are very famous."

"Really?!" he asked, like a child fishing for affirmation.

"Yes, of course," Mad offered, but Baron's countenance didn't seem like he was appeased, forcing her to humor him. "My ex-boss always talked about you and told us how the day you consigned jewelry to her would be the happiest day in her life—even happier than her wedding day!"

"Really?!" Baron's eyes widened to the size of gleaming saucers.

Of course, she didn't mean it! She thought everyone should kiss her ass, not the other way around.

"I'm surprised you didn't hear of it! She always said you were on her dream list! Just like the founders of Tencent . . . Alibaba . . . SaSa."

Baron burst out laughing, clearly loving the pleasantries being offered. Fully convinced and satisfied, he ultimately continued.

"Well, I actually contacted you because I've decided that it's time for me to sell my jewelry—slowly."

Music to my ears.

"Oh, why so?" Mad asked innocently.

"When too many people start buying something, it's time to start selling. Just like Hermès bags. Back in the days it was all about quality and exclusivity, the Birkins and Kellys. Now *everyone* has one! It's no longer chic! People don't buy it for the quality—not that it's that great anymore—people buy it because it's expensive, it's a status symbol. They want to show off and fill up whatever emotional hole they have in their lives."

"Well, I wouldn't go that far. It's still a perfectly exquisite handbag."

"Yes, but honestly, how many bags do you need? Do you really need a Birkin in every color?"

"Well, if you put it that way." Mad shrugged her shoulders and wondered why they were talking about handbags.

"I'm completely disappointed in the quality! Ghastly! It's become so commercial; it's no longer what it stands for."

"Right," Mad replied nonchalantly, but knew she had to bring Baron back on topic. "And so, what does that have to do with jewelry?"

"That's what I see with the jewelry industry too! It's a money-making machine; all about profits. It's no longer about craftmanship, passion, and integrity! It just makes me sick to think about it."

"OK . . ."

"So, I just want to get rid of these things that remind me of what the world has become. The materialism of it. It's so passé. It's time to lead a simpler life."

"OK . . ." Mad repeated as she wondered when he'd finish his tirade.

"You know, one person told me years ago, when she sold off all her Birkins and Kellys, that it was liberating. Ever since, she's been living the life of a nomad; bouncing from hotel to hotel, country to country with no possessions. She could be where she wanted to be anytime, everywhere. How free is that?!"

No doubt luxury hotels . . .

"*So!* How can I help you?" Mad said firmly, hoping this would reel him in. Her patience had expired, and she felt more anxious as each minute passed.

"So, as I was saying, I want to sell some of my jewelry pieces. Maybe your prince would be interested. I heard he lacks some contemporary pieces in his collection, and you are actively filling that void."

"Well, yes. News does travel fast."

"Let me show you what I have."

About time!

Baron stood up from his armchair, but he didn't leave the room to fetch the pieces. Instead, he turned around and started rummaging through a big brown cardboard box directly behind him. It dawned on Mad that he kept his jewelry in a cardboard box! Usually, her clients, or any sane person, kept their items in a much safer and secure place. So odd yet so entirely befitting of the strange character. Nonetheless, she had heard that he had a good collection of JAR pieces bought from the grand maestro himself, which meant that no one had seen them before—or thought of searching in a cardboard box!

Maybe he has some Bhagat pieces too. The flair and modernity! How fabulous! Wouldn't it be nice to add some modern Indian pieces into the prince's already extensive Mughal collection? Or if his reputation really holds true, maybe some pieces from Hemmerle or Sabba . . . That would be wonderful!

Interrupting her train of thought, Baron deposited packs of jewelry inside transparent ziplock bags on the table. Mad shouldn't have been surprised at all. That was how they kept their jewelry at Minos too. It definitely cheapened the whole polished image of luxurious goods marketers wanted you to see, which was why they were always repackaged in velvet pouches and glossy boxes before being given to clients.

Mad stood up and hovered over the bags, shuffling them back and forth, like she was shopping at a flea market. As if that wasn't depressing enough, the jewelry itself sure was. There were none from any grand contemporary masters. As a matter of fact, there were only a handful of pieces made by "designers" *imitating* other designers. Some well-known in the industry for even thinking they were the next "JAR." Some she recognized from her auction days, made by dealers combining their stone collections together to make a jewelry piece sold under a more marketable pseudo brand name. No creativity, no passion, and no credibility—just plain disappointment.

"What do you think?" Baron asked anxiously.

"Um . . ." Mad replied hesitantly. "Do you have more?"

"More?!" Baron was taken aback, his ego noticeably hurt. "Yes, of course I have more! But as I was saying, I'm going to sell slowly, and I think these are the best for the current market conditions."

Mad doubted he had better pieces. Despite his reputation, it was indeed all rumors.

"Look at these pieces," Baron pursued. "His jewelry is sold in all the auction catalogs nowadays. And look at this one! She's the next JAR, you know."

I'm pretty sure if there's a "next JAR" it might be Emmanuel Tarpin and not whatever he's showing me now.

"And here, how about this?"

Baron held in his hands a necklace mounted with a line of diamonds and a line of emeralds. Each gemstone was connected by tapered baguette diamonds and emeralds in zigzag formation. The necklace was contemporary, but was it a masterpiece? No. Mad could tell it was not made by expert craftsmen, but it offered a false perception to the untrained eye. As a courtesy, though, she took the necklace from Baron's hand and began to inspect it. It would be rude if she didn't at least spend some time on it. She peered at the gemstones; the diamonds scintillated with fire and flashed beams of white light, complementing the lush greenish emeralds. Yet, the colors were not spellbinding, breathtaking, attention-grabbing enough to warrant a second glance. She placed the necklace on the back of her hand, letting it drape and caress the natural curvatures. Yet it didn't. As she expected, it lacked fluidity, sitting stiff and unyielding. On the neck, it would pass for an Elizabethan collar radiating hideous tastelessness, deformity, and erring. This was clearly made by someone lacking passion who probably worshipped money.

How ironic. He's clearly missed the mark on everything he's collected.

"They're all Muzos," Baron said, unrelenting.

"Right, yes, they're beautiful." Mad wavered, but she knew it was not wise to dismiss him completely. He didn't look like he took criticism lightly. It was better to do it softly and gradually. "These pieces are very modern and contemporary. I'm not sure if they're exactly what the prince is collecting. Would you mind if I take some pictures and discuss it with him first?"

"Well, of course! Yes, yes! You and the prince have probably never seen these pieces before. They're exclusive and one of a kind, you know." He laughed proudly.

"Yes, yes. They are all so . . . unique," Mad muttered as she took pictures with her phone, which also alarmingly indicated that it was 8:00 p.m. and she had a slew of missed calls and messages.

I better hurry up and leave!

As she snapped and scribbled notes, Baron rambled on about the importance of each piece and of course, himself. Oblivious to Mad's hurrying, he was obviously caught by surprise when he finally noticed that she had finished and packed up her tools. Bag on her shoulder, Mad stood up, readying to make a run for the door.

Baron looked bewildered. "You're done?"

"Yes!" Mad replied, power walking out the door. "I'll let you know if the prince is interested in anything."

"How about close-ups?" he shouted from the room.

"Got them!" she hollered back from the hallway.

"How about your drink?"

"It was greeeaattt, thaaaaank yoooou!" Mad answered even louder as she left the building, unsure whether Baron had heard her last words. She jumped into her waiting car and slammed the door shut.

"Hong Kong Club! ASAP! Ben! Speed!" Mad ordered.

The car sped out of the driveway, shrieking fiercely as it made a sharp turn to the right, onto the main road. Ben knew exactly what to do. Her phone flashed 8:30 p.m. but immediately jumped to 8:31 p.m. as Mad scanned through the distressing number of missed calls and unnerving messages, mostly from

Steve. Her heart raced as she called him back and thumped wildly to the obnoxiously slow and deafening ringtone, until it went to voicemail. Seemed like he was adhering to the club's no-cell-phone-usage policy. Some excruciating minutes later, at 9:00 p.m. sharp, they arrived at the front steps of the Hong Kong Club. Mad zoomed through the entrance and ran up the spiraling staircase to the private rooms. Without hesitation, she pushed through a set of doors, barging into what seemed like the finale of a dinner party.

Small clusters of men and women were dispersed about the room, chatting and laughing around the slightly stained white-clothed round dinner table. Placed on top were petit fours and various desserts, surrounded by wine, champagne, and miscellaneous alcohol glasses that were either empty or close to. Among the disarray, one table setting still remained, and sitting next to it, guarding it, was a man sipping on a glass of whiskey, chatting with a group of men. Recognizing the silhouette immediately, she knew it was Steve. At that moment, as if he felt her presence, he turned around and spotted Mad as well. His flicker of a smile was encouraging, but as quickly as it appeared, it disappeared. It dissipated into a frown, casting a cold draft in the space between them. With fortitude and certainty, she walked towards him, ready to face the music—only to be blocked by a waiter.

"Champagne, Mrs. Lam."

"Oh, no, it's OK," Mad declined. It wouldn't look good if she walked up to Steve, at the brink of a storm, with an alcoholic beverage in her hand. Nonetheless, the waiter kept the glass in midair, waiting for her to take it.

"Mad!" One of Steve's aunties slurred and wobbled towards her direction. "Here you are! Where have you been?"

Smoothly, the waiter deftly slid the glass of champagne into Mad's hand and walked off briskly.

"Oh! Hello, Auntie Marge. I just finished my work—"

"Work?!" Auntie Marge shrieked, characteristically of someone drunk. "At this ungodly hour! Who is your boss? Let me have a word with—"

"Auntie Marge!" Steve whisked in just before she launched into a diatribe. "I'm so sorry for breaking up your conversation. But my poor wife hasn't eaten yet. The club has to serve her before the kitchen closes."

"Oh! Poor thing! Run along and quickly get something to eat, my dear."

Placing his arm protectively around Mad's waist, Steve ushered her over to the table. His friends, shrewdly, had left. Upon seeing them seated, the waiters swiftly brought over a hot bowl of lobster bisque and the roast beef main course. The food smelled and looked delicious, but Mad couldn't help but stare at Steve's clenched jaw instead. He was clearly upset.

"I'm so sorry for being late," Mad said softly; but he didn't answer.

"Steve?"

"You could have called. Left a message!" he said under his breath. "Do you know how it feels when you can't find someone? Especially your wife!"

"I'm so sorry! I wanted to get out of the meeting as soon as possible! And I couldn't check my messages until I left!"

"If it wasn't for Ben, I would have thought something happened to you," Steve said, with a tinge of relief, but no sooner returned to restrained anger. "You should have called. If you were in my position, I don't know what you would have done."

I would have gone ballistic!

"I'm so sorry!" Mad pleaded.

"You know how important this dinner was to me? Business dinners, I understand. But this is a family dinner! Nothing is more important than family!"

"I'm so sorry," she repeated. But even she was tired of hearing herself say those words. It seemed like no matter how many times she repeated them, she was just digging a deeper hole for herself. The silence, though, was unbearable. "I totally mishandled the situation, and I know you're upset and—"

"Mad!"

Both snapped their heads up and saw Steve's mom and her friends descending on them.

"You're here! *And late!* Drink up!" Steve's mom cried as she towered over and shoved a glass of red wine filled to the brim in front of Mad's face.

Mad wondered how her mother-in-law always looked impeccable, even slightly red-faced from the alcohol she had consumed. No smudges around her eyes nor lipstick smeared; her hair perfectly curled and coiffed to a length covering her ears but slightly above the 8-carat circular diamond ear studs. Dressed in the latest fashion, there was nothing old-school about her. Tonight, she wore fitted black leather pants and a Balmain military jacket over a gold-lettered "It's Versace, not Versachee" T-shirt. Her entourage of friends circled around her, all wearing similar outfits with a few adaptions, but none without either a bottle of wine in hand or a wineglass. Some with both.

Noticeably annoyed at the intrusion, Steve sternly said, "Mother, we're talking."

"You can talk later! How often do I get to see my daughter-in-law? Now bottoms up!" Steve's mom insisted and pushed her son aside, but not without giving Mad a little split-second smile that only she could see. The ones that the Lams had perfected so well and Mad had seen Steve using when he had something mischievous in mind.

Like mother, like son. She's trying to save me from Steve!

However, Mad wasn't sure if that was a good idea. If postponing the talk with Steve meant consuming a lot of alcohol, then it really didn't seem that alluring at all. But it seemed she had no choice. The ominous crowd, which had now surrounded her, like picketers around a bonfire, chanted, "Drink! Drink! Drink!" With no other option, Mad obediently did so, taking breaths in between each gulp, drinking until the very last drop. Without skipping a beat, her mother-in-law filled up the empty glass, which could only mean there was more drinking to come.

"Mad! Remember Auntie Bella? We went to Miss Porter's together."

"Hello, Auntie Bella," Mad said, simultaneously clinking glasses with her. Mad took a sip, but Auntie Bella didn't. She downed it! If Mad wanted to be polite and not embarrass her mother-in-law, she would have to do so too. Taking a deep breath, she poured the contents of the glass down her throat. It was brutal! She felt the cool wine trickle down her esophagus and into her empty stomach. The effects of the alcohol instantly shot through her blood, accelerating her heartbeat and filling her with a sudden warmth. She actually felt a little better, happier, looser, giddier.

"Now, Mad, this is Auntie Naomi. We've been friends forever!"

"Oh! I remember Steve when he was a baby!" Auntie Naomi said. "He's such a lucky boy to—"

Mad didn't hear the last few words. Her glass had magically been refilled. Her hand holding the glass automatically moved forward, clinking with the others before rising to her mouth, which took another giant gulp.

"This is Auntie Vivian. Remember? She went to your wedding?"

And another gulp.

"This is Auntie—"

And another.

In the dizzying disarray of alcoholic debauchery, frenzied laughter, and high-spirited banter, Steve had been pushed outside the circle of women. His furrowed eyebrows exhibited concern, but soon men circled around him, and within moments, it all became a blur. There was more red wine and uncontrolled laughter until Mad felt the inevitable sickness of a stomach that had had enough. The room swerved as she felt herself losing complete control. The last bits of memories she had were of the smell of soft leather seats in a car, the gooey redness of the acrid substance ejected from her throat into the toilet bowl, the muscular arms carrying her up the stairs, the softness of her pillow, her comforter, and then she was gone.

A few weeks before, Mad had promised herself she would never be in that position again. The one where she drank so much that the next day ensured a merciless splitting headache, dehydrated, nonfunctional, fatigued body, and a bottomless black hole of remorse. But there she was, hands grasping her thumping temples, scowling at the pain she had inflicted on herself, again. Still in bed, but only half awake, she recalled the shuffling noises from Steve's closet and splashing water from the bathroom. He had woken up and gotten ready for work. She remembered his hand touching her forehead before he left the room. The smell of coffee brewing from the kitchen downstairs and the gentle but still audible click of the front door closing. Then she passed out again and awoke to this.

What a disastrous night.

Moving gently to her side, she felt the softness of her silk pajamas gliding on her skin. Steve must have changed her last night. Slowly getting out of bed, she walked over to the bar cart at the side of the room to get some water. Placed delicately next to an already filled glass of water was a note.

Panadol will help with the hangover.
Chef will deliver soup.
I'm off to Shanghai this morning but I will see you in Australia.
Miss you already.
Love, Steve

Carefully placed on a small dish and taken out of their packaging were two Panadol pills. Mad sighed as she reread the note and felt terrible about what happened last night. Still, she was extremely relieved that her mother-in-law's plan had worked and Steve didn't seem upset at her today. Putting the pills in her mouth and taking some water to wash them down, she scanned the room for her cell phone. Without fail, it sat connected to the charging cable on her bedside table. Steve had charged it for her. She walked back to the bed and picked up the phone. It was 12:30 p.m.

12:30 p.m.!

Shock waves shot through her body!

12:30 p.m.! OH MY GOD! I'm in deep shit!

She was supposed to have lunch with Jackie today and go over the Maldives trip! Panic seized her as she hastily called

Jackie. Mad held her breath as the ringtone seemingly graduated in volume.

"Hello, Mrs. Madeleine Lam," Jackie said sarcastically. She only used full names when she was pissed off.

"I'm soooo sorry, Jackie! I had dinner with Steve's family last night, and you know how they get when they are all together. I got really drunk and blacked out. I just woke up and realized it's 12:30 p.m.! I'm so so *so* sorry about it!" Mad rambled on.

"I can't believe it! You stood me up!"

"I'll rush down right now! Give me like thirty minutes!"

"Don't bother coming!" Jackie shot her down.

"I'm so sorry, Jackie. You know I've never done this before! You know no matter how drunk I am, I'll still crawl out of bed and meet up with you. This is *really* an exception. They were *really* vicious last night!"

Silence.

"Jackie?"

"Well yes, Auntie Lam can be quite vicious—and relentless."

"See! You know what I mean! I barely got out of there alive! You have to forgive me! I'm *soooo* sorry!"

"Fine! But, I'm still very angry at you. It's so irresponsible! You know I hate people disrespecting my time."

"Absolutely!" Sensing that the tide was turning, Mad added, "Steve was upset at me, and his mother was trying to save me by making me drink. It was just chaos and bad decisions one after another. But I'm not excusing myself for my bad behavior. It is my fault, and I'm truly sorry about it."

"You and Steve got into a fight?" Jackie asked, sounding slightly concerned. She was her best friend, after all.

"Well, I've had to cut my time in Hong Kong short, and we basically only had last night together, which ended up being a total disaster! Anyways, it's not something I can deal with at the moment. I'll come see you now?"

"No," Jackie said sternly, but her tone did not sound angry anymore.

"Then, tell me what I can do to make it up to you."

Silence.

"Jackie? Please."

"All right! I'm not angry at you. You do sound like you had a horrible night and you're suffering immensely from it, not that I feel sorry for you. You deserve it."

Mad's whole body relaxed. "Yes, I do," she concurred.

"If you want to make it up to me, we were supposed to go through our Maldives trip at lunch today, but I don't think you can operate in your condition anyways. So, you might as well give me full rein."

"You mean . . . ?"

"I choose everything we do there. Maybe an input here or there from you. *Maybe.* But basically, I choose everything we do, eat, drink, etc., OK?"

"Yes! Yes! Of course!" Mad acquiesced promptly.

That's even better! I don't really have the time to go over the details anyways.

"OK then." Jackie sounded pacified. "You better get some rest. I can enjoy a quiet lunch by myself. I haven't had that liberty in a long time."

She sounded weary.

Is there something wrong?

Jackie always had an abundance of social events to attend. Mad never understood how she had the energy to do all those seemingly frivolous things, run her family business, date, and still look gorgeous all at the same time. Now, with Stuart, an equal in terms of the number of social engagements, her hectic life had only been compounded. But Mad never thought the all-invincible Jackie would crack.

"Have you been busy?"

"Yes, quite busy actually," Jackie replied but quickly changed the subject. "Don't you have to pack for New York? You're going tomorrow morning, right?"

"Yes, I do," Mad said, taken aback but deciding not to push her. "I'm excited about the Maldives!"

"I hope you are, and even if you're not, you better pretend that it's the best trip ever! You owe me bigtime!"

"Jackie, I don't need to pretend! I know I'm in good hands. You're always the best."

"And don't you ever forget that!" Jackie laughed jokingly.

But Mad knew her too well; she wasn't joking.

◇   ◇   ◇

New York was even colder this time around. Mad leaned closer to the window, where the temperature felt like it instantly dropped a few degrees. It was a crisp wintery morning. Even with her sunglasses on, she could see the bright yellow rays of the sun reflecting off the thin sheet of fresh snow that had blanketed the city overnight. She peered down at the bustling traffic; the yellow cabs and black sedans driving around Columbus Circle, some exiting onto Fifty-Ninth Street, cutting through the snowcapped greenery of Central Park and the stoic skyscrapers of New York City.

What a magnificent view.

As the warm moisture of her breath fogged up the glass, she pulled away, back into the comfort of her seat, facing the high ceilings and extended windows of the plush, handsome restaurant. Warming her hands on her second cup of cappuccino, she reflected on how she got here. How a nobody like her, once entrenched within the suffocating auction house rat race, escaped, flourished, and now basked in a life she never thought she would a while ago. She was extremely grateful and couldn't help but break into a smile. She felt unusually tired today. The thirteen-hour time difference would affect anyone, but she thought it was probably the long, sleepless plane ride yesterday that was taking a toll on her this time.

Bringing the cup to her mouth, she took a much-needed sip of caffeine. The mere smell of the nutty aroma helped awaken her senses and alleviated the arid air in the room, which, if she hadn't noticed before, she noticed now that it smelled slightly of jasmine, or was it sweet narcissus? She closed her eyes and took a deep breath, fully inhaling what she was sure was a combination of both flowers and more underlying complicated notes that somehow fit perfectly together. Yet oddly, the strength of it suddenly intensified.

"Mad?"

Her eyes snapped open. A woman in a Max Mara camel cashmere wrap coat stood before her. Her flowing lush dark locks and Van Cleef & Arpels orange cabochon coral ear studs, accented by pear-shaped amethysts and circular diamonds, framed her dainty face, and the sunglasses she had just taken off revealed big doll-like eyes and long lashes. Mad remembered the first time she saw her, she thought she was the most gorgeous lady she had ever seen in her life.

"Fiona!" she cried, gathering herself together. "Please sit!"

"Good morning," Fiona said as she took off her coat and sat in the seat across the table.

"Good morning to you too," Mad returned, taking off her sunglasses. "How are you?"

Fiona gasped.

"Fuck! You look like shit!" she cried, comically startling the waiter standing next to their table, who undoubtedly did not expect such an elegant woman to curse.

"Oh, excuse my language," Fiona said sweetly, redeeming herself. "I'll have an espresso and the smoked salmon and cream cheese bagel, please."

The waiter turned to Mad. She hadn't even thought about what to order yet and couldn't be bothered.

"The same, please. But cappuccino, not espresso."

"I love bagels in New York City," Fiona commented.

"Do I really look like shit?"

Mad pulled out her little pocket mirror from her bag. Her eyes did look droopy and puffy, and indeed there were dark bags underneath. The concealer she applied this morning had actually managed to make her skin drier. Her eyeliner wasn't crisp but rather messy and smudged. All in all, she looked rather dehydrated, jet-lagged, burned out, and as Fiona stated ever so bluntly, "like shit."

Mad frowned, which made the lines on her face even more apparent.

"Is there something wrong? Everything OK?" Fiona asked.

"What?!" Mad jolted up, feeling a little vulnerable and exposed.

Is there something wrong that I'm not aware of?

"No, nothing is wrong. Why?"

"Oh, just checking on you," Fiona replied. "Don't worry, I think it's just . . . winter. You need a nice hydrating mask and perhaps some time to take it easy? Get some rest? I could have my team help—"

Mad knew where she was heading and cut her off.

"No, no, don't worry. I'm OK. As you said, it's the weather. A hydrating mask will do. Plus, after the exhibition, I'll take a rest."

Fiona didn't look convinced. But Mad charged through.

"I'm super excited about the exhibition!"

"Talking about the exhibition"—Fiona finally relented—"I just got this in my email."

Mad peered at Fiona's phone.

"The designs for the exhibition hall. Look," said Fiona, pointing. "Here's the entrance, the stage, and backdrop. The different sections for Mughal jewelry, Belle Époque, Art Deco, contemporary, hall of extraordinaries. We'll place the colored stones here, and the ruby and sapphire necklaces you just acquired here. And here are the showcases for the jadeite and the centerpiece carving . . ."

As Fiona continued, her voice began to trail, sounding like a hypnotic buzz, administered to relax and loosen. Mad's eyes became heavier as a warm hearty glow reverberated from within her body, her mind slipping away to a state of elevated cushy comfort.

". . . to the diamonds, the colored and the colorless . . ."

Falling deeper and deeper, Mad just managed to keep herself upright.

"Which reminds me . . . *andddd* here you go!"

Mad jolted and whipped her eyes open.

Oh my gosh! Again! Just like Myanmar! I've got to stay awake! What is wrong with me?

Fiona had placed two transparent jewelry membrane cases, each containing a diamond, on the table. They were the reason Mad had made this strenuous detour to New York City, instead of flying directly to Australia. She was going to have them recut in time for the Venice exhibition. One of them Mad had discovered a few months ago while rummaging through the prince's colored-diamond collection. She had come across the 14.09-carat marquise-cut fancy blue diamond, and upon examining where the color was concentrated, she knew instantly that with some recutting and polishing, the potential of the stone could be amplified to a fancy intense blue, making it much more valuable than it already was. At the moment, the stone was worth US$500,000 per carat. Even after the process and losing a few carats, it could easily be worth US$1.2 million per carat, increasing the total value by millions.

The other box contained a 35.09-carat D color, Type IIa, potentially internally flawless rectangular-shaped diamond. Again, with just a little nip and tuck, getting rid of the needle on the side, it would lose a little weight but then escalate the diamond's stature to an exquisite clarity of internally flawless. Worth US$120,000 per carat now, it would then be worth US$145,000 per carat, increasing the total value to a little less than US$900,000.

"Wonderful, I'll deliver them to the cutter," Mad said, fully awake now. "We've talked before, he knows what to do."

"He'll have it done before the exhibition? On time?"

"Yes. He's the best in the industry."

"All right then. We're in good hands. When are you leaving New York City?"

"I'm leaving tomorrow morning and heading to Australia."

"Do you want to grab dinner tonight? Just something cozy at my friend's near here."

Cozy?! Again?!

"No! I better not!" Mad declined quickly. "I'm going to order some room service and have that hydrating mask you were talking about."

"You sure you don't need some help with all this?" Fiona looked worried. "I mean, all the traveling must be super tiring."

Why does she keep on asking me? Of course I can do it.

"Trust me, I can handle it. It's just jet lag, and honestly, winters here are not my forte."

Fiona stared at her, opened her mouth to say something, but then closed it and paused for a moment before speaking again.

"All right, but do let me know if you change your mind. Now where is my coffee?! Waiter!"

Mad exhaled a sigh of relief. She did feel unusually fatigued, but she was sure it was the combination of the frigid weather and the additional amount of traveling. Brushing that all aside, she looked forward to the exhibition that was coming together quite well. There was absolutely nothing to worry about.

All I need is some rest, and then I'll be on top of my game again.

CHAPTER SEVEN

Down Under

It had to be the longest flight ever, *period*. With a brief stop in Singapore, it took more than thirty excruciating hours to fly from New York City to Sydney, Australia. The good thing was, Mad slept for a full twelve hours straight and got the rest she desperately needed. As a matter of fact, she slept so much her back muscles ached when she finally crawled out of her seat-bed, showered, and put on makeup before landing. She changed from her polar-arctic apparel to a sunny ensemble of a white T-shirt and miniskirt befitting the hellish Australian summer, known to jump up to 40-plus Celsius, equivalent to 104-plus Fahrenheit. Having freshened up, she didn't need to head to her hotel first and could dive straight into work, which involved acquiring Argyle pink diamonds and South Sea pearls before meeting up with Steve in two days for a rendezvous in the Blue Mountains. With her sunglasses and Speedy bag in tow, she left the airport, headed to Chinatown in downtown Sydney, and within minutes, found herself surrounded by trays and trays of Argyle pink diamonds, in an office situated right above an unassuming abalone-selling kiosk.

Australia is a country with an abundance of natural resources, contributing to the vast mining operations of minerals and gemstones since the colonial days. One of the most famous mines had been the Argyle. Located in Western Australia and discovered in 1979, the mine had been known to produce the most stunning array of pink, red, and purple diamonds in small sizes but large quantities. Since its opening, it had become the largest producer of fancy pink diamonds, quenching the insatiable thirst for these extraordinary stones by supplying more than 90 percent of the world's demand. However, all good things must come to an end. Argyle finally had to close down when it became so deep that further operations and rising costs overwhelmed revenues. One person had the hindsight and wisely stocked up on these precious diamonds over the years, knowing that one day they would be as rare as Kashmir sapphires. Although his main line of business was selling abalones, since the closing of Argyle, it had become his side business, appropriately changing his moniker from "Abalone Tom" to a rather glitzy "Pink Diamond Tom."

"Are these what you wanted?" Tom inquired as he and Mad hovered over a table filled with plastic boxes containing his prized possessions in various shapes and sizes.

"Ummm . . ." Mad said, shuffling the boxes around. She was searching for some pink diamonds to mount around a cushion-shaped green diamond. Pink on green was all the rage now as the color juxtaposition accentuated and emphasized the center stone's intensity, *if done right*.

"You wanted some seven-pointers for your green diamond, right?" Tom asked. "I wasn't sure what shade of green you had, so I just organized a spectrum of pinks for you to see."

"How can I explain it? It's more of a bright green, not a pastel green, so not baby pinks but maybe—"

"Hot pinks."

"Precisely."

"Got it! Give me a few minutes."

Tom left and returned a bit later with several plastic transparent boxes of circular pink diamonds lined in rows.

"Happy hunting," he reveled.

"Eh—" Mad began to say, wanting to chat with him—after all, she hadn't talked with anyone for more than two days—but Tom had already disappeared.

Mad sat down alone at the table and exhaled deeply. She took out her tools and turned on the diamond light.

Here we go.

Summoning all her efforts, she went through each box and sorted out the "hottest" pinks. She then eliminated those with major clarity issues (too included that you could see without a loupe) or with table dimensions that differentiated too much from the others (diamonds could weigh the same but differ in pavilion depth and table width). She needed to make sure all the diamonds were uniform in color and size, while clean enough that they didn't deflect from the beauty of the stone. As straightforward as it sounded, it took Mad seven hours to choose fourteen suitably well-matched hot-pink diamonds. By the time she was fully satisfied, the sky was dark and her eyes so tired, her vision so blurred, that she couldn't differentiate what was pink enough anymore. Placing the diamonds in a new transparent plastic box, she sealed it shut with tape and handed it to Tom, who promised to have it shipped promptly to her workshop in Hong Kong, where the diamonds would be mounted in time for the Venice exhibition.

Normally, after visiting Tom, Mad would walk back to the hotel, taking advantage of the dry coolness of the Australian summer. But the same unfamiliar exhaustion had engulfed her again, so she instead decided to take the car and call it an early night. It was not until she reached her hotel room when a sudden urge propelled her to frantically switch on all the lights in the room, check behind the curtains, underneath the bed, and in the closets to make sure no one, *or nothing* was there. Content, she switched on the television to CNN before ultimately falling asleep to the monotonous voice of the news anchor.

It was wishful thinking on Mad's part, but she really thought she could sleep until her alarm rang at 6:00 a.m. Regrettably, her eyes popped open wearily at 2:00 a.m., and alas, after enduring several hours of tossing and turning, which she attributed to jet lag, she gave up, got up, made herself a coffee, and waited for the sun to rise. Mad knew it was going to be a long day, but perhaps she could take a nap on the flight to Broome that morning. The plan was to arrive in the early afternoon and meet with the Luna brothers, hopefully acquire some of their famous South Seas pearls, return to Sydney in the early evening, back to the airport in time to meet up with Steve the next morning, then head to the Blue Mountains together. Ambitious, but certainly doable. And she hoped the day trip to Broome would be worth it.

The prince had previously only acquired "natural pearls," those created spontaneously and accidently in nature, without any human intervention. Due to increased pollution in the oceans and other adverse factors such as climate change, natural pearls had become one of the rarest and most valuable gems on earth. Cultured pearls, on the other hand, were pearls formed by humans deliberately inserting a bead in the mollusc, causing a pearl sac to form around it. The ease of cultured pearl production caused the proliferation and commercialization of it, ultimately deteriorating the value and falling off any jewelry connoisseur's radar. However, there was one breed of cultured pearls that still stood strong within the collectors community, and that was produced by the *Pinctada Maxima*, the largest pearl oysters in the world that could create the largest pearls, called South Sea pearls. Of the multitudes of companies that produced South Sea pearls, only one surpassed Mad's discerning eye and exceeded all expectations. That was Luna.

Situated in the remote wild unspoiled waters of Northwestern Australia, the Luna pearl farms produced the crème de la crème of South Sea pearls. Adamant tenaciousness in sustainable aquaculture practices, combined with generations of experience, had earned them a reputation for creating pearls in exceptional sizes hardly seen in decades. In addition, their pearls were characterized by phenomenal luster and highly sought-after pinkish overtones induced by thick nacre conceived through years of immense patience. If there were cultured pearls worth acquiring for royalty, they would be from Luna. Consequently, Mad found herself, a couple hours later, getting off a private jet at Broome International Airport.

"Welcome to Broome!" said a man with "Luna" embossed on his shirt pocket, simultaneously opening the door to the car parked on the tarmac. "Mr. Luna is expecting you."

"Oh, thank you," Mad said as she slipped in the car, where she noticed fresh cold towels and glass-bottled water on the seat separator.

"Let me know if there's anything else you need other than water," he offered. "We also have chilled wines in the back."

"Oh gosh, no thank you! Water's fine!"

"Maybe later!" He chuckled and drove out of the tarmac.

"Maybe!" Mad replied dubiously.

Once out of the airport parameters, the car sped past a beautiful coastline of clear blue waters, white sandy beaches, and dramatic red sandstone cliffs. The sun beamed down on the dancing waves, forging glistening sparkles seemingly appearing ubiquitously and to no end. Mad couldn't help but lower the window and let the cool wind blow on her face, whipping her hair in a frenzy. She closed her eyes and took deep breaths of the crisp clean air mixed with a tinge of saltiness that calmed and relaxed her senses. Fully immersed in the moment, she didn't open her eyes until she felt the car stop longer than a traffic-light cycle. They had arrived in front of a house, or rather a mansion on the beachfront. Mad got out of the car and took in the magnitude of the multifloored suave white and glass-paned contemporary building surrounded by tropical plants and dozens of palm trees. The sounds of the nearby waves crashing, birds hospitably singing, and a wind chime faintly ringing in the distance suggested that this meeting might be more sociable than expected.

"Mad!"

She swung her head around. It was Logan. He ran down a flight of stairs hidden by a myriad of exotic greenery. Once he reached Mad, he gave her a Herculean hug that swept her off her feet before setting her back on the ground like she was a weightless feather. He promptly kissed her on both cheeks, bringing her intimately near the traces of sand on his earlobes and the ocean scent lingering on his neck from perhaps a morning swim or, as his toned physique suggested, most likely from surfing in the sea.

"I've been waiting for you!" Logan gushed. "How was your flight, everything OK?"

"Oh, yes, yes!" Mad caught her breath, still overwhelmed by his unorthodox welcome.

"I'm so glad you could make it here this time." He smiled. "There's so much I want to show you."

"Is this your house?" Mad asked, slightly disoriented. "I'm assuming this is not your office?"

"Oh yes. This is more appropriate for our relationship."

Our relationship?!

"Logan! Don't keep our guest out in the sun!"

Mad glanced up at the two older Luna brothers, Alexandro and Philippe, descending the same flight of stairs. The oldest brother, Philippe, was dressed in a blue suit, tie, and white shirt that seemed a bit too warm for the weather. Alexandro was more casual in his khaki suit without a tie, and Logan, Mad only now realized, was wearing jeans and a white T-shirt. As different as their styles were, they all radiated the same tanned, rugged, Hemsworth-brothers wholesome good looks. Blond, brown eyes, unceasing smiles, and unbelievably fit, they were the quintessential Australians depicted in movies, and with their accents, Mad could only imagine how many clients they had enchanted and mesmerized.

"Welcome to Broome, Mad," Alexandro said. "Please, let's go inside."

They led her up the stairs; the two older brothers walked in front while Logan, with his unfaltering smile, accompanied her by her side. At the top of the steps, the greenery opened up to a magnificent infinity pool that flowed and blended fabulously into the vast blue ocean and baby-blue skies. The waving palm trees, glowing afternoon sun, and inviting white-and-black striped sun chairs and umbrellas beckoned her to stop and perhaps take a dip. Mad thought they would head into the house, but instead they brought her straight to a crisp white cabana. A white marble-and-glass bar stood to the side of cushioned lounge chairs, facing the nearby sandy beach.

"What would you like to drink?" Alexandro asked as Mad took in the view and savored the moment.

"Oh, um—"

"A mojito? Gin and tonic? Wine?" Alexandro quickly suggested.

"Oh! I thought maybe an iced cappuccino!" Mad replied, surprised at the offering, although at second thought it was quite befitting of the current ambience.

"We could do that too, but you absolutely have to try our white wine," Philippe insisted. "We grow the grapes ourselves in our vineyard down south. It matches the oysters perfectly."

Their own wine? Their own oysters? What else do they have?!

"Um, sure," she replied, facing the three brightly smiling brothers. "I would love to try that."

Clearly glad that Mad accepted his offer, Philippe subsequently pulled out a bottle of white wine from behind the bar table.

As Mad settled down on the lounge chairs, a woman appeared with a towering platter of oysters and plates of cheese and cold cuts of all sorts. Mad's mouth watered at the number of delicacies placed on the table, barely taking her eyes off the display, even when Logan handed her a glass of white wine.

"Right, thank you." She took a sip of the refreshing wine. It was indeed a good choice.

"We're glad you could make it down here this time," Alexandro said. "We have something really special for your exhibition. As a matter of fact, it's so special, Logan wouldn't let anyone near it."

"I wanted you to see it first," Logan said with a twinkle in his eye.

Philippe walked over with an azure box and placed it in front of Mad.

"Tell me what you think." Philippe's brows furrowed. He seemed concerned with the reaction the box would invoke.

Logan, like a little boy, looked anxiously at Mad, waiting to see if she would be pleased.

Well aware of the scrutiny, she carefully lifted the lid, revealing the most gorgeous *and largest* strand of cultured pearl necklace she had ever seen in her life. Her eyes widened as she stared at thirty completely round white pearls, each glowing with highly coveted natural pink overtones, only seen in pearls that had not been enhanced with coloring or polishing. That itself promised it would last for generations. She took the necklace out of the box and examined each pearl. No blemishes, dimples, or spots—just pure perfection. And the luster! So fine and exquisite! Mad could see her own reflection on each and every pearl, like a mirror. Only the highest-quality nacre could achieve such magnificence.

"It's nineteen point five to twenty point one millimeters. Took us a whole decade to match. We only found the final pearl in the last harvest."

"It's . . . it's . . ." Mad stuttered. The necklace had rendered her speechless.

"We find that our pearls are best viewed out here in nature and natural sunlight—the atmosphere, the senses it evokes. But if you wish, we could go inside too."

"Oh no! This is perfect," she replied, longing to stay in the moment.

"And we have a pair of earrings to match them." Logan beamed.

He opened a second, smaller azure box. Inside were a pair of ear studs, equally stunning in color, shape, luster, and overtones. Mad reached out for them, but was stopped instantly.

"Here, let me do it." Logan took the ear studs out of the box and gently put them on her ears, his fingers lightly brushing her earlobes, sending a startling tingle through her spine. He then took the necklace and placed it around Mad's neck, delicately caressing her hair as he secured the clasp. She looked in the mirror, which had been placed in front of her by one of the brothers. She couldn't speak. The brothers waited in silence and held their breaths.

"Like a bride on her wedding day." Logan broke the moment of stupor.

Mad instantly blushed.

"Oh gosh!" she finally blurted out. "You guys are making me blush! I'm speechless! I'm sold! Please send it to the exhibition."

Philippe exhaled a big breath of relief. "Thank you for your business!"

"And many more to come." Alexandro laughed, infusing the moment with levity.

Mad laughed too and took off the necklace while Logan helped her with the ear studs. He gave her a wink, and she returned it with a smile.

"Thank you," she said quietly to him.

"Anything for my Madeleine."

"Careful, other girls might get jealous," Mad joked.

"There are no others in my life."

"No girl—"

"Now that our official business is done," Philippe interrupted, "how about a little spin around our pearl farm?"

"Where?"

"Our pearl farm? Up the coast. You can see how we run our operations, meet the technicians. Logan can bring you."

"Oh, I shouldn't." Mad hesitated. "I need to get back to Sydney."

"When do you need to get back?"

"By the morning."

"It'll only take a few hours. Thirty minutes seaplane, one to two hours tour, thirty minutes seaplane back, and off to Sydney. You'll be back before the morning with plenty of time to spare."

"Hmmm."

In all honesty, Mad had always wanted to visit the world-renowned Luna pearl farms. The waters where it was located were famous for being so pristinely unpolluted that marine wildlife, such as whales, sharks, and dolphins, flourished. The family-run company operated at such a massive scale, and yet so intricately and successfully, that it was suggested they be featured in one of those Harvard Business School case studies. She knew Luna offered tours for their VIP guests, prestigious gem laboratories, and even the Boss was once invited on an all-expenses-paid trip. Now, it was her turn. There was just one caveat. She was supposed to meet Steve at the Sydney Airport when his flight arrived in the morning and then head to the Blue Mountains together.

But I really want to go! It'll only take a few hours. I'll be back in Sydney in time. Plus, this is a once-in-a-lifetime opportunity! When will I ever make it down to Broome again? Even the Boss has been here. I must take this offer!

"Right, so maximum three hours?"

"Yes! Since you're here anyway," Philippe said. "Alexandro and I will take care of the necklace and ear studs. We'll email you the details. Logan will take you on a tour. Kill two birds with one stone."

"All right then," Mad said, persuaded that she should go on the detour. "I just can't be late."

"I'll make sure of that!" Logan said, delighted, and jumped out of his seat. "You won't regret it. Let's go!"

Mad wasn't sure if it was the wine she had consumed, but the next several hours flew by pleasantly as she giggled like a child and laughed with Logan. There was the exhilarating seaplane ride, where they flew over a beautiful open bay with jumping pods of dolphins, the landing on a patch of sea with rows of yellow bobbing balls used as markers for the pearl farm, and the thrilling speedboat ride. He introduced his team, diligently described the operations in detail, and peppered the tour with jokes, innocent flirtations, and gentlemanly gestures.

There were a few moments when Mad was caught off guard. Like when he helped her board the seaplane and held her hand a little longer than she thought necessary. And when he caught her from losing her balance as she got off. Oh, and when he held her close on the jolting speedboat ride to one of their many massive pearling vessels. But he undeniably gave her 100 percent of his undivided attention and patiently answered all of her multitudinous questions, explaining that their farm was located in waters with plankton-rich nutrients that oysters fed on and that even though they had to expand operations due to the increased Chinese demand for high-quality South Sea pearls, they still maintained their modus operandi, preserving and sustaining the uninhabited coastline. Among the many seeding, harvesting, cleaning, and support ships that they retained, they boarded one with over fifty technicians in white lab clothing and hairnets, who were carefully cleaning the oyster shells of harmful parasites, and with their special twee-zers, meticulously implanting a nuclei seed into the mollusc.

"We bring our highly trained technicians to the oysters," Logan explained. "Not the other way around, so there's min-imum harm, stress, and trauma. Not only can we then reuse the oyster, but also, we strongly believe that the healthier and happier the oyster, the more beautiful the pearl."

"And that is what sets you apart from your competition," Mad chimed in.

Mad hadn't felt such engagement, ease, and spontaneity in a long time. It was actually nice to talk to someone who was as passionate and knowledgeable about gems and jew-elry as she was. She hadn't realized until now that working by herself could be such a lonely experience. The detour was a much-needed break from the daily grind and was the right decision—until the storm clouds approached. Cyclones were frequent in this region, meaning that although the crew was prepared for such sudden conditions, it still made flying back to the mainland impossible. They would have to take cover in a protective bay on one of the islands.

"We're probably going to have to stay overnight," Logan said gingerly.

_OH NO . . ._

Dread and gloom swept over her.

"You're kidding, right?" she muttered.

"I'm so sorry, Mad. The storm's rolling in. It's going to be at least a few hours till it clears. By then it'll be dark. We can't fly the seaplane until the morning."

Mad knew it was true. The menacing clouds were closing in, and the waters were getting precariously choppy. The shuf-fling about and anxious looks of the crew on board, as much as they tried to hide it, only revealed that the situation was not to be underestimated.

"We have shelter on a nearby island in case of these storms." Logan held his hand out and waited for Mad to take it. "Come with me."

She stared at his outstretched hand. The rain was going to start any second now, and there was no time to dwell on anything else but escaping to safety. Mad finally placed her hand in his. He gripped it tightly.

"Lead the way," she replied.

They took the speedboat to a nearby island and ran up the beach to the safe house. The rain had started pouring. They were soaked by the time they reached the door. Mad brushed the residual rain off her clothing as Logan slammed the door shut just before the wind pounded on the wooden walls. Switching the lights on, he ran into the other room and returned with towels.

"Thank you," Mad said, quickly wiping herself and her bag. She hastily fished out her phone. It was still working, but there was no reception.

Logan looked to be reading her thoughts. "There's no reception here, but we can communicate with the mainland through the satellite phone. I'll call Philippe and Alexandro. They can contact anyone for you."

There was only one person she needed to contact, and that was her husband, Steve. But what was she going to say? That against better judgment, she decided to take a detour, and now she wouldn't return to Sydney in time to meet him. Or that she followed her heart, went on a once-in-a-lifetime tour of Luna's pearl farm, and now she wouldn't make it to see him. Either way, she was stuck here *alone with Logan* and was either going to be late meeting up with Steve or, the worst-case scenario, miss the whole Blue Mountain trip. Mad gulped.

"Could you tell them to inform a passenger, Steve Lam, arriving on the flight to Sydney from Hong Kong in the morning, about the situation we're in? That I'll contact him once I have a cell phone signal. Maybe I can still meet him at the airport, or a hotel in Sydney. Or the Blue Mountains? I could take a helicopter from Sydney Airport and fly directly to the resort . . ." Mad rambled on, trying to untangle her jumbled thoughts.

Logan stared at her as she struggled with the alternatives.

It took a few minutes, but then she finally made her decision.

"Yes, I'll do that! I'll meet him at the Blue Mountains," Mad said, determined. She had persuaded herself that it would work out. *It has to work out.*

Logan nodded and left the room. But Mad kept on pacing around, relentlessly trying to find a spot that might have cell phone reception. Her mind whirled with how she could rectify the situation or just mitigate Steve's disappointment. After what had happened in Hong Kong, she couldn't believe that she'd managed to put herself in this position. She wasn't sure how long it had been when she realized Logan was standing by the doorway, staring at her in silence.

"Oh, you're back!" Mad gasped. "I'm just trying to find a place with reception. Maybe I can still send him a message?"

Logan opened his mouth to say something, but a sudden blast of thunder interrupted him. They looked out the window. It was completely dark outside, and the rain thrashing the glass pane had obscured their vision.

"I'm afraid it's going to be a long night." Logan shifted his attention over to the fireplace. "I'll start a fire and warm up the place. It's not ideal, but maybe some hot coffee?"

Mad checked her phone. There was still no reception. It was time to give up.

"Yes, please."

Moments later, the fire had started, and they settled down over mugs of hot coffee. Her mind had calmed down a bit, but she was in deep thought when Logan spoke again.

"He'll be OK," he said.

"What?" Mad asked. "Sorry, I didn't hear you."

"Steve will be OK. Don't worry."

"Oh, I don't know about that . . ."

"Why?" Logan sat up from his seat.

"I've been disappointing him a lot recently."

"How so?"

"Just been late a lot, not seeing each other enough, work and stuff. Shit happens, I guess . . ."

"Are you and Steve drifting apart?" Logan asked, his voice gentle, yet clearly curious.

That hadn't occurred to Mad.

Are we? So soon?

"I imagine it's hard with all that traveling and busy schedules," Logan commiserated. "To balance your personal life with work."

"It is," she answered somberly, then added as she stood up, "but can't we have it all? Do we really have to sacrifice something?"

Have we really come to this? I have to give up something?

"I think some things are worth fighting for. I don't know about you, but when you've found the one, you know she's the one, and no one else could replace her. Your heart skips a beat when you see her. You have butterflies in your stomach. You just want to see her smile and hear her laugh. And when she talks to you, you feel a little dizzy, like you're seasick on a boat. That's worth fighting for."

"Lovestruck." Mad laughed.

Logan laughed too. Likewise, he stood up from his seat. He walked closer and closer to Mad, staring deep into her eyes. "And when she can talk all day with you about gemstones and jewelry, you know that girl is special because no one else can do that. You know she's the one, and no one can compare to her."

Mad didn't know what to say. She was afraid that if she said anything at all, it would lead to something risky. The rain banged on the window and walls of the house, filling in the void brought on by the escalating tension.

"And you can only hope she feels the same about you too." By now Logan had stopped, his lips all but a few millimeters away from hers, trying to solicit permission.

Mad could feel the warmth of his skin as he waited for her response. She knew any move or glance, delicate or subtle as it may be, might trigger an immediate response. Something had to be done quickly, or she might regret it for the rest of her life.

Alarmed, she jumped backwards, creating space and thwarting his advances.

"I hope you find her someday."

She took another step backwards, hoping he understood.

Logan smiled softly. "I hope so too."

"So, shall I take the bedroom tonight?" Mad said, changing the subject promptly. "Sir, you can take the couch."

"Yes, ma'am!" He chuckled.

Mad grabbed her bag, turned swiftly around, and charged into the bedroom. She closed the door lightly and let her knees surrender, dropping her face down on the bed. She was physically and mentally exhausted, but her mind was riotous over what just happened. Steve always had his doubts about Logan, but he was so young, Mad never thought that it would materialize into anything more than a harmless infatuation. She was wrong again. Her head ached as she tried to think of solutions to the problems that had sprouted up all at once, but to no avail. Succumbing to her tiredness, she inevitably passed out to the splashing of the torrential rain and howling wind.

True to the laws of nature, the more violent the storm, the more gorgeous the next day would be. The sky had cleared, the sun had come out, and the birds were chirping, discarding all signs of the previous night's elemental outrage.

Nonetheless, the mood between Mad and Logan had been altered, permanently. Other than small talk, they kept silent as they headed back. As awkward as it felt, Logan still insisted on accompanying her to the jet. On the tarmac, they said their goodbyes. Logan gave Mad a prolonged hug that surprisingly felt relieving and comforting.

"Steve would be silly to let you go," he whispered.

"Thank you," Mad said as they pulled apart.

"But if he's that daft"—Logan smirked and squeezed her hand—"you know where to find me!"

She laughed and couldn't help but give him a peck on the cheek.

Logan playfully grabbed his left chest, comically pretending he was having a heart attack, and laughing as he fell on the ground. Mad chuckled, but there was no time to spare, so she turned around, ran up the stairs, and into the private jet. The plane flew as fast as it could back to Sydney, where a helicopter waited for her at the airport. She had been sending messages to Steve, apologizing for the delay, but all she received in reply was a terse message:

> Arrived Wolgan Valley
> See you later

At dusk, her helicopter arrived at the Wolgan Valley Blue Mountains Resort, hovering over little wooden cabins and carefree kangaroos, wallaroos, and wallabies jumping out of their bushes to graze on the grass. Steve and Mad had made plans for the day, which had included going on a wildlife safari, massages at the couples spa, swimming, and relaxing at their private cabin pool as they enjoyed the serenity of the Blue Mountains. Most of all, they had planned to hit pause and just be together, but the precious hours had passed, and they had to leave the next morning, back to the reality of their busy schedules.

Once the helicopter landed, Mad jumped out of her seat and ran towards their cabin. Flinging open the front door, she caught her breath and walked briskly into the hallway, entering a living room where a waiter was setting up a candlelit dinner for two. She didn't immediately see Steve, but through a window, she recognized a familiar silhouette standing out on the porch, one hand holding a glass of whiskey. She wanted to run towards him, but thought it more prudent to approach calmly and cautiously. Slowly, she pushed the porch door open, and her foot stepped onto the creaking wooden floor panels, stirring the pensive man.

Steve turned around, clearly relieved to see Mad, but just as quickly, all expression vanished, revealing no emotions. She couldn't read him.

"Dinner is ready, may I get you a drink, Mrs. Lam?" the waiter interfered.

"Water is fine."

"Still or sparkling?"

"Sparkling, please."

Subdued, Mad and Steve sat down at the table, where the waiter recited the courses and inquired about allergies as he poured wine in their glasses.

"No allergies." Steve spoke for the first time since Mad's arrival. "But make sure my wife's steak is medium and not too rare."

Her heart skipped a beat upon hearing his voice.

"Noted," the waiter replied.

Ironically, the first course was oysters. Mad didn't have the appetite but forced herself to take one so that she could avoid explaining why she wasn't in the mood for them. Then their mains, Wagyu steaks, arrived, and the waiter cordially excused himself so that they could enjoy the meal alone. The door closed with a deafening click, magnified by the suffocating silence in the room.

Should I start talking?

She didn't need to.

Steve put his right hand on top of hers. It felt warm and soothing. Mad looked up at his gentle gaze, trying to uncover his thoughts and emotions. He didn't seem angry or upset— just tired.

"These few months, being with you, have been the happiest in my life," Steve finally spoke. "But it's also made me extremely and excessively anxious. I'm terrified when you don't answer my messages or phone calls. I don't know where you are. I don't know if something has happened to you. I'm not possessive. I give you space and let you do what you want. But I never know if you're going to show up anymore! I find myself constantly waiting and waiting in fear."

"I'm so sorry! I can explain! Luna—"

"I love you, Mad. But we barely see each other. We're becoming strangers—one of those couples with hardly any time for each other. We're drifting apart."

Logan's words.

Mad's breathing quickened as those words echoed in her head, only to be interrupted by the untimeliest intrusion.

Ring.

Ring.

Ring.

Mad gawked at her phone in horror. She hadn't realized she had placed it on the table.

"Have you seen my phone recently?" Steve asked calmly.

It just occurred to Mad.

No.

"I've had my fair share of busy, but I make it a point to give you all of me when we're together. I understand that you love what you do, and I love the passion you have for gems and jewelry. It's how we met, after all. You shouldn't have to choose between me or your job. I love that smile on your face and how you sparkle when you talk about jewelry." Steve paused. "But where does that leave us?"

Those last words hung in the air.

"I don't know . . ." Mad said helplessly, unable to process everything Steve had, rightfully, off-loaded onto her. The key to a healthy relationship was communication, although she was caught off guard and was unprepared for the gravity of it all. She opened her mouth but couldn't conjure up anything useful. Agonizing minutes passed as they remained at a stalemate.

The waiter eventually returned. Realizing they hadn't finished their main courses, he refilled their wineglasses and stationed himself out of sight, but within earshot.

They ate in silence. Mad was lost in thought.

Why haven't I noticed his phone wasn't in sight? I did that night in Courchevel, but I didn't think much about it. Do I really need to sacrifice something? What should I do?

Even after they finished their dinner, and the waiter had gone, the silence endured. The intense moment had passed but left Mad's thoughts and feelings in disarray. She was taken aback at the severity of the situation and reeled from something she didn't fully grasp or know how to resolve. It was just easier not to talk at all.

Steve did the same. Like strangers, they drifted to their routines, only convening at the bed, where they slept apart on either side.

The sunny skies did not improve their mood the next day. They headed back to Sydney Airport, where Mad had a flight to the Maldives. They were fully aware of the elephant in the car, sucking up all the air and suffocating them, but both chose not to address it. At the airport curbside, while a porter helped Mad with her luggage, she stole a glance at her husband. He wasn't looking at her. Dejected, she started to follow the porter into the terminal when Steve suddenly grabbed her and gave her a long and intense hug.

"Enjoy your holiday with Jackie," he said gently.

Tearing up, Mad was afraid if she spoke, she would start bawling. She gulped and ended the embrace. Turning quickly around so that Steve wouldn't see the tears roll down her cheeks, she walked into the terminal.

Is it over?

CHAPTER EIGHT

The Maldivian Atolls

"Mad! Mad! Maaaaaaaaad!"

Even with the door and windows closed, and the loud buzzing motor still running, everyone on the seaplane could hear Jackie squealing on the jetty outside. Her humongous floppy straw hat bobbed up and down over her blue-rimmed sunglasses, flowing Pucci silk kaftan, a pair of multicolored semiprecious cabochon gemstone Bulgari bangles worn on each wrist, and gold gladiators as she jumped repeatedly with glee—in addition to balancing iced cappuccinos in each hand.

Mad couldn't help but smirk at how ridiculous and hilarious Jackie looked, but also thought how sweet her best friend had always been to her.

It had been hours since she left Steve at the airport curbside and had subsequently felt nothing but utter misery and bleakness. Her thoughts and emotions were in turmoil, but rather than broadcast how disturbed and upset she was, she covered half her face under her large sunglasses. The last thing she wanted was to have someone ask if she was OK, because she clearly wasn't and didn't feel like talking about it either. As the seaplane flew over the Maldivian atolls of tiny islands and reefs outlined by pure white sands and surrounded by vibrant shades of shallow blue water, other passengers eagerly took photos of the incredibly beautiful spectacle, while Mad just sat, stoic and indifferent in her seat, her mind worlds away from it all. Steve had messaged her, but she couldn't muster up a decent reply.

Steve:

Enjoy your holiday

We should talk in Venice

Mad:

Ok

She decided not to tell Jackie about what had happened between her and Steve. Not that she had much to say or wanted to talk about it. Like an ostrich, she felt it was better if she just buried her head in the sand for the moment, until later when she felt ready to make sense of her thoughts and figure things out. So, she summoned up all her efforts, got off the seaplane, and flashed a megawatt smile.

"Jackiiiieeeee!" Mad screamed. They hugged and squealed like teenagers that just scored tickets to their favorite boy band's concert, overly excited and too obnoxious to care about what everyone else around them thought.

"Just the way you like it." Jackie handed Mad her iced cappuccino.

"Thanks, J! You always know how to make me happy."

"Come on, let's go! We've got a busy day," Jackie said, hopping on a buggy.

Mad followed, and they sped away, flanked by the most amazingly clear turquoise waters she had ever seen in her life. The rays of the tropical sun illuminated the ever-changing hues of the water, from electric blues to neon greens; they reminded Mad of Brazilian Paraibas, the most luminescent and prized tourmalines in the world. Guests in fluorescent masks and flippers snorkeled with kids on zooming Seabobs next to the carefully manicured white sand beach that led to an equally welcoming kidney-shaped pool decked out with inviting white beach chairs. Waiters in crisp white linen shirts and pants and leather sandals, balancing trays of tropical drinks and freshly cut coconuts, strolled over to effortlessly tanning guests.

Past the pool and into a tropical jungle, their buggy sprang between vacationers in designer sunglasses, panama hats, vibrant swimwear, and kaftan coverups as they biked under the shade on the winding sand path. As they crossed the island and left the jungle, the sunlight beamed brightly again. They then embarked on the delightful wooden planks, ubiquitous in all tourist brochures, connecting the main island to the individual over-the-water villas. Mad relished again the stunning twinkling blue waters, feasting her eyes on the beauty of it, until the buggy reached the end of the path and stopped next to the farthest villa, which they would be calling home for the next few days.

All the while, Jackie had been talking nonstop about what she had planned. Distracted by the enchanting scenery, Mad hadn't exactly been listening. All she'd heard was something about snorkeling in the ocean, fishing, swimming, and dining on a sandbank.

"Are you OK with it?" Jackie asked, annoyed that Mad hadn't responded.

"What?"

"With the arrangements! Were you listening?"

"Jackie! It's beautiful here! Whatever you have planned is fine by me. I can't wait! It's going to be spectacular!"

Jackie smiled from ear to ear. She clearly couldn't wait either.

"OK, I'll let you change, and then we can head out."

Using her keyless-entry card, Jackie unlocked and pushed the villa door open to reveal a beige-and-cream sanctuary furnished with accents of blue fabric, white marble, and mahogany wood. A sleek flat-screen TV stood to the side of the room along with an iPad for contactless access to the many services and amenities. Immense floor-to-ceiling glass windows enveloped one whole side of the villa, displaying the breathtaking Indian Ocean. Mad beelined over to the sliding door, pushed it open, and walked onto the terrace deck, appointed with a plunge pool, sun loungers, and a plush day bed underneath a wooden gazebo. She dashed over to the edge of the deck, where a ladder led down to the house reef, teeming with an abundance of fishes. A row of enticing over-water hammocks hung neatly in a line, completing the enchanting picture.

All I need are some pillows and a good book.

"Come on, Mad! Change, and let's go! We'll come back later anyways."

"OK! OK!" she said, tearing her gaze away from the hammocks. "But I need to unpack too!"

"Just change! The butler will unpack for you!"

Of course, why didn't I think of that?

▽ ▽ ▽

"One! Two! Threeeeeee!"

Mad and Jackie screamed as they jumped off their privately chartered yacht into the middle of the Indian Ocean with their snorkeling gear on. Following a marine biologist, they ducked their heads underneath the water into a dazzling world. Along a deep trench was a reef blossoming with a kaleidoscope of wildlife: tropical fishes with stripes and spots of all different colors and shapes swam with schools of silver sardines amidst the orange, yellow, green, and purple corals. Mad and Jackie glided past sea turtles foraging on the seagrass and spotted giant clams, starfish, and dozens of Nemos and Dorys. Like amateurs, they froze at the sight of a nimble reef shark whizzing above the corals, minding its own business. It was all too marvelous!

Nevertheless, even with life vests on, the strong currents of the open sea finally took their toll. Exhausted, they returned to the yacht and basked in caviar and Bellinis, foie gras pâté, and sushi while they reminisced.

"Remember Mademoiselle Charton? How she would scream at you in class?" asked Jackie.

"She screamed at everyone! Not just me!" Mad giggled. "I always wondered when that vein in her neck would pop."

"Yah, she was great! I've never had a French teacher like her."

Mad raised her eyebrows. "She was great? You used to pretend you had a fever so you could take the day off and study longer for her tests! Remember you gargled hot water in your mouth before the nurses took your temperature?"

"Worked like a charm! I heard Jackie O used to do that. I learned from the best!" Jackie laughed. "Can't believe the nurses still fell for it."

"Remember?" Mad continued. "You once used that absurd poltergeist excuse to skip her class."

"Oh! That was classic! The baby ghost crying throughout the night!" Jackie laughed even louder. "Come on, Mad! How could I not take advantage of the fact that our room was known to be haunted! That girl hid her pregnancy, gave birth secretly, and left her baby in a shoebox to die in the closet."

"It's a myth!" Mad cried and rolled her eyes. "I can't believe Charton believed you, though!"

"She was kind of into those supernatural things. But yes, I was surprised she believed me too!"

"Remember how all her papers smelled like cigarettes? I saw smoke come out of her window several times."

"Specifically, like French cigarettes," Jackie added.

"Because only something made in France would do for her and anything else was inferior!"

"I would bring her cigarettes whenever I came back from Paris. Did you know that?"

"No way! How?"

"I had my ways." Jackie winked.

"But she still screamed at you in class. She loved saying—"

"Stupid girls!" they chorused together, mimicking a French accent.

"Well, old habits die hard, and I wasn't a particularly good student," Jackie admitted.

"I still can't believe you didn't fail her class," Mad scoffed.

"I wonder how she's doing? If she's still terrorizing those girls."

"She passed away a few years ago. You know, we graduated years ago."

"Oh, time does fly," Jackie replied solemnly.

They both raised their glasses.

"To Charton!" they cheered, happily intoxicated, and emptied their drinks.

The sisterly tête-à-tête with Jackie had been long overdue and frankly, to Mad's gratification, much needed. Not once did she even reach for her phone or even think about it. Her mind was at ease, and it felt strangely liberating. Even when the next item on the schedule was "fishing for dinner," a task that sounded unnecessarily tedious, she went along with it. Besides, it didn't take long before they both caught three fish each. With their bounty, they were transported to a nearby white powdery sandbank, smaller than the size of a studio apartment, where a chef and his ad hoc kitchen awaited to cook the fresh catch, meters away from another bottle of chilled champagne and a white-clothed table.

Barefoot, they strutted to their seats and waited for nature's phenomenal show to begin. So relaxed, they propped their feet up on their chairs as they sipped champagne and watched as the magical orange, pink, and purple sunset unfolded, amplified, then engulfed itself into darkness. Glowing candles lit up their little island haven. Like lapis lazuli gemstones, with the dark-blue surface and gold dusts, billions of scintillating stars appeared before their eyes in the expansive night sky. It was a magical spectacle to end the day. Like two drunk teenagers, they staggered back to the yacht, laughing comically at nothing in particular.

"I hope I don't throw up on the boat," Mad shrieked.

"If you do, I'll hold your hair back. Just like our old clubbing days. Remember our road trip in the south of France? You threw up all the way up to Saint-Paul de Vence."

"You threw up all across Vendome! When we walked from the Mandarin back to the Ritz! That was worse!"

"I'm sure I wasn't the first!" Jackie howled.

"Girl trips are the best!" they both squealed as they held on to each other on the yacht, wind whipping their faces and hair as they sped back to their hotel.

Mad managed to say, "Thank you, Jackie," despite her drunken stupor. "I had so much fun today."

"Awww, anytime, my dear!"

"I needed it. Steve and I had an argument. We both need to figure things out," Mad blurted out. "Balance family and work, I guess . . ."

"*And,*" Jackie yelled, eyes drooping shut. "Friends too!"

"Oh, yes, yes, that too. Jackie?"

Jackie had passed out.

Mad pulled her bag over and rummaged for her phone. There were no messages from Steve, but two from Logan.

> I just wanted to check up on you and see if
> you are ok
>
> I miss you

Mad dropped her phone back into her bag and closed her eyes.

◇ ◇ ◇

"Rise and shine!" Jackie screamed, tearing open the curtains, letting the morning sun explode into the room and every corner with its bright warm rays.

Mad grunted and pulled a pillow over her head, trying to block the sunlight and the dastardly effects of the previous day's alcohol consumption.

"Why is it you never get a hangover?" Mad groaned.

"Cuz I'm Jackie, bitch! Now wake up! We're having break-fast at the restaurant, then going to the beach club today! We can tan, swim, and do all those fun water activities! I can't wait to go jet skiing!"

Silence.

"Mad!"

"All right!" she replied reluctantly. "Give me five minutes. No, ten minutes."

"Mad!"

"All right! Five minutes."

After fifteen minutes of diddle-daddle, Mad finally wiggled out of bed, but by habit, reached for her phone to check her emails and messages. Her eyes instantly popped wide open. Frantically, she scrolled through the inboxes.

Holy cow! There's literally hundreds of emails and messages!

Within the past eight hours, Raj had sent more than ten emails of updates and suggestions for the polishing and mounting of the Burmese rubies and sapphires. Hailey and Hazel had sent high-resolution images of the jadeite carving, which would take hours to upload on Mad's phone! The New York lapidary, on the other hand, had sent images of the blue diamond with such low resolution that Mad couldn't even tell what she was staring at. Fiona had bombarded her email inbox and WhatsApp messages with exhibition designs, rundowns, and checklists. In addition, there were countless tracking emails from Malca-Amit, Brinks, and Ferrari for the Argyle diamonds, Luna pearls, etc. And this was just the tip of the iceberg.

From the buggy ride to the restaurant through breakfast, Mad barely glanced up from her phone, only pausing for a triple-shot iced cappuccino. Time was of the essence, and she needed to respond ASAP. She read and replied to each email and message as fast as she could, typing expeditiously. Though some of her responses could be rendered with an "OK," most could not and had to be pursued with further questions. Which in return, meant even more back and forth before the issues could be resolved and concluded—for the day.

When they reached the beach club, Mad bolted for the nearest chair, slumped down, and continued tackling her task.

"Are you coming or not?" Jackie asked.

"Just give me thirty minutes," Mad said as she typed furiously, eyes glued to her phone.

By the time thirty minutes had passed, Mad hadn't budged. She was knee-deep in work, and no one could possibly pull her out from the trench she had dug herself into. Although Jackie, albeit unsuccessfully, did return and attempt several times.

"Do you want to go kayaking with me? They have those transparent kayaks where you can see all the marine life below."

"Ummm," Mad responded, hearing every word but obviously not listening at all.

Jackie rolled her eyes and went off by herself. Returning later, she tried to lure Mad away from the screen.

"Mad! There were so many rays! They were like dark shadows underneath! You want to come and check it out with me?"

"Ummm," Mad said, unmoved from her position.

"Do you want to go jet skiing, then?" Jackie coaxed.

"Ummm."

"Fine." Jackie turned around and left Mad in her chair. She came back later in high spirits and gave it another try.

"Mad, that was so much fun! I think I saw this fin right behind me! Could have been a shark!" Jackie laughed.

"Ummm."

"Want to go snorkeling in the house reef?" Jackie persisted.

"Ummm."

"OK, I'll be back," Jackie said, obviously discouraged. She went off by herself but returned later, endeavoring again.

"The reef conditions are so nice here too! Lots of fishes and corals—no coral bleaching. You want to come and see?"

"Ummm."

"Do you at least want something to drink?" Jackie offered.

"Ummm."

Jackie shrugged her shoulders and left Mad alone. She came back and placed an iced cappuccino on the side table.

"What do you want for lunch?" Jackie asked, sitting on the chair next to her with a menu in hand.

"Ummm."

"A burger? Maldivian curry? Pasta?"

"Ummm."

Mad didn't know what she said or if she even ended up eating anything at all. By the time she finished all her work it was already 5:00 p.m. The whole day had been a blur of emails, messages, and calls.

Did I eat today? Did I even have water? I don't remember.

The beach club was closing, and it was time to return to their room. When they got back, Mad surrendered herself to the sunbed on the deck and closed her tired, strained eyes, allowing her mind and body a moment of solitude. Slowly the tension from her shoulders, neck, and hands dissipated. She felt a warm sluggish glow reverberating within as she levitated to a dreamy realm in between consciousness and unconsciousness. It felt like thirty minutes of bliss but in actuality had probably only been five when her phone's sharp ring hit her like a violent blow to the head. She sprang up from her reverie and swung around, frantically searching for the culprit. It wasn't on the sunbed, nor on the side table. The ringing was coming from indoors. She ran inside and ransacked her bag. It wasn't there either!

"Jackie!" Mad yelped, throwing the cushions on the sofa up in the air. "Have you seen my phone?"

Jackie's silence only made the ringing increasingly aggravating.

"*Jackie!*" Mad screamed. "Have you seen my phone?!"

The ringing abruptly stopped, but in place was Jackie's deafening roar.

"*No!*"

Shocked at Jackie's sudden outburst, Mad hollered, "What's wrong with you?"

"I can't stand it anymore!" Jackie yelled. "The whole day! All you did was work, work, work! It's all about your phone! This is supposed to be a girls' trip, our holiday!"

"It's important! I have a deadline to meet!"

"Everything is important! Everything is more important than me! I don't matter to you anymore!"

"It's just this time! I promise!"

"It's been like this for months! Can't you see? There'll always be work. There'll always be projects. There'll always be deadlines. That's not the problem. The problem is how you set your priorities! What is more important to you? Work?! At the end of the day, family and friends are the only things that are forever!"

"You don't know anything! I have dreams, and I need to work hard for them. As a friend, you should be more supportive, not make it harder for me. You just don't get it because you never had aspirations."

"You think I have no aspirations or dreams? That's because you never asked me. When was the last time you asked how I was doing or what I have been up to lately? Have you thought about that?!"

"Uh." Caught off guard, Mad was stunned. Speechless.

When was the last time? I don't remember.

"That's right," Jackie sneered. *"Never."*

She grabbed her bag and stormed out the front door, bellowing, "This whole thing sucks! Bye!" before slamming the door shut.

Mad collapsed on the sofa. She was furious at Jackie's outburst.

How dare she blow up at me! Can't she be more accommodating? Less selfish? What dreams and aspirations could she have? All she does is jet around vacationing, partying, and attending those charity dinners. But Jackie's far from being an airhead. What has she been up to lately? Has she been OK? I guess I could have asked her. She always asks me . . .

Beep.

Mad tilted her head towards where the sound was coming from, over at the small coffee table, next to the sofa she was sitting on. It was her phone, letting her know that she had a missed call. She remained still until the butler rang the doorbell and walked into the room.

"Sorry for disturbing you, Mrs. Lam. Ms. Fu wanted me to pack and deliver her luggage."

Fine. Let her be. I don't care.

It only took the butler a few minutes to pack up Jackie's things and leave the room, leaving Mad to sit alone in silence again. Refusing to waste any more time thinking about Jackie, she decided to retire to bed. Except, she couldn't fall asleep. It was the first time in their lives they'd had such a nasty fight. Even when they fought before, they would make up within a few hours. But this time it felt different, and Mad couldn't help but feel puzzled and disturbed.

Trying to untangle her thoughts but making no progress, she was lost. Finally, in the early morning, she fell asleep— though her mind remained restless and unrelenting. Drifting into darkness, she dreamt of running and running. But no matter how hard she ran, she couldn't escape and stayed in the same spot. Frustrated and angry, she reached her boiling point and was about to scream when suddenly the floor opened up, and she fell into a bottomless pit. She tried to scream for help, but nothing came out of her mouth. Without any control of the situation, she kept on falling and spinning, until a loud bang mercifully jolted her out of the nightmare.

Covered in sweat, Mad gasped and caught her breath. A bolt of lightning flashed outside the window, and thunder struck. Rain came down hard, splashing on the rooftop. The clock on the bedside table read 11:00 a.m. She sighed and reached for her phone. Old habits die hard. There were hundreds of messages and emails, but none were from Jackie. She threw her phone down on the bed. Her stomach growled, urging her to freshen up and head to the restaurant for some food.

Perhaps today, I should eat before working.

When she got on the buggy, the thunder and lightning had stopped, but the rain persisted.

The driver attempted to chat. "How are you today, Mrs. Lam?"

"Fine," Mad replied noncommittally.

"It's good that you're not leaving today," the driver continued. "The weather conditions have been so different these last few years. It's still constantly changing too. Just this morning it was all nice and sunny, but all of a sudden a storm appeared from nowhere."

Mad couldn't think of a response, and so she remained silent.

"We had a seaplane fly out this morning, but it hasn't arrived in Male yet. We're all hoping nothing happened to it."

"Oh," she offered.

When Mad reached the restaurant and waited patiently for the hostess to bring her to a table, whisperings of the missing seaplane buzzed around her. As she followed the hostess, the conversations only got louder and more unsettling.

"I heard from my butler only one family boarded the seaplane."

"My butler said one family and one single female—maybe hotel staff."

"They still haven't found the plane yet?"

"They shouldn't have flown in such conditions."

"But it was sunny this morning."

"Do seaplanes have GPS or something?"

"The clouds came in fast."

"Global warming."

"Climate change—"

"What would you like to have, Mrs. Lam?" A waiter interrupted Mad from listening further.

"An iced cappuccino and a chorizo mozzarella omelet."

"Is there anything else you would like?"

Her curiosity spiked, she asked, "Do you have any news about the seaplane?"

"Oh! I'm sorry, I don't know too much. The last I heard was that we lost contact. We have guests on the plane, and we're doing everything we can to find them."

"Do you know who boarded the plane?"

"From our hotel? A family of four and one lady, not related to the family."

"Oh." Mad paused. "OK, thank you."

She peered at the table, staring at nothing in particular, just the blank space between her fork and knife. Gradually a strange sensation crept over her, prompting her to check her phone and see if she knew what Jackie was currently up to. Her WhatsApp indicated that Jackie was last seen online early this morning. She held her breath as a suspicion formulated in her head, and in the spur of the moment, she gave Jackie a call.

Her phone was turned off.

Could it—? Is it—? Is it possible?

She stood up from her seat and headed towards the lobby, trying hard to suppress the fear blooming within her. When she arrived at the reception, it was evident that the mood was far from what she experienced the first day she arrived. Somber and grave sentiments were apparent.

Please don't be her. Please don't be her. Please don't be her.

Mad scanned the room; staff trying hard to hide the severity of the situation whispered sternly on their phones, despite their wrinkled foreheads and dark eyes betraying them. One of them put his receiver down.

At once, Mad took the opportunity and sprinted over.

"Hi, could you tell me who was on the seaplane this morning?" she asked hastily, not even trying to hide the distress in her voice. "Did they find the plane yet?"

"Sorry, madam, we're still trying to figure out the details of the wreckage," he replied, eyes all watery and sweat rolling down the sides of his face. He obviously wasn't doing too good himself.

"What?!"

"The seaplane lost control and fell into the ocean. We got an SOS from the pilot."

"And did the people survive?!" Mad shrieked.

"Rescue boats are out searching for them. We're all hoping for the best. We have the location already—we're doing everything we can."

Mad's heart stopped. In a split second, her mind flashed to a deep bottomless hole, where just like her nightmare, she kept on falling and falling, plunging uncontrollably. Physically, she felt herself swerve and clenched the side of the reception desk before she toppled over.

It's all my fault. It's all my fault. If I hadn't pushed Jackie away, if I had asked how she was doing, if I had just put my damn phone down, she would still be alive. How am I going to live without her? Who's going to cheer me up, support me, ask if I'm OK? I haven't done anything close to what she had done for me. And now she's gone . . .

Mad's face must have been as pale as a ghost as employees once consumed with the phones now shifted their attention towards her. Even those lingering around stopped what they were doing and gaped at her sickly appearance.

"Mrs. Lam, are you all right?" It was her butler, appearing deeply alarmed. "Please, come sit down."

He held her hand and led her to the nearest chair, ordering someone by his side to go get the doctor.

"Are you OK?" her butler asked again. "Let me get you some water."

Am I OK?

That was when Mad's floodgates opened. Tears burst out of her eyes. "Oh, it's all my fault!"

"This is no one's fault. No one could have predicted this weather! It was perfectly sunny this morning."

She collapsed into the chair, sobbing uncontrollably, and her body shook violently as remorse and guilt engulfed her.

Helpless, the butler didn't know how he could pacify someone seemingly in so much pain. He could only stand there and watch.

"Madam! What is it?" The doctor had arrived. With his furrowed brows, he looked extremely concerned about her current state and the escalating situation. "What happened?" the doctor asked the butler. A woman kneeled down, trying to comfort Mad by patting her back and saying over and over again that it wasn't her fault. Another woman handed her tissues to blot the tears on her face. The more people consoled her, the more hysterical she became. Drowning in her own grief, she wailed and sobbed even louder, captivating an audience that grew like wildfire, audibly sympathetic and mournful.

"She has a friend on the seaplane."

"Oh! Poor thing!"

"Yah, she thinks it's her fault."

"What a catastrophe."

After what felt like an eternity, her butler grasped a moment in between her sobs and gently suggested, "Mrs. Lam, would you like me to call Ms. Fu? Maybe, she could come back from the Cheval Blanc?"

"What? Chev Blanc?" Mad asked, sniffing at intervals.

Not sure if he heard her clearly, she repeated in a full sentence, "What do you mean, Cheval Blanc?"

"Well, it's not too far away. It took our yacht less than three hours to bring her there last night. Because of the storm, our yacht is still there. You're not well. We would be more than happy to accommodate your wishes."

The butler's words struck her hard, echoing over and over again. She held her breath as she deciphered the information and bit by bit, pieced together a gradual realization.

It dawned on her. "You mean, Jackie went to Cheval Blanc last night?" Mad squeaked.

"Ms. Fu couldn't take the seaplane. No seaplanes after 3:00 p.m. So, she took the yacht over. You didn't know?" the butler asked, then it clearly dawned on him as well and his eyes widened to the size of saucers. "*Oh! Oh! Oh!* You thought, she was—"

"She's not, right?"

"I assure you, Mrs. Lam! She wasn't on the seaplane!"

Mad's heart leapt out of her chest and hurdled back into place, defibrillating her body to life! She was a cocktail of emotions: relief, elation, disbelief, and finally embarrassment for the commotion she caused.

"*Oh, thank God!*" She slumped down on her chair, her face blotchy, swollen, and red, and her body exhausted and limp from the emotional roller coaster she put herself through.

No one knew how to react next, but the doctor, who knew a thing or two about remedies, barked: "Tequila, she needs a shot of tequila!"

The butler nodded and sprang into action, leaving Mad to her own thoughts and a welcome twist of perspective.

I can't have that happen again. There are people that are too important in my life. I need to stop dodging the problems and face them. I need to be a better person—to change. If I don't, there's too much at stake, too much to lose. I just need to figure out how.

Several feet away, another form of elation erupted from the reception. They had found the wreckage, and everyone was alive. People who didn't know each other hugged, clapped, and cheered together, bringing the day to a fortunate conclusion.

CHAPTER NINE

Home Sweet Home?

"Honey! I'm home!" Mad said, walking through the foyer, into her apartment, where it seemed darker and colder than usual. She knew Steve was on a business trip in Shanghai and would meet her in Venice, but something in her wanted to say those words out loud. Even though no one could hear her, it still felt comforting.

"Ma'am, did you call for me?"

Startled, Mad shrieked and dropped her bag, all the contents falling out onto the floor.

"Oh! I'm so sorry," her part-time housekeeper said, rushing over to help Mad pick up the mess. "I didn't mean to frighten you! I thought you called me."

"I didn't know you were here!" Mad said, embarrassed by her blunder.

"I wanted to do a deep cleanse of the place before you arrived. I heard you're staying a bit longer this time."

"Oh, yes, yes, thank you," Mad replied, shoving everything back into her bag. "I need to check up on the jadeite carving at the workshop. I won't be leaving for Venice until next week."

"Will you be eating dinner at home tonight? I'll make arrangements with the chef?"

"Oh, no, no. That won't be necessary. I have engagements tonight."

"OK then, ma'am. I'll just finish a few more details in the toilet, then I'll leave you alone," her housekeeper said as she turned around to leave.

"Liliana?"

"Yes?" Liliana turned back.

"Feel free to stay as long as you want. Have a coffee or some snacks if you have time," Mad said. "It's nice to have someone else in the house."

Liliana looked surprised at the offer, but slowly smiled. "I would love to."

It *was* nice to have someone else in the house. Liliana's busywork and occasional singing, albeit off tune, were a warm welcome instead of the lonely silence Mad had come to accept. Mad hadn't felt so relaxed and unhurried in a while as she lit candles and allowed herself to take a long hot bath before getting ready to go out. She even had time to go through her jewelry safe and choose a pair of Sterlé stylized feather ear clips for the night. Donning a new Persian-blue turquoise minidress, gold high heels, and her signature red lipstick, she walked into the Aubrey, where she was to meet up with Liam, Susan, and Henry for drinks before heading to Clarisse's atelier opening, where she hoped to bump into Jackie—and apologize to her.

Dev, previously the mixologist from the Michelin-starred restaurant 8½ Otto e Mezzo Bombana, had recently moved to the Aubrey, curating chess-inspired signature cocktails with sustainable ingredients. Located on one of the top floors of the Mandarin Oriental hotel, the bar, with its dark wooden interior and dimmed chandeliers, perfectly accentuated the intoxicating night lights of the central business district.

"Oysters, but no champagne?" Mad said, plopping down on the plush velvet chair next to a table already bursting with drinks in different colors and platters of sushi and oysters.

"We got you the Queen's Gimlet," Liam said, giving Mad two kisses on the cheeks. "And I'm guessing you're going to need it, because you look like you've been hit by a train!"

"Thanks!" Mad said sarcastically, but she knew it was true. Stress from the past few months had taken a toll. Her skin was dry and patchy, and no amount of concealer could cover those dark circles and bags from Liam's scrutinizing eagle eyes. "Things have been spiraling out of control."

"What happened?" Susan inquired, her tone tinged with concern.

"Well, Steve and I hit a rough patch. Jackie and I got into a huge argument in the Maldives. And I get it. I haven't been able to balance work and my personal life! There's never enough time, and no one is getting enough attention—so now we're all suffering," Mad said in one breath before taking a sip from her drink.

"Strained relationships, inefficiencies at work, lousy physical and mental health are all symptoms of poor work-life balance," Henry lectured. "You need to do something about it for sure."

"So, it's true, there is no such thing as women with successful careers and perfect families!" Susan scoffed.

"Remember hearing about Nicole Kidman and how she won her Oscar but when she got back to her hotel room, there was no one she could celebrate with?" Liam pointed out. "Do you really want that kind of life?"

"That's true." Susan nodded her head. "What is the meaning of work and accomplishments when you come home and have no one to share it with?"

"You need to set boundaries," Henry said sternly, putting his drink down on the table. "You need to step back. You can't try to do everything."

"And it's probably not a bad thing if you delegate some responsibilities. You can make it a win-win situation." Susan nodded in agreement.

"But how?" Mad asked. "I know I need to change, but I don't know what to change!"

"Change can be good," Henry replied. "Accepting that you need to change is always a good start."

"Darling." Liam finally jumped in. "The first thing is to set your priorities."

Mad shrugged her shoulders. "That's exactly what Jackie said."

"And then set your boundaries," Liam continued. "Everyone needs boundaries. We're all different; do what works for you. Then you know what you need to do next. And if you need help, ask for it! Hang up the ego! There's no shame in asking for help."

"That's what friends are for," Susan added. "We help each other out."

"Even if we can't," Henry said, holding his cocktail up. "We're all ears—and drinks."

Mad lifted her drink and clinked Henry's glass. She took a sip, pondering her friends' advice.

Priorities. Boundaries. Help.

It was beginning to become clear to her what she needed to do. Her next steps were slowly taking shape as a rough plan of salvaging what was important in her life formed in her head. She hadn't figured out the details yet, but now she knew how to start.

"Enough about me!" Mad smiled and looked at each one of her friends. "What is going on with *you*?"

Susan swiped her long black hair back. "Since I opened my own painting studio, my old clients have been buying nonstop from me. I can't keep up with the demand!"

"Oh! Boss lady!" Mad cried with glee and gave Susan a high five.

"So, you know how I went on that sabbatical on the old Silk Road in Dunhuang?" Liam said.

"Yah. How was it?" Mad asked.

"It was magnificent! Such an eye-opening adventure! People were so into what they were doing. So passionate . . . so—"

"Unlike Minos?"

"Yes!"

They all burst out in laughter.

"You know me," Henry said. "Just getting ready for the next sale."

"Record-breaking again!" Mad lifted her glass and took another sip.

"Well, yes, and, Irene is pregnant!"

"What?!" Mad and Susan sat up from their seats and yelled, "Congratulations!"

Liam gave him a big hug. "You baby-making machine!"

"Shots on the house." Dev, who seemed to have been waiting for the perfect moment, dropped a tray of yellow liquids on the table, winked, and left.

Henry took the first shot glass and lifted it in the air. "To welcoming changes and new beginnings!"

"Changes and beginnings!" they all agreed and took the shot, gladly.

◇ ◇ ◇

"Welcome, Mad! How have you been?" Serena asked as she escorted her into Clarisse's atelier opening at the überposh Tai Kwun building. Located in the SOHO (South of Hollywood Road) area, the building was formerly the Central Police Station before it was redeveloped into a heritage and arts center. Trendsetters had opened boutiques and restaurants in the building, forging a community of chic trailblazers unafraid to showcase their limitless ideas and talent.

"I've been good," Mad replied. "How are things treating you? I think the last time I saw you was—"

"Ages ago!" Serena laughed. "You're hardly in town anymore! My PR firm sends you all these invitations."

"And I'm extremely sorry I'm never able to make any of them! You know I would support you if I was in town."

"I was psyched when I saw you RSVPed to this event. Finally, we have something worthy of your presence."

"Oh! Now you're teasing me!"

"Just kidding, I'm glad you could make it."

"There's no way I would miss this one. It means too much to me. Where's Clarisse?"

"She's over there with the reporters. Here's your glass of champagne. Just the way you like it."

"Thanks, Serena," Mad said, taking the stem of the flute. "I know you're busy, I'll let you go, but let's catch up tonight. I promise I'll go to more of your events in the future."

Serena smiled genuinely. "Sure," she said and gave her a hug before turning back to the front desk.

Numerous reporters and photographers surrounded Clarisse and her team at the middle of the venue. From afar, Mad gazed at the confident woman, undaunted as she answered questions, smiling graciously as she posed for pictures, and fearless as she instructed her team. How much Clarisse had grown and matured this past year! From the eager, innocent, and naive little girl Mad met at Minos, to the strong, sophisticated, and self-assured woman of grace and certainty. She worked hard and believed in herself; within a short amount of time, she'd built her own jewelry atelier, showcasing her talents, thoughts, and opinions. And not once did she use what she'd observed at Minos, where people trampled over others to get what they wanted. Instead, she rejected the Minos culture and rose above her painful experience.

I'm so proud of her.

Clarisse turned her head and spotted Mad. Her eyes instantly glittered, and she waved excitedly at her. After whispering something in her assistant's ear, Clarisse walked across the room. Her entourage followed closely behind.

"I miss you!" Clarisse cried, giving Mad kisses on the cheeks. "You busy queen bee!"

"What are you talking about?" Mad hugged Clarisse. "You're busier than bees!"

"Picture, please!" the photographers shouted, to which the two obediently smiled and posed before returning to each other.

"I'm so proud of you," Mad said.

"Thanks. Come! I want to show you my collection." Clarisse led Mad towards the showcases. "It's nothing compared to what you were used to at Minos or what you collect for the prince, but I find this more fulfilling.

"This is my animal collection. Something fun!" Clarisse said, hovering over a showcase of yellow gold jewelry, each mounted with colorful gemstones. Mad moved closer, peering at a necklace of a whale inside a pond, ear pendants with monkeys and bananas, a necklace, a ring and earring set of zebras with rainbow stripes, a brooch of a penguin in a suit with turbo boosters, and another brooch of a deer with headlights on its head. Everything was indeed whimsical and fun.

"After working at Mino's," Clarisse explained. "I realized that those big-ticket items don't necessarily make people happy—because it probably doesn't have any meaning to them. Remember how clients would come and pick up their jewelry without a smile on their faces?"

"Countless clients. It was as if they didn't take any pleasure in what they bought."

"I always thought that was just sad! So, I wanted to make pieces that tell a story, and that people will actually respond to. I wanted to make small pieces that people could wear on a daily basis and enjoy! Put a smile on their faces! It's so much more fulfilling than seeing money in my bank account for selling something people don't actually even like!"

Something in the corner of the showcase caught Mad's attention. "Can I see that?"

"That? Sure! That's my 24 Karat Magic collection."

Mad raised her eyebrows, giving Clarisse an are-you-serious look.

"Oh! Come on, have some fun! Remember how we used to sing that song together when we worked through the night at Minos? Cuz it's us against the 'bad bitches and ya ugly ass friends'!"

Clarisse burst out laughing. Mad couldn't help but follow. Clarisse had an infectious, booming laugh.

"Here." Clarisse took out a pendant shaped like an hourglass. Inside, instead of sand were tiny faceted rubies. "I call this 'Too Much Time.' But of course, it's satirical. We never have enough time, and one day it's going to all run out! So, don't keep on putting things off, saying you'll do it and you don't, because one day it'll be too late, and you will regret it!"

"Tempus fugit. Time flies."

"Exactly!" Clarisse clapped Mad on the back. "I know it's cliché, but you know what? Life's too short. Do what is truly important and truly makes you happy."

There was a small carving on the bottom of the hourglass, reading:

It does not do to dwell on dreams and forget to live

"What a beautiful quote. When did you become a philosopher too?"

"Oh! I didn't! I'm quoting Dumbledore!" Clarisse burst into her booming laugh again.

"Thanks, Clarisse."

"For what?" She stopped laughing while her assistant handed her a tissue to blot off the tears streaming down her face.

Mad smiled. "For being yourself! I'll take this."

"Really?!"

"Yes, of course! I've always wanted an hourglass with priceless rubies dripping through it rather than sand," Mad joked. "Of course I want it! It has special meaning to me."

"Thanks, Mad!" Clarisse hugged her, then handed the hourglass over to her assistant. "They'll wrap it up for you."

At that moment, a blur of shimmering yellow gold material flashed before them. It was Jackie in a long Grecian goddess dress, radiant with a dozen diamond stars clipped into her hair like Empress Sisi in that famous Franz Xaver Winterhalter portrait.

"Hey, Jackie!" Clarisse kissed her on the cheeks.

"Congratulations, dear! It's wonderful and fabulous! I love everything here!"

"Awww, thanks, Jackie! Coming from a fashionista like you, that means a lot to me."

"Jackie! Jackie! Picture, please!" the photographers cried, already swarming around them. Mad stood out of the way while the women posed. As the flashes waned, someone whispered in Clarisse's ear, and she nodded.

"Hey, girls, I've got to talk to *Prestige*, but enjoy yourselves and don't cause any trouble, you two!" Clarisse said.

"Oh, please, we won't do anything you wouldn't," Jackie said, rolling her eyes playfully, sparking one of those infectious booming laughs from Clarisse that echoed throughout the room as she left the two alone.

Mad and Jackie hadn't spoken since that fateful day in the Maldives. For all Mad knew, Jackie was still furious at her, and rightfully so. But Jackie hadn't fled or appeared disgusted with her after Clarisse left, so perhaps this was a good chance for her to apologize. Mad made her move.

"What could we do this time?" Mad said, facing Jackie and putting on her best smile.

Jackie didn't respond but took a sip of her champagne and scanned the room.

"Maybe we can pull a 'Manolo' here, just like we did in Barcelona," Mad continued, not giving up. "Or look at that guy over there." She pointed towards a man standing in one corner of the room. "Terrorizing that group of girls. Look at his hands, touching them from behind. It'll be fun to 'Naomi Campbell' him."

That did it for Jackie. She swung her head towards him, and her eyes narrowed on the greasy-haired man in a purple velvet suit, shirt unbuttoned down to his belly button, exposing everything you didn't want to see. Jackie choked on her drink as she clearly tried to suppress her laugh, splashing champagne all over her face.

"What did you make me do?!" Jackie squealed.

Mad laughed as she quickly grabbed a napkin from one of the waiters circling with trays of drinks and hors d'oeuvres.

"Here, let me help you with it," Mad said as she carefully blotted the champagne off Jackie's face, making sure her makeup was intact and not smudged.

"There!" Mad giggled.

"Thanks," Jackie whispered.

"You know you can't stay mad at me forever."

"I know," Jackie admitted.

"I'm sorry. You know I am. And you're right. I haven't been there for you, and I should have been. I've been very selfish to everyone who cares about me. It's not right."

"Damn right, you obtuse bitch."

"I'm going to change," Mad said sternly.

Jackie looked straight into her eyes. "How?"

"For starters, I would like to know what you have been up to? Seems like you have something going on, but I haven't had the chance to ask you about it. If you're free, my whole night is yours."

Jackie's eyes slowly softened, and a smile of relief curled the corners of her mouth.

"Perfume. I've been wanting to share with you, but you've been so busy and—"

"Difficult. I know. Guilty!"

"I've been making farm-to-bottle perfume for clients. I travel around the world searching for ingredients from organic farms that use sustainable resources. I combine the different aromas and bottle them myself, creating bespoke fragrances for each individual client. It started out as something fun that I did when I had time, but word got out, and now it's kind of exploded into a full-fledged business. People want to feel special and want to smell unique."

So that's what Fiona was talking about on the phone when I was in Courchevel! And oh, that heavenly scent that hit me at the restaurant in New York City before I even noticed Fiona standing there.

"Wow! That is amazing!"

Mad couldn't stop staring at her best friend; she was thoroughly, absolutely, and genuinely in awe of her.

"You free for lunch tomorrow?" Jackie asked.

"Lunch?" Mad sneered, sounding like Jackie just asked a stupid question. "Tomorrow?"

Jackie dropped her eyes, waiting to hear the inevitable "No, I can't," but instead Mad asked, "How about the next several days?"

Jackie's head snapped upwards, eyebrows raised.

"For real!" Mad cried. "I'm all yours. We have loads to catch up on."

"Can I choose the restaurants?"

"I would pack my bags, slam the door, and leave on the next boat out if you didn't," Mad quipped.

"Oh! That stung! That was good, Mrs. Lam."

"Oh, but you only know the half of it." Mad giggled. "I'll tell you at lunch."

"All right," Jackie said, content with their reconciliation. She shifted her gaze over to the front of the room. "Hey, aren't those the girls who—"

Mad turned her head around. Standing in front of the event backdrop, smiling, and posing up a storm for the photographers were two of Mad's ex-colleagues, Elena and Lolita. Infamous social climbers and opportunists, they terrorized Mad when she used to work at a smaller auction house, belittling, bullying, and ostracizing her because to them not only was she a "nobody" in society, but also someone who never kissed their asses.

Among other shame-intended incidents, Mad vividly remembered how they would lead the whole office out for long hearty lunches but had her stay behind to answer phone calls and man the reception. She remembered starving, but she couldn't leave because she didn't want the auction house's reputation on the line. Or when they would invite everyone to a party and purposely leave her out but made sure she knew about it. It wasn't that she wanted to join them anyways, but she wished she had stood up for herself and said something, instead of just smiling and acting like nothing happened.

"Yaaa." Mad turned away; she couldn't stand their fake laughs.

"Well, you know what," Jackie said, taking out her cell phone to make a call, her eyes fixated on Serena at the front desk. "They need to be updated."

"On what?"

"Not them! The List!"

"What 'the List'?"

"There's a new movement—as a matter of fact, a global movement—that started with Olivia Wilde. It's her nice-people-only policy. The List is updated constantly." She paused to talk to Serena. "Hi, dear, it's Jackie. I've got two more names for that list we've been working on."

Serena nodded as Jackie spoke.

"Thanks, dear." Jackie ended the call. "It's done; come on, let's get closer. You don't want to miss this."

Jackie led Mad to a pillar behind and in close proximity to the front desk. She leaned on the side of it, drink in one hand, just in time to hear Serena say:

"Sorry, you're not on the RSVP list."

"What?" Elena yelled at Serena. "Do you know who I am? Of course we're on the list."

"Check again!" Lolita cried, tapping Serena's iPad with her finger repeatedly and furiously.

Serena politely pulled the iPad away and checked the RSVP list again. "No. I'm pretty sure you're not on the list."

"Do you know how many times I've been to *Tatler* parties? Just this month?!" Elena yelled again.

"Oh, wait!" Serena interjected, eyes widening as if she saw something on her iPad that would change the circumstances.

"See! Now let us in!" Lolita demanded.

By now, they had garnered a crowd, all wanting to see what the commotion was about.

"You are on a list," Serena said.

"See!"

Serena slowly shifted her head upwards, away from the iPad, and announced, deadpan, "on the asshole list."

"What?!" Elena and Lolita cried in disbelief, their faces turning red with anger, probably thinking to themselves how a "nobody" could have the nerve to say that to them.

"We uphold the nice-people-only policy strictly here. You'll find that your infamous names are already on our global network. I suggest you consider some changes in your overall behavior," Serena said in one breath, without pausing.

"Johnny?" She turned to the security guard, who seemed to have had a hunch from the shouting that he would be needed and had conveniently situated himself next to her. "Would you escort these ladies out of here?"

Beyond stunned, Elena and Lolita followed Johnny out like mindless zombies as guests stared at their indignant exit.

"Oh, I see someone on the List tried to take advantage of my press event," Clarisse said, appearing right next to Jackie.

"Yup," Jackie said.

"It's all about good karma here. Not that pretend KYC shit that Minos likes to pull. I hope this gives mean girls a warning! Did you girls know that it was going to happen? Is that why you're stationed here?" Clarisse asked.

Mad and Jackie burst out laughing.

"Tell you later," Jackie said, tears coming out of her eyes from laughing too hard. "Mad and I have to go pull a 'Naomi Campbell.'"

Clarisse scowled at them, mouthing out the words "Oh no you don't!" but they scrambled away, laughing and holding on to each other, just like old times.

CHAPTER TEN

Venice

> *Mr. and Mrs. Steve Lam,*
> *Welcome to the St. Regis Venice!*
> *My sincere appreciation and gratitude for your patronage.*
> *My team and I remain at your disposal for any*
> *assistance you may need. Please do not hesi-*
> *tate to contact us any time of the day or night.*
> *Have a wonderful stay!*
> *Giovanni Bruni*
> *General Manager*

"Riggghhhhtttt," Mad mumbled sarcastically to herself, throwing the thick greeting card back on the table, next to the sizable flower arrangement and bottle of Dom Pérignon chilling in the silver bucket.

I don't even know when Steve will be here. Come to think of it, we haven't even talked about it—or anything substantial. Unless you call "hi," "bye," "good morning" substantial.

Mad dismissed her cynical thoughts and stepped outside onto an impressive terrace furnished with an enticing assortment of cream lounge chairs, orange cushions, and spring flowers, directly facing the glorious Grand Canal and the imposing Baroque Basilica di Santa Maria della Salute. The busy buzzing and splashing of the vaporettos, gondolas, and water taxis were worlds away from the whirlwind past few days that she'd had, reconciling with Jackie. It had been hours of catching up on lost time; they tried out new restaurants and cafés, shopped for their spring and summer wardrobes, and had sleepovers where they ended up chatting into the early hours of the morning. It was a gratifying interlude. But now, Mad was in Venice, staying conveniently at the very hotel where the exhibition would take place, about to dive into the final preparations. Fiona's dynamic marketing efforts had elevated the exhibition to "the event of the year" to be at or be seen at. Mad absolutely had to be on her A game and avoid all distractions in order to deliver above the bar that global expectations and anticipation had set.

And that was what she did. The next two weeks were chaotic, but Mad was in her element, and loved every minute of it. She worked amongst the hollering, hammering, and sawing of the contractors and crew as they built the venue from scratch, erecting makeshift walls, showcases, and backdrops, installing security cameras and motion sensors, arranging and blending in furniture and fixtures, etc. It was when this framework was nearly completed that Mad could actually start working her magic: displaying each gemstone and jewelry piece to perfection. Each had its own unique display stand and designated showcase with specially crafted descriptions that tied into the theme of "unity." Starting with where the stone originated, the artisan who cut and polished it, the designer who envisioned the conception, to the craftsman who mounted and fused it into the final masterpiece that it was, all were fully credited and displayed for the world to see that each aspect was equally important in the equation.

With her notes and jewelry cloth in hand, Mad hung, rested, fastened, pinned, and wiped while adjusting the lighting to bring out the best in each piece. Chosen highlights and pieces with significant provenances from different periods were placed in their own themed rooms, such as a maharajah's *sarpech* at the Mughal room, an old-cut diamond *devant-de-corsage* in the Belle Époque room, and an Egyptian-motif brooch in the Art Deco room. A plethora of Bulgari Serpentis, Cartier panthers and tigers, and Van Cleef & Arpels mystery-set jewelry bedecked the designer room, which led straight into the colored-stone suite, aptly named "The Big Three," that burst with boundless shades of red rubies, green emeralds, and blue sapphires. Under Raj's skilled and expert polishing, the Burmese sapphire and ruby necklaces danced and sparkled in their showcases—the fire of the gemstones and the majesty of the yellow gold mounting only augmented by the deliberate incandescent spot lighting. The pigeon's blood ruby from the Russos juxtaposed brilliantly with Vikram's flawless emeralds and the emerald rings from the Geneva auctions, which were sure to cause frenzied curiosity. Just to shake it up a bit, Mad placed Raj's purplish-pink sapphire in the mix. Like an exotic flamingo basking within its lush green habitat, it complemented the other stones fantastically.

The prince's famous rainbow arc of colored diamonds obviously occupied an entire room. The latest members of the distinguished collection included the fancy vivid blue-green diamond and the blue diamond, freshly recut from New York City. It had been reborn into an impressive fancy intense blue, with a color so saturated that it was borderline fancy vivid blue;

even industry pros could be fooled. Having just shaved 2.53 carats off to 11.56 carats, the lapidary effectively increased the value of the diamond by a remarkable US$6,827,000. Aware of how extraordinary this stone was, the GIA even issued an expedited report and appendix certifying its qualities.

Situated conveniently beside the colored diamonds was the room of colorless diamonds, illuminated by expert white lighting and reflective mirrored panels. The Pandora's box of limpid Golcondas dominated the space, scintillating elusively in wonder, above a pond of water. Mad purposely placed several D color flawless or internally flawless non-Golconda diamonds in the exhibit, just to show the optical differences between "first water" diamond material and those that were not. The lapidary delivered the 35.09-carat diamond, now reborn into a splendid 35-carat D color internally flawless stone, which had increased in value by a fine US$864,200.

Across the hallway was the modest but exhilarating room of modern contemporary pieces by grand masters and up-and-coming stars of the industry. Deserving of their own highlight case were the Luna pearls, glowing with pride among the sculpted avant-garde jewelry of JAR, Bhagat, David Michael, Wallace Chan, etc. The final yet most intriguing room was the jadeite parlor that led back to the entrance of the exhibition. The display morphed from old mined jadeite pieces into newer material that included the recently acquired jadeite bead necklace. With its freshly minted diamond clasp, the stunning jewel had been provocatively named "The Superstar." Mad couldn't wait to hear what the jewelry industry had to say about that.

The last and final allotment arrived via private jet just in the nick of time, the day before the exhibit began. Mad held her breath as the crew pushed the large wooden crate through the entrance, disassembled the box, and unveiled the monumental jadeite carving. Gushing in vibrant green with white mottling, it was a vision to behold. Carved amidst a natural landscape of towering mountains, splashing waterfalls, and budding foliage were numerous delicately depicted figurines in different cultural clothing. Each stood with their hands in the air, releasing the ultimate symbol of peace, the dove, into the sky. The title of the piece was simply *Unity*. Hazel and Hailey had indeed outdone themselves this time. The crew hauled the massive carving onto a wooden pedestal positioned in the entry rotunda. Mad must have spent an hour climbing up and down the aluminum folding ladder as she adjusted a set of soft glowing lights and spotlights, until finally she was satisfied.

"Perfect," she said with a smile on her face.

"It is."

Mad swung her head around. Standing in a white T-shirt, jeans, and a backpack behind his back was Logan!

"What are you doing here?!" Mad exclaimed.

"Well, the last time I checked there's a jewelry exhibition here, no?" he joked. "I heard it's going to be the event of the year. Everyone's dying to see those Luna pearls."

"Oh yes! I wasn't aware of it being 'the event of the year'!" She laughed. "It's just a little jewelry exhibition and *just* some cultured pearls. They're not that big, really."

Logan swooped in to give Mad kisses on the cheeks. "I wanted to make sure everything was OK."

"I just finished setting up the last piece. You want to go check on the pearls?"

"I mean, are you OK?" Logan treaded carefully. "I haven't heard from you. Have you and Steve sorted things out? If you need me, I just wanted you to know I'm here for you."

Mad smiled. Logan was the sweetest thing, but Steve would always be the love of her life.

"We've got to work things out," she replied honestly. "But that's what a relationship is all about. We're not perfect, but it's *our* perfect, and I love him too much to give up on it."

Logan, clearly crestfallen, dipped his head down, hiding his disappointment momentarily before looking up again with a genuine smile.

"I wish I'd met you sooner, Mad. I'm happy and extremely jealous of Steve for having someone like you."

"You will meet someone much better suited than me!" she reassured him. "When you meet her, you will know for sure she's the one. Plus, frankly speaking, I'm not really the nature, camping, surfing type!"

Logan exploded into laughter. "Awww! I love surfing! And camping! Not that glamping thing that city folks do."

"I can tell," Mad said, eyeing his bulging biceps.

"Oh, great. Thanks for ruining that perfect goddess pedestal I put you up on!"

Mad laughed and stepped in to give him a hug. He wrapped his arms around her, savoring the last few moments before beginning a new chapter in his life as well.

"I'll see you at the opening, my goddess," he whispered in her ear.

"Don't be late," Mad whispered back.

Logan turned and left. She watched as his silhouette dwindled in the distance. She was glad she'd sorted things out with him. Even more, she was relieved she'd finally said it out loud— that she was going to salvage her relationship with Steve. Something about voicing it made her even more determined to make it happen. She took a long deep breath, inhaling the aroma of wood and fresh paint, but also registering a draft of jasmine and narcissus.

Fiona tapped her on the shoulder. *"Bellissima,* Mad!"

"When did you get in?" Mad asked as they kissed each other on the cheeks. "How long have you been here?"

"Long enough to be blown away! You did it! The prince will be so impressed when he sees it," Fiona said, her eyes scanning their surroundings.

"Well, yes! Just in time for the opening reception tomorrow."

"I knew you could do it."

Mad flinched, but Fiona didn't seem to notice. If she did, she didn't say anything.

"So, shall we?" Fiona asked, glancing towards the exit.

"Sure, let me grab my bag. I'll see you in the lobby."

With her bag in hand, Mad walked towards the exit, but before leaving she turned around and took one last glimpse at what she had achieved. The dust had settled, the jewelry and gemstones gleamed in their showcases, and the events team were huddled together, going through tomorrow's rundown. She smiled. It was perfect. She was proud of herself.

I'm going to miss this.

"Are you seriously telling me that you, and everyone in your family, have never lost money horse racing?! Like never?!" Mad asked incredulously.

"Yup, that's true," Fiona replied, pushing her finished plate of linguine vongole to the side.

"How? How do you know which horse to bet on?" Mad inquired, in awe of what she just learned of her friend.

"Well, it's all in the genes. The parents, the sire and the dam, already determine 90 percent of the results."

"But then you would need to know the names of all the 'parents' in the world and if they're any good."

"Yup."

"So, you memorized all the names?"

"Yup."

Mad sat back in her chair. "You never fail to amaze me."

"You never fail to amaze *me*!" Fiona replied. "Now tell me what you wanted to talk about."

Mad had asked to meet with Fiona privately so that she could tell her face-to-face what was on her mind. Fiona chose to convene at a small cozy Italian restaurant within the maze-like passages of the water city.

Mad cleared her throat.

"Fiona, I'm ready for a change—actually, I need to change."

Fiona looked a little confused but let Mad explain herself.

"Working for you and the prince—"

Fiona corrected her. "Working *with* me, not *for* me!"

"Thank you." Mad smiled appreciatively. "It has been such a growth experience for me. Professionally and personally. I've learned so much about myself in the process, and it's forced me to start making conscious decisions. Things are falling apart, and I'm losing important people in my life. It shouldn't be like this. The truth is, and I'm not afraid to admit it, I just can't do it."

Fiona didn't say anything. Mad couldn't read her, so she continued.

"I've learned the hard way that my priorities should be my family and friends. And because of that, I need to establish limits and boundaries. Don't get me wrong, I love my job! But I need a balance. I can't keep on answering calls and replying to messages instantly during the day or at insane hours or when I'm on holiday!"

"That's right. I understand," Fiona finally replied.

"Really?" Mad said, not expecting that response at all.

"Yah, of course. I always wondered how you managed to answer your emails and messages so quickly. It's not necessary."

"Oh! So, you don't expect me to?"

"Of course I don't!"

Wow! That was easy!

"Well, another thing that I realized was that I really need to let go of my ego and seek help. I need a team. I know things can be done quickly and efficiently with me working alone, but as much as I thought I had things under control, my life was actually falling apart. It's true, you can't go far without a team to help you."

Fiona nodded, but her face was impassive.

"I need people to support me and work with me. For productivity and definitely a healthier lifestyle. I know that's not what you envisioned, not why you hired me—and that it's not even possible—so truth be told, I'm not right for this job. I'm not who you need."

Mad lowered her eyes and gazed out the window, bracing herself for the inevitable.

"Why didn't you tell me sooner?" Fiona chuckled.

"What?" Mad swung her head back, surprised at her reaction.

"I always thought it would be great if you had a team," Fiona explained. "But after all that you went through at Minos, I thought you needed time to heal before you could trust and depend on other people again."

Was that why I was so adamant about doing things myself?

"That could be the reason. I never realized it!"

"I was just waiting for you to let people into your life again. Whatever you want to do, whatever you need, the prince and I will be 100 percent supportive. Plus, wouldn't it be beneficial if you could train and teach new talent? The industry needs more honest and passionate gemologists out there. While you're at it, please go hire yourself a personal assistant too. You need one."

"I would like that. I could actually talk to someone at work!"

"Honestly, I don't know how you survived talking to yourself on those solitary business trips." Fiona shook her head. "Mad, you're like family to us, and I want nothing more than to see you healthy and happy. So please go assemble your team ASAP! You should have told us sooner. You look miserable!"

"I will! I will! Thank you," Mad placed her hand on Fiona's. She was deeply touched and relieved.

"So, you and Steve OK?"

"We're going to be OK." Mad smiled. "It's my turn to take the wheel—make things right again."

"Well, let me know what the prince and I can do to help. We're here for you."

"Thank you! I'm feeling good about this."

Mad was feeling anything *but* good the next day. With the cocktail reception starting in a few hours and the whole world about to scrutinize, dissect, and critique her work, she plunged into extreme anxiety. Until today, she had been confident that the exhibition would be well received, but as the minutes drew nearer, she couldn't help but question her choices and doubt the decisions she'd made. Moreover, physically, she hadn't been feeling so well either. She was nauseous and agitated, and her stomach had been doing somersaults all morning; so intense was the acid reflux that she couldn't even take a sip of her iced cappuccino without regurgitating the nasty combination of bitter bile and coffee back into her mouth. Forsaking any attempt of ingesting food, she simply spent the rest of the day working on an empty stomach. She double-checked, cleaned, and adjusted everything in the exhibition until the very last second, when she absolutely had to return to her suite at the urging of her glam squad or risk having guests see her in such a disheveled state.

Her glam squad was fortunately a dream. Within an hour, they had her hair blown out and curled to old-Hollywood flowing waves. Her makeup was flawless and impeccable, glowing with sultry nude shades, highlighted by her signature red lipstick. Though the butterflies in her stomach hadn't waned, and the bloating tightened the sheer bustier, the Atelier Versace aquamarine draped gown with a dangerously sexy slit to the upper left thigh still made her look spectacular. The final touches of a pair of 1950s earrings of a stylized knot of marquise and baguette diamonds cascading into three graduating lines of circular diamonds, long white gloves, and her red diamond engagement ring completed the ensemble. She was ready.

By the time she reentered the venue, the party was in full swing. The DJ had set up shop at the far corner on an elevated stage, spinning the latest international top hits; the waiters and waitresses in smart black-and-white outfits circled around with trays of fancy hors d'oeuvres and alcoholic or caffeinated beverages; the photographers and paparazzi, sprinkled throughout the venue and camped at the entrance, snapped photos at every opportune moment. Guests ranging from *Tatler* favorites and celebrities to jewelry designers mingled with aspiring jewelers, specialists, and gemologists that Mad had specially invited to attend. From the laughter, "oohs," and "aahs," it was apparent that the guests were truly enjoying themselves.

"Mad!" Fiona, in a hot-pink tulle dress, called out and waved. She beckoned Mad towards the flurry of reporters and security detail surrounding her and the prince.

"You look like a goddess!" Fiona proclaimed as Mad approached.

"Thank you, Fiona. You look amazing yourself too. Love those conch pearls." Mad pointed at her pink conch pearl and diamond cluster earrings.

"Ah! Here's the star of the show!" the prince declared out loud. "May I introduce my one and only jewelry advisor, and dear friend, Madeleine. She is the brainchild of this exhibition. Without her expertise and advice, this would not be possible."

"A few words, please!" the reporters shouted as they shoved their microphones and recorders towards her.

Mad took a deep calming breath. She wasn't caught off guard or the least unprepared. As a matter of fact, for the past year, she had wanted to address all the negativity she had experienced at Minos and turn it into something positive. This was her chance to broadcast her vision for the future of the jewelry industry. It had been long overdue.

"Let me make it clear that it was your Highness and my dear friend here," Mad said, turning her gaze and smiling at Fiona before turning back to the reporters, "who gave me this wonderful opportunity to showcase the most extraordinary jewelry in the world, all under one roof. Not only that, but they've also made my dreams and the dreams of many deserving of opportunities come true. Without strings attached, all proceeds from this exhibition go to educational funding, internships, and support of anyone aspiring to a career in the jewelry industry. I want all the dreamers and believers out there to know that, just like me, if you put your heart into your passion and stay true to yourself, with a little inspiration, anything is possible for you too."

"Well said." The prince gave Mad a wink.

"Picture! Picture!" the reporters shouted.

They huddled together and smiled for the sea of cameras and flashing lights. It was hard not to feel like a winner.

"Now, please excuse us," the prince interrupted, after patiently giving the reporters plenty of time for the photo op. "We've got to get this party started!"

Satisfied with the interview and shots, the reporters laughed and let them through.

Noticing someone familiar, Fiona nudged Mad and directed her eyes towards the entrance. Dressed in a handsome tux, one hand in his pocket, was Steve.

"Go," Fiona said.

"We'll talk to you later," the prince added.

Mad nodded and made her way towards Steve, stopping a few centimeters in front of him, not exactly knowing how she should handle the next moments. She studied his face, trying to pick up some signals, but was distracted by the fact that he'd lost weight and those frown lines on his forehead were even more pronounced than the first time they'd met.

Had he been as anxious and worried as I have been these past weeks? Does he miss me as much as I miss him? Why does he still smell so good?!

Breaking the ice, Steve handed her a glass of chilled champagne. "You look breathtaking."

"Thank you." Mad smiled.

That was a good start.

"The exhibition is astonishing. You did such a wonderful job—"

"Could we perhaps go to the balcony and talk?" Mad blurted out.

Steve nodded, and they made their way through the crowd. She was eager to talk to Steve and make things right, but also confounded by apprehension.

What if it's really over? What if he thinks it's too late?

As they walked out onto the balcony, a cold blast of frigid air hit Mad in the face, reminding her of the ominous feeling she had felt over the past few months.

Is something still amiss?

Swiftly, Steve took off his jacket and covered her bare shoulders. His gentle gesture prompted her to make the next move.

There's no time to waste. It's now or never.

Mad looked into Steve's eyes. "I—"

"I'm sorry," he cut her off.

But she wouldn't have it. "No! I'm sorry! Let me own it!"

Steve hesitated but clearly decided it was best to let her talk.

"I've been awful, insensitive, and selfish, and I need to apologize for it. I've been taking us for granted, and things were getting out of control. I love what I do—my passion for jewelry and gemstones will never change. But it's all meaningless if I don't have you with me."

Steve's hand touched Mad's face gently, giving her the boost and reassurance needed to continue.

"I won't lose you. I'm not going to let you go. You're too important to me. I'm going to make changes. I'm going to assemble a team to help me out at work, and I will establish boundaries. It took me almost losing you to realize that I've been doing it all wrong. That I really need to find balance in my life for both of us—for our future."

Mad searched his face for a sign, but wasn't certain of what she saw.

Does he agree? Does he forgive me?

"Steve, what are you thinking?"

"Well," he said as his right hand swung behind her waist holding her tight, "that I will never let you go too." He moved in close and kissed her desperately and eagerly, completely taking her breath away.

Mad melted into his arms, abandoning all her doubts as she kissed him back longingly. This kiss was also long overdue. Though, they hadn't reconciled long enough before Jackie, probably intentionally, barged in.

"There they are!" Jackie cried, approaching with the prince and Fiona close behind. "You two lovebirds! I see things are sorted out!"

"Always impeccable timing, Jackie," Steve grumbled.

"Hey, J." Mad gleamed. "You made it! Where's Stuart?"

"He's rushing over from Marco Polo now. He made a pit stop in Kuala Lumpur to pick up some *kuehs* and pandan cakes for you. Thought you would be craving some Asian delicacies after two whole weeks of Western food."

"How sweet of him!"

"Isn't he?" Jackie gushed.

"Am I sensing an enga—"

"I don't want to disturb you guys," Fiona interjected sheepishly, "but I just wanted you to know that the reviews are out of this world, and everyone is raving about the exhibition! Katerina even told the *New York Times* that if there is one jewelry exhibition to attend in one's lifetime, it is this one!"

"For real?!" Mad cried, thrilled that her hard work had paid off.

"Congratulations, dear." Jackie hugged Mad. "I propose a toast, to Mad!"

"No! To family and friends!" Mad corrected, holding her glass of champagne in the air.

She took a big gulp, finally relaxing from all the stress that she had put herself through. The liquid slid down her throat comfortably, just as it had happened countless occasions before. But this time, inexplicably, something was different. An invisible force abruptly ejected the hostile liquid back up her throat, rather than it settling nicely in her stomach. Her hand quickly clamped her mouth shut as it burst into the cavity, threatening to pry her lips open.

Avoiding an imaginable humiliation, Mad fled the premises for the nearest toilet, which fortunately was a single stall right next to the balcony doors. She unceremoniously kicked the door open, fell to her knees, and threw up into the toilet bowl.

"Are you OK?!" Jackie screamed from behind as she locked and secured the toilet door.

Mad couldn't answer. The violent outbursts wouldn't stop. It was like once it started, the force relentlessly pushed and pushed, trying to expel all the contents out of her body—of which there was none since she hadn't eaten anything at all today. Jackie crouched down beside Mad and held her hair up as she retched and gagged, using tissues to wipe the spit from her face.

"I should never drink on an empty stomach," Mad managed to say in between expulsions. "It's all that anxiety and buildup to the event—"

She vomited bile again.

"Are you OK?!" Steve knocked anxiously on the door.

"She can't stop throwing up. We need to get a doctor!" Jackie yelled back.

"Fiona, call our doctor," the prince's muffled voice came through the door.

After a few more exhaustive bouts, Mad stood up with the help of Jackie lifting her by the side. Jackie opened the door, and Mad felt herself collapse into the familiar stronghold of her husband's body. She could hear the prince's security detail talking into their comms as she was transported through the back entrance, up the elevator, and into her room.

"Oh, you guys don't have to come with me," she said faintly. "I'll be all right. Please go and enjoy the party."

"Nonsense!" The prince refused.

"The doctor's here," Fiona said as Mad was placed on the bed.

Feeling weak and delirious, Mad closed her eyes.

"Don't worry, he's my personal doctor," the prince said to Steve, who Mad knew by now must be extremely distraught.

"She's been throwing up uncontrollably," Jackie hastily reported to the doctor.

"I'll be all right. It could be a bug. Please, could you guys go and enjoy the party," Mad muttered, trying hard to talk louder so someone would actually listen to her.

"We're not going until we know you're all right," Fiona asserted definitively.

"Yah! That's right!" Jackie shrieked.

"Come, let's wait outside," the prince said, enforcing the voice of reason. When no one moved, he literally pushed the hesitant Fiona and Jackie out the door. "Give them some privacy."

"Thank you," Steve said appreciatively.

The doctor knelt down at the side of the bed and took Mad's pulse.

"Are you feeling better?" Steve asked tenderly.

"Better," Mad whispered, reading his distressed face.

Thank goodness he's here. What would I have—

Without warning, the doctor's head suddenly snapped up. His stern eyes terrified both of them. "Have you been drinking?"

"Well, yes—only a sip! On an empty stomach, though. If I knew the reaction I would have, I wouldn't have done it!"

"When was your last period?"

"What?" Mad spat out, not even hiding how stunned and annoyed she was.

What a rude question to ask! How is this even relevant?! But yes, come to think of it, when was *my last period? I simply can't remember!*

She had been so busy traveling, working on the exhibition, and figuring things out that she just couldn't remember something so mundane. Then it dawned on her. It all made sense! She slowly looked up at Steve's face; his eyes were as large as saucers.

"Really?" he asked the doctor, incredulously.

The doctor stood up; his face displayed no expression at all, but he patted Steve on the shoulder.

Mad exploded with joy! She opened her mouth, unable to contain her happiness, and began laughing hysterically. Steve burst out laughing too, so hard he visibly had tears in his eyes. For their friends waiting nervously outside, they must have sounded insane! But they couldn't care less. Steve climbed into bed and embraced her.

"I love you, I love you, I love you," he whispered repeatedly.

The doctor took the cue and left the room as quietly as possible, although the happy couple had completely forgotten about his presence anyway.

The tranquility didn't last long. Upon hearing the incredible news, Jackie screamed bloody murder and, from the very audible crash-bang, must have flung something accidently, such as her phone, on the wall. Her heels clicked vigorously on the marble floor as she ran towards their room, with two more sets of pitter-pattering close behind.

"How is it that we're always around for these moments?" the prince uttered gleefully out loud.

Mad closed her eyes, waiting for her friends' imminent arrival and well wishes. She was about to embark on a new adventure with her family and friends. And she thought to herself, before opening her eyes again, that it was *perfect. Everything was perfect.*

ACKNOWLEDGMENTS

Words simply cannot express my gratitude. Since the launch of *No Reserves*, I've received countless congratulatory messages, immense support, and inexplicably amazing book sales. This would not be possible without my family, friends, and fans. I am truly, truly blessed.

Thank you to my core, my no-questions-asked, my inspirations, Angela, Christine, and Tina. My life would be very different without your fabulous presence. To my wonderful group of friends, who risked their lives attending my *No Reserves* book signing: Jenny, Jeannie, Sandy and Simon, Christine and J. J., Elizabeth, Teni and Harold, Carolyn and Simon, Kelly and Kelvin, Teck and Lorraine, Jasmine, Rosa, Sandra, Karen, Anabella, Stevenson, Hazel and Howard, Esther, Peter C., Gillian, Lina and Jason, Carol, Peter, Phillip, Randy and Gabby, Kay, Othniel, Aaron, Joy, Rebecca, Elaine, Geraldine, Lil, Kathy, Renee, Chris and Selwyn, Della and Kelvin, Vincent and Sofie, Joyce, Raphaele, and many, many more! I'm sorry if your name was not mentioned, but please know that from the bottom of my heart, I am eternally grateful. To the wise Chris,

Koboer, Emmy, and Gerald for your invaluable advice. To my fiery hype man, Clarisse (yes, you!), thank you for being my conscience and for having my back. To my amazing friends: Rebecca Y., Christine F., Jennifer, Tisha, Maryrose, Claire, Denise P., Central Library, Jen L., Winky, Jaime, Elizabeth, Andrew M., Annie, Jeffrey, Alicia, Jean, Angela, Nancy, Teming, Carolyn, Wen Li, Li Xin, Ada, Lisa, Carina, Lillian, Andrew K., Sandy, Ah Mei, Tiff, Yvonne, Sam and Lambert, Dan, Maha, and many more for supporting me in your way. To my jewelry industry and auction house friends (you know who you are!), thank you so much for your unbelievable support and unrelenting friendship all throughout the years. To my indestructible Helene, thank you for all that you have done for me in front and behind the scenes. To my kickass friend Joanne, who started all of this by giving me a bottle of Believe. My sweet Denise, for your insights and experiences in Myanmar and most importantly, for giving me one of the best decisions I've ever made in my life. To my army of alma maters: Hong Kong International School, Miss Porter's School, Babson, and Bentley for broadcasting my work throughout your networks. To Bookazine Hong Kong, for giving me a chance. Thank you again to Girl Friday Productions for putting up with me and being so patient along the way. To my awesome fans, *White Glove Life* is written for you!

To my wonderful family, you mean the world to me! Thank you for your boundless love, for always believing in me, and most important, for allowing me to be me. I love you . . . I love you . . . I love you!

GLOSSARY

Burmese ruby: The most sought-after rubies are from Myanmar, where the most highly saturated red rubies can be found. Under UV light, the rubies glow a red fluorescence, giving them extra redness.

buyer's premium: The commission the auction house makes from the buyer. The charge added on top of the hammer price.

cloisonné: A technique in which enamel, gems, or glass is outlined with metalwork.

colored diamonds: Diamonds containing substantial impurities or structural defects within their chemical composition resulting in color. For example, boron gives diamonds the color blue, nitrogen the color yellow, radiation turns diamonds green, and crystal lattice defects turn diamonds pink. Yellow and brown diamonds with saturation beyond the GIA Z color.

colored stones: Gemstones other than diamond. For example, the "Big Three" are rubies, sapphires, and emeralds.

condition report: Report describing the quality of the lot. Gives essential information such as additional certificates, cataloging mistakes, or stones missing.

cultured pearls: Pearls created by artificially inserting a nucleus into the mollusc, which coats the irritant with layers of nacre and eventually forms a pearl.

en tremblant: Used to described jewelry with a part attached to a trembler to create movement when worn.

fire: When white light hits a gemstone and results in the dispersion of spectral colors.

GIA: Gemological Institute of America. A highly reputable nonprofit educational institution and laboratory. GIA certificates are the industry standard for grading diamonds. Its Graduate Gemologist (GG) training program is world-renowned and provides comprehensive knowledge of diamonds and colored stones.

Golconda diamonds: From the now depleted mines of Golconda in India, the diamonds are famous for their exceptional translucency. The material of the diamond is so pure and limpid, it's often called "first water."

hammer price: Price at which the lot is sold, not including the buyer's premium.

ICAC: Independent Commission Against Corruption. Anticorruption organization in Hong Kong.

internally flawless: Diamonds with minor external blemishes but no inclusions.

Kashmir sapphires: Sapphires from the depleted mine in Kashmir. Famous for their velvety-blue color.

KYC: Know your client. A process where the client identity is verified in addition to potential legal risks.

La Peregrina: One of the largest perfectly symmetrical pear-shaped natural pearls in the world. Once owned by the Spanish royal family and also Elizabeth Taylor.

lot: An individual or group of items offered for sale in an auction. Each lot is given an estimate.

loupe: A small handheld magnification tool used to see gemstone details, usually at 10x magnification.

maker's mark: Brand signature or initials stamped on jewelry.

natural pearls: Pearls created naturally without artificially inserted nuclei. With increased ocean pollution, high-quality natural pearls are extremely hard to find.

origin: Where the gemstone was found. Important for determining stone value.

Paraiba tourmaline: Gemstone in the tourmaline family known for its electric-blue and neon-green colors.

Persian turquoise: Turquoise from Iran. Top-quality turquoise is pure blue in color with minimum matrix.

pigeon's blood: Rubies with a highly saturated red color from Burma. Often compared to the first drop of blood from a slaughtered pigeon. Considered the highest-quality color and commands the greatest prices in the industry.

pleochroism: Different colors appear when observed at different angles.

plique-à-jour: An enameling technique where no backing is used, allowing light to shine through.

price per carat: The price of a gemstone per one carat, usually in US dollars.

provenance: A record of previous ownership. Exceptional provenance usually increases a piece's value and popularity.

refraction: The bending of light as it passes from one medium to another. Double refraction is when light is split into two rays when it enters another medium. Single refraction is when light is not split and remains a single beam.

saturation: The intensity of the gemstone's hue.

specialist: Expert in their respective field. A jewelry specialist's job consists of finding consignments, appraisal, obtaining bids for the sale, etc.

SSEF, or Swiss Gemmological Institute: Schweizerische Stiftung für Edelstein-Forschung. Swiss laboratory known for its expertise in colored stones and pearl testing. Also renowned for its gemological educational courses.

sugarloaf cabochon: Cutting style where the gemstone is polished into a smooth four-sided pyramid.

telephone bid: A bid placed by a client indicating which lots they would be called on to bid on the day of the sale. Telephone bidders bid on the client's behalf.

Type IIa: Most chemically pure diamond. Almost or entirely devoid of impurities. Often displays exceptional optical transparency.

unheated gemstones: Natural gemstones that are not enhanced with heat to improve aesthetics.

white glove sale: An auction where all lots are sold.

ABOUT THE AUTHOR

M. L. Wright worked in the jewelry auction business for over ten years, including the prestigious auction house Christie's, where she helped lead the Asia Pacific department to a Market #1 status for years. Expertly trained as a gemologist, she has a passion for all things jewelry. She currently lives in Hong Kong with her family and spoodle, Mushroom, and continues to work in the jewelry industry. *White Glove Life* is the highly anticipated sequel to her hit debut novel, *No Reserves.*